Game OVER

BOOKS BY BELLA NORTH

OAKWOOD RANCH

Score to Settle

Game OVER

BELLA NORTH

Bookouture

Published by Bookouture in 2026

An imprint of Storyfire Ltd.
Carmelite House
50 Victoria Embankment
London EC4Y 0DZ

www.bookouture.com

The authorised representative in the EEA is Hachette Ireland
8 Castlecourt Centre
Dublin 15 D15 XTP3
Ireland
(email: info@hbgi.ie)

ISBN: 978-1-80550-472-6
eBook ISBN: 978-1-80550-471-9

If you've ever stayed up until 3 a.m. screaming, "JUST KISS ALREADY," this one's for you.

GAME OVER PLAYLIST

If She Wants a Cowboy – Zach Bryan

Dress – Taylor Swift

Back in the Saddle – Luke Combs

Country Boy's Dream Girl – Ella Langley

Man I Need – Olivia Dean

Wood – Taylor Swift

Oops (I Think I Love You) – Savannah Jade

So Easy (To Fall In Love) – Olivia Dean

Lover – Taylor Swift

End Game – Taylor Swift ft. Ed Sheeran, Future

Listen to the playlist on Spotify!

ONE

DYLAN

The moment I jam my foot on the brake and hear the dull thud of my brand-new Ford Raptor nosing the vehicle in front, I know I'm gonna be late for the most important meeting of my life. Of all the days! Who the hell stops like that? The light turned green. The traffic was moving. I glanced at the clock—one quick check—and then bam. The old silver compact ahead slammed the brakes. I hit mine too late, and the seat belt yanked me back, hard.

The driver's out before I've even thrown my car into park. She's tall. Long legs, black tank top, denim cutoffs that should be illegal. Hell, they'd be stopping traffic if we weren't already jamming it up. The kind of athletic build that says she's no stranger to hard work, her tanned skin glowing like it soaks up the sun on a daily basis. Dark blonde hair flies down her back as she stalks to the bumper like she's ready for a fight.

Just watching her makes my dick stir in my jeans, like it's forcibly reminding me that I've spent the best part of two years focused on recovering from the knee injury that's kept me from playing in the NFL for the Denver Stormhawks. Women—dating—have been the last thing on my mind.

I climb out, biting back a curse. My meeting with Coach Allen starts in ten minutes. I don't have time for this. The woman blows out a long sigh, raking a hand through her hair. She must be a few years younger than me—twenty-six or twenty-seven, I'd guess. Her face is free of makeup and I find my gaze snagging on the cute spray of freckles that run across the bridge of her nose. But it's the green eyes that grab me. Bright and sharp—sunlit leaves after a rainstorm. The kind of eyes that on any other day might make me wonder if this is a sign I should prioritize dating again. The thought is cut short as those green eyes fix on me.

"Seriously?" Her tone drips with sarcasm. "Were you trying to climb into my backseat or is tailgating just your style?"

Frustration pulses through my veins. It's the first day of the rest of my life and I don't have time for this. I rub a hand over my jaw, expecting to feel the scratch of my dark beard and connecting instead with smooth skin, remembering the clean shave and haircut I got this morning, now I'm finally back to full strength and ready to play pro football again. I'm ready to get my life back, and the high-altitude Stormhawks training camp in Arizona in two weeks is my ticket back to it.

I force my tone to stay even. "The light was green and you stopped."

"And you were way too close." She jerks her thumb at my truck. "Maybe ease up on the gas next time, big guy."

Big guy? I'm thirty-one, six five, built like a defensive line-backer, and she makes me sound like I'm a clumsy kid with their first trike. If I weren't seriously annoyed at how late I am right now, I might laugh.

"Maybe don't stop without warning, little lady," I shoot back, not even bothering to hide my smirk as her eyes narrow. She must be five eleven, with curves in all the right places, but if we're resorting to name-calling, I'm all in. Whatever charm and magic with women my younger brothers, Jake and Chase, inherited, it skipped right over me.

On the road behind us, a truck blasts its horn, and a second later the traffic starts to move, vehicles weaving around the blockage we're causing.

The woman jams her finger at me again. "This is on you."

I follow her gaze to where the nose of my truck is jammed up against her car, and for the first time, I look beyond the bumper hanging loose and take in the rest of the vehicle. "Hey, I've seen more life in a junkyard. This thing was on life support long before it met me."

She lets out a short laugh. "Wow. Way to own your mistake. Did they teach you that kind of charm in jerk school, or is it just natural talent?"

The first ripple of annoyance pulses inside me. I bite it back. No way am I letting some stranger get under my skin. I woke up this morning with a buzz in my veins and a smile on my lips. No doubt a welcome change for my family. Even I know I've been grumpy as fuck these past twenty-two months, but who can blame me? As the oldest Sullivan boy, I've grown up leading the plays. I spent my teens hauling Chase from parties and Jake out of trouble, making sure their sorry asses got to every practice and class on time. Then nine years ago, all my dreams came true when I was drafted to the Stormhawks. Wearing the red jersey for my home team was everything. Until one bad tackle took it all away. To go from being top of my game to standing on the sidelines, watching my little brothers carry on playing the best football of their lives without me, hurt as bad as my injury. But all that changes today.

I can already hear Coach Allen's voice in my head: *You're back, Dylan. You've made the team.* They're the words I've lived for. No way am I missing this meeting. If I leave right now, I can still make it.

I pull two hundred-dollar bills from my wallet and push

them into her hands. "Here, blondie. For the damage. It should be more than enough."

She looks down at the money then up at me, those green eyes still blazing. "You can't just..." she starts. "This isn't about the money, you—"

But I'm already walking back to the truck, my mind on the meeting with Coach Allen. The past few months of practice have gone well. It felt damn good to lace up my cleats, feel the weight of the pads on my shoulders again. Even if Jake and Chase didn't hold back, knocking me flat on my ass a few times just to prove I was ready.

Now I finally am. I won't be returning to tight end. That's Jake's position now. Watching Jake—just a year younger than me—step into my old role as tight end after my injury nearly killed me. But I've been training in my old college position as fullback and it's working for me. I'll be the lead blocker, clearing a path for the running back, taking hits, protecting the quarterback too sometimes when the defense comes charging. A fullback is less speed but more grit. And that quarterback I'll be protecting? My little brother, Chase.

His move from the Kansas City Trailblazers was one of the biggest trades of the offseason—a headline-grabbing deal that brought him home to Denver, to the Stormhawks. Now the three Sullivan brothers are suiting up for the same team for the first time.

Yeah. It's perfect.

The roar of my V8 engine fills the air, and I swear it sounds like freedom. But as I drive away, I can't help a final glance in the rearview mirror. I feel a tug of guilt that I should've stayed to make sure blondie's engine started. I'm about to pull over and reluctantly offer to help quickly when she raises her hand and flips me her middle finger. A smile tugs at the corner of my mouth. Looks like I'm not the only one who went to jerk school, but right now I'm late for the start of the rest of my life and nothing is going to hold me back.

"I'm sorry, Dylan."

The words hit me like a blindside tackle—vicious and impossible to swerve. Coach Allen's gray hair and matching handlebar mustache blur before me as I dip my head. The floor feels as though it's crumbling beneath my feet. Not just the floor —my whole world. Obliterated.

"I'll cut the crap," Coach Allen continues, his usually gruff tone edged with regret. "Your fitness is good. Your strength is good. I've never seen anyone recover from an ACL tear like you have. But you've lost your speed, and you hesitate for a fraction before a tackle. That fraction matters. I can't give you the fullback position or any other space on the team. It kills me to do this, but your time playing for the Stormhawks is over."

A roaring noise builds in my ears. My mouth is as dry as the dirt track leading to the ranch. The silence draws out. I know I should fill it. Tell Coach I understand. It's what he wants to hear. But football is my life.

I still remember how alive I felt in that last game against the Indianapolis Riverrunners. As tight end, my job was to stir up plays, make the win. I was unstoppable. Right up until I wasn't. Until the third quarter and the moment their linebacker made a late tackle. I tried to swerve and jump, but his helmet connected with my knee and I went down, the pain blinding. The diagnosis was a complete ACL tear that meant operations, physical therapy, and months of sitting on my ass.

Every grueling stretch. Every icy bath in the lake on Oakwood Ranch last winter. Every vitamin and superfood smoothie. I did it. All I cared about was getting back to football. I don't know who I am without it.

Coach leans forward from where he's perched on the edge of the desk in front of me, his strong hand clasping my shoulder. "I'm truly sorry, son. I know this isn't what you wanted to hear."

Despite the crushing weight of disappointment, I force my head up. This is Coach Allen—the man who played a decade as a Stormhawks offensive lineman before joining the coaching staff and making his way up the ranks to head coach. He's a man who commands respect, and he's got mine.

"You had a great run," Coach continues, moving around the desk and returning to his chair. It squeaks with his shifting bulk.

"Nine years," I reply, ignoring how the last season and most of the one before were spent injured. "Your first draft," I add.

Coach nods, the regret evident in the lines of his face. Like me, he's probably thinking back to the year he took over as head coach. The year I was drafted in the first round, pick twelve. Fresh out of college. Coach Allen has been on the sidelines for every win and every loss of my pro football career. He's the closest thing to a father figure I've had since Dad died in a ranching accident when I was eleven. Even now, as Coach crushes the last of my dreams, I respect the man. Which makes seeing the pity in his eyes like salt rubbed in an open wound.

"Dylan," he says, softer now, "the Stormhawks will always be your team and your family. You know you're welcome here and at Stormhawks Park anytime."

"Thanks," I mumble over the roar in my ears. I can't breathe. Can't think. My body moves on autopilot. I push back the chair and leave his office.

The walls in the hallway feel like they're closing in. The smell of sweat and dirt and cleaning products claws at the back of my throat. That unforgettable scent of the locker room—the place I've lived and breathed for so many years. I feel like someone's slammed a helmet in my gut. Everything I've ever wanted is gone. For good this time.

All those months of rehab. The hours of practice, getting my fitness back. The bruising drills with Jake and Chase on the football field Mama built at the back of the ranch after Dad died, when she threw us into football to give us something to focus our grief on. Even in the darkest moments of the last couple of years, I've clung to a whisper of hope. But it was all for nothing.

I hit the parking lot. The heat of the afternoon and the bright July sun sting my eyes. I don't know where I'm going, only that I have to get away from here. My phone buzzes in my pocket. I don't need to look to know it'll be Mama. I imagine Coach Allen picked up the phone to call her the second I left.

Mama isn't just the woman who raised us single-handedly after Dad died—she's one of the best NFL agents in the business. She took on the job the moment the college scouts came knocking for me first, then Jake the year after, and Chase two years after that. "No" isn't a word in Mama Sullivan's vocabulary. She's negotiated every contract, every bonus clause, every sponsorship deal. She's the reason the Sullivan name means something. She built our careers from the ground up, while still managing to cook our dinners, call us out when our egos got too big, and pick us up through illness and injuries. Last year, when Jake's reputation as a bad boy got out of hand, it was Mama who fixed it with a huge profile piece in *Sports Magazine*, written by Harper, now Jake's fiancée.

And right now, Mama will want to tell me all the reasons it's going to be OK. She'll pull out a game plan. TV appearances. Commentating. A new kind of career. But anything she'll suggest is a life on the sidelines watching others live my dream. I can't face it. I can't face her. The phone stops ringing. A second later, it buzzes again and I turn it to silent and shove it in the back pocket of my jeans.

~

I don't remember the drive. One moment, I'm pulling out of the stadium parking lot. The next, I'm parked outside The Hay Barn bar and pushing through the doors with a baseball cap pulled low to hide my face. The smell of beer and fried food hits me. Country tunes carry from the jukebox in the corner. The place is familiar and cozy. Wood panels and dim lighting. Stormhawks memorabilia covers the walls, and over the bar sits a set of bull horns. It's the only bar I drink in. Usually with Jake and Chase in tow, the three of us tearing apart our games, ribbing each other over our mistakes.

The Hay Barn's owner, Flic, raises a questioning eyebrow as I approach, already reaching for my usual light beer as I slide onto one of the barstools. Her long, white-blonde hair is pulled back into two braids, and as always, she's dressed in a black tee and tight black jeans, her sharp eyes missing nothing. Her hand stops as I shake my head.

"Bourbon," I say. "And keep it coming."

She slides an empty tumbler across the bar and pours in a generous measure of amber liquid. "Rough day?"

I ignore the question and her worried frown as I knock back the glass in one gulp. The smoky liquid scalds its way down my throat before settling into a warm burn in my chest. The sensation doesn't dull the hollow ache inside me, but it numbs the edges.

I motion at the empty glass, forcing out a thanks before gulping it back like the first. It burns a little less but still heats my veins.

Flic shoots me a concerned look before stepping away to serve another customer. The bar is quiet at this time on a Thursday afternoon, and I feel her staring even as she pours drinks for other customers. I know I need to say something. Flic isn't just the owner of the unofficial Stormhawks team and fans bar, and a fan herself: she's a friend. More like a sister considering the amount of time she spent hanging out with me and my brothers on the ranch while her parents ran this place.

"Don't call them," I say when Flic moves to refill my glass. "Please," I add.

"Who?" she asks with an innocence that two shots in is almost funny.

"Jake, Chase, or Mama. I'm fine. I just need some bourbon and some time to myself."

She assesses me for a long moment before she nods. "OK. But hand over the keys to your fancy new truck."

"I'm not stupid, Flic," I reply. "I'm not gonna drive it."

"So you don't need your keys then." She waves the bottle at me with one hand, holding out the other.

I shrug, throwing her my keys. A second later, my glass is full. I take a sip and finally the alcohol settles like a warm blanket over the sting of disappointment. I might as well keep drinking. Nothing can make this day any worse.

TWO

IZZY

"And the guy's still alive?" Flic's voice rings with surprise.

"I know, right? Who calls someone over the age of ten *little lady*?" I huff, taking another sip of my beer. My mind flashes back to the moment the truck door opened and out stepped arrogance personified: dark, cropped hair, massive shoulders, towering height, dark eyes, and that damn smirk. Like he knew just how sexy he was.

"Why are all the hot guys absolute dicks?" I ask, gripping the bottle tighter as I breathe in The Hay Barn's aromas of wood polish and beer and try to let go of my frustration. I'm no football fan like Flic, but I like the small-town vibe at The Hay Barn and the old country tunes playing on the jukebox. It helps that my only real friend in the world owns the place.

"I'm surprised you didn't give him your number." Flic grins. "I thought hot guys who treated you like shit were your type."

I laugh. "If he hadn't ditched faster than a one-night stand realizing it's Sunday morning church time, maybe I would have. Or maybe I'd have put his ass on the ground. He didn't even apologize for rear-ending me." I try to laugh, but the noise comes out strangled as I remember the scent of his aftershave—

like worn leather and cedar—as he pushed those bills into my hands.

Of course it happens to me.

Of course just when I'm about to be out of a job and a place to live at twenty-seven, my car breaks down in the middle of traffic. Of course the person who hits me is a jerk.

"But he gave you two hundred bucks," my friend says, her long blonde braids brushing the top of the polished bar where she's leaning over. "For a piece of junk older than I am? Hey, maybe this is your new career."

"What?" I groan and shift on the barstool. It's worn smooth and warm where the skin on the back of my thighs meets the leather.

"Breaking down in front of rich assholes who'll throw you cash and drive away—sounds lucrative."

I shoot her a glare, but she's clearly pleased with herself, her smile wide enough to light the room. Flic is effortlessly cool and gorgeous inside and out. Dressed in all black like a rocker bartender goddess, she's the kind of person who knows how to read a room without breaking a sweat. It's infuriating how she always looks put together. But I know her too well to be intimidated. I've seen her sprawled out on the couch in my trailer in mismatched pajamas, crying over Hallmark Christmas movies in the middle of July.

The mention of my career—or what used to be my career—hits harder than I want to admit. For the last eight years, I've had the best damn job in the world: working for Bill, my granddaddy on my dad's side, breeding and raising rodeo horses on his ranch east of Denver out near Shamrock, just off Route 36.

He's never let me call him Granddaddy. Just Bill. The man with the weathered hat, sun-lined face, and a faint limp to his step. He taught me everything I know about ranching. As a kid, I spent every weekend and summer I was allowed out there. And when I came crawling back to Denver at nineteen—

divorced, broke, and dragging more baggage than a rodeo trailer —he took me on as a ranch hand without a moment's hesitation.

Over the last few years, we've both ignored how his health was slipping. Pretended we didn't notice the coughs or the way his steps slowed. But just before Christmas, the doctor gave it to him straight. Told him to sell up and rest or not expect to see many more New Years. After that, every phone call, every meeting he took, felt like a countdown. And the truth is, deep down, I'd always known my time with Bill wasn't permanent. I just didn't realize how fast the clock would run out. I lived with the weight of it pressing down daily, knowing I'd be jobless again, back to square one. No savings. No security. Just more uncertainty in a life already full of it.

I don't blame him for selling. He wants to travel and see the world, and I'm happy for him. I just wish it was me buying the ranch. Instead, with no money to do that, I'm back dodging my parents' calls and their "what next?" questions I can't answer. Because thinking about what's next means thinking about Mad, and I can't go there right now. I have more than enough to be freaking out about.

I force another laugh, but it sounds wrong. My eyes squeeze shut for a moment, betraying more than I'd like. Without Bill's ranch, I'll have no paycheck and no place to live.

"Too soon to mention your career?" Flic asks, her tone softening.

I open my eyes to find her watching me with concern. "Just a bit," I say, managing a smile.

Flic flashes me a sympathetic look as she steps away to serve a couple of guys at the other end of the bar. Behind me, the corner table erupts in laughter. Glasses clink over the music. A group of men in red football jerseys and baseball caps are throwing back beers. I catch one of them elbowing his friend and jerking his chin in my direction. I don't bother flipping them the finger. I've had enough of men and their opinions for one day.

I stare absently at the job postings on my phone until Flic returns. "It's a shame you didn't get that guy's number for 'repairs.'" She makes air quotes around "repairs," her expression as suggestive as her tone.

I laugh despite myself, loving Flic for trying to cheer me up. "Did you forget the part where he was a jerk?" I ask.

"Come on, Izzy. Jerk or not, in the three years we've known each other, you haven't had a single date."

Sometimes I forget we've only known each other three years. It feels like I've known Flic forever. We met at the county rodeo. She was running the beer stand and I was watching the show, checking out a mare I knew was coming up for auction soon. The owner swore up and down she had "the heart of a champion," but for a barrel racer, she wouldn't stop spooking at every stray sound. Flic handed me my first drink that night, and we've been friends ever since.

"Oh, and you're swiping right and out there every night of the week now, are you?" I shoot back.

Flic shrugs. "I've got this place to run. What's your excuse?"

"With my track record? I'd rather be single forever." For a split second, it's not my present situation tugging at my gut; it's the weight of my past and my mistakes and what a disappointment I am to my family.

"But it's such a waste. You're gorgeous, Iz, and the annoying thing is, you have no idea. I bet you just threw those clothes on this morning without a second thought and you still look like that."

"It's July. It's too hot for more clothes than this." I glance down at my black tank top and cutoffs and shrug. "Besides, the only men I meet are either total dicks or overachievers, and I've already got enough of those in my life."

Flic falls silent. She knows I'm talking about my family. Just as she knows it's a sore subject.

"My parents know Bill's selling up. They want me to come home," I admit quietly.

Flic leans closer, her hand resting on my arm, offering me the support she knows I need. "Will you go?" There's no judgment in her question and I love her for it.

The thought of going back to live in the house I grew up in sends a shot of dread straight through me. The house itself is nice enough. One of those cookie-cutter homes in Aurora Hills, East Denver. And it's not my parents, either. Not really. They're good people, always offering to help me. But they're doctors. They live their lives by structure and routine.

Living under their roof again would mean returning to a life that once felt like it might suffocate me. A life where every step I had to take to become the daughter they wanted was mapped out for me. It doesn't help that I'm the youngest in the family. Where my sister, Amelia, and my brother, David, followed the plan—med school, white coats, perfect families, picket fences—I've always been the wild card in their otherwise pristine deck. The one who never felt like they belonged.

I even tried to play their game. I got the grades. I followed them into med school. But it wasn't for me. One month in, I dropped out to marry a country singer. I was eighteen and in love, and when he promised me freedom and fire and forever, I believed him. But of course, that all fell apart faster than a cheap buckle at a rodeo.

I start to shake my head at Flic's question, about to tell her I don't know what choice I have, when movement at the far end of the bar catches my eye. The guy in the black baseball cap, lost to his bourbon, turns on his barstool and stands, heading in the direction of the restrooms. I didn't pay him any attention when I first arrived, but I'm hardly going to forget those impossibly broad shoulders. That half-hidden scowl.

I shake my head. "Unbelievable."

Of course he's here. Of course the universe would drop this man back in my path for the second time today, on the same day Bill's ranch sale is going through. The horses—Moonlight, Rusty, Bramble, Logan, and so many more. I love them all. I know they'll be well cared for by the ranch out in Dallas that bought them, but saying goodbye this morning broke a piece of my heart I don't think will ever heal.

Suddenly I'm irritated as hell, like no time has passed since those bills were shoved in my hands.

"What?" Flic asks.

"That's the guy," I say under my breath. "The dick driver."

She frowns, and then barks a laugh. "Dylan Sullivan called you 'little lady'? That's hilarious."

Dylan Sullivan? I know who he is. He's Flic's friend, along-side Jake and Chase. She spent so much time at their ranch growing up, she talks about them like they're her brothers. They're regulars here, but with no interest in football players or their egos, I've always kept out of their way. The last time I saw Dylan Sullivan, he was full-bearded, shaggy-haired, and walking with a knee brace. It's no wonder I didn't recognize him earlier.

I watch him as he stalks toward the restrooms at the back of the bar. He doesn't so much as glance my way. What does a guy like him—a professional football player with money and fame, and no doubt every woman in Denver swooning at his feet—have to look so pissed about?

"I'll be right back," I murmur, slipping off the stool and striding after him, my annoyance pounding in my ears. The door to the restrooms swings closed just ahead, and I push through, letting it thud behind me. The hallway is narrow and dimly lit, the kind of place where more than a few bad decisions have been made.

He's standing halfway between the men's room and the

hallway exit, looking like he's taken a wrong turn. He shifts at the sound of the door, his eyes locking on mine.

For a second, neither of us says anything. Then I break the silence. "You," I hiss, hand digging into the pocket of my shorts for the bills he shoved at me earlier. "You think you can just throw money at me and drive off like some big-shot hero?"

Beneath the baseball cap, his jaw tightens. "I paid for the damage, didn't I?"

"That's not the point." I close the gap between us and thrust the bills at his chest. "Take your damn money back."

He doesn't move. Doesn't reach for it. Just looks at me with those brooding eyes that somehow manage to be both infuriating and unfairly hot.

"You really want to do this in a bar hallway?" he replies, voice low and rough.

"I didn't start this," I fire back.

He shifts closer. I don't back up.

We're toe to toe, the bills still pressed against his chest, crumpled between us, but I don't drop my hand. His breath is steady. Mine, not so much. His leather and wood aftershave fills my senses, making my head spin like I've drunk ten beers instead of one.

His eyes drop slow and deliberate like he's drinking me in, and when they drag over my body, I feel something low in my stomach clench tight. His eyes settle on the curve of my hip, then flick back to mine, and that ache between my legs roars to life, and oh my God, I've forgotten this feeling. This fierce, fiery want I haven't felt in years.

And the look in Dylan's eyes right now? It isn't hunger—it's need. It leaves me feeling both exposed and somehow powerful too. My life is a mess. My job's about to disappear. My entire future is uncertain. But none of that exists in this moment, and suddenly all I want to do is lose myself.

I'm not sure who makes the first move. All I know is one

moment we're staring at each other, both gunning for this fight. In the next, there's a shift. A spark. I don't know which of us moves first, but suddenly, his mouth is crashing into mine.

It's not soft. Not gentle. It's as furious as the anger between us just moments ago. It's his hands gripping my waist, his body pressed to mine. It's fire in my core and the hottest, most infuriating kiss I've ever had. Dylan's mouth claims mine like he has something to prove, and my back hits the wall with a thud. He cages me in with his body, one hand fisting the hem of my tank top, the other tangled in my hair. And all I can do is pull him closer.

His tongue sweeps into my mouth, and I meet him with every stroke, matching his intensity. His hands are everywhere —running down my body, over my hips, around my ass. His touch is possessive and a little desperate. And fuck, I've never wanted anything more.

Then reality crashes back into my thoughts. My life is imploding. And like a cherry on top, I'm kissing a pro athlete asshole like it's the best idea I've ever had.

Typical, Izzy, absolutely typical.

I pull back, breathless and furious, with myself as much as him. "What the hell are you doing?"

Dylan's eyes narrow. "You kissed me."

"The hell I did. You're the one who stepped into my space."

He shakes his head, looking ready for another fight. His lips are still parted, like maybe he wants to say something else, and I shove the crumpled bills into his chest again, harder this time.

"I don't want your damn money," I say.

He rolls his eyes, finally taking the bills. "Fine, don't have it then."

"Great."

"Good," he fires back.

We stare at each other like we're both daring the other to say one more word. I don't trust myself not to open my big mouth. I spin on my heel and march back toward the bar, heart pounding and heat still thrumming through every inch of my body.

Everything about this man screams jerk. I'm certain Dylan is just like every other man I've been drawn to in my life. And right now, that is the last thing I need.

Note to self: Never kiss Dylan Sullivan again. Not if he's the last man on earth. Not if the world is ending. Not if my life depends on it.

With any luck, I'll never see him again.

THREE

DYLAN

I don't know how the kiss happened—if it was her or me or both of us—only that in the moment, with the bourbon swimming through my veins, cloaking my thoughts in the best way, I didn't want to stop. And the woman with the smart mouth and legs for days? She gave as good as she got. The way her fingers dug into my shoulders like she hated me and wanted me all at once. Right up until she pulled away, green eyes flashing and ready to fight.

I stare at the door she disappeared through, my dick still hard and my blood still hot. I've kissed my fair share of women, but nothing like that. That was... fire and something raw that I poured every last drop of my frustration into.

There has been no room in my life lately for anything that wasn't getting me back to playing football. But it's not like I had women lined up before the injury. I don't flirt. I speak my mind, and more often than not, it lands too harsh and gets me in trouble.

My love life has never been a priority. When I wasn't at practice or playing football, or helping out with the Stormhawks youth coaching outreach program, I kept busy on the ranch.

Fixing up the paddocks. Repairing the fences when storms took them down. Painting the barn every offseason. Keeping things looking nice for Mama, even if the ranch wasn't being used for work and hadn't been since Dad died twenty years ago.

I guess there was Kate, a fitness instructor who lived a few blocks from me in the city. We met six months before the Indianapolis Riverrunners linebacker took out my knee. She didn't seem to mind that football came first, didn't expect grand gestures or romance. We got along... fine. But I didn't miss her when I ended things the day after my injury. Didn't think about her once when I was laid up at the ranch. There was no spark with Kate. Nothing close to what flared just now with blondie. And I don't even know her name.

Hell, I don't even like her. And she clearly hates me. I must be more buzzed than I realized if I'm even thinking about women.

Fuck. I need another drink.

I push through the doors into the bar, pulling my cap lower. The Hay Barn's filling up with the after-work crowd—ranchers, mechanics, football fans. It's the usual noise of boots on hardwood, country music, talk, and laughter. I keep my head down and pray no one recognizes me. I don't want small talk with a well-meaning fan. I don't want sympathy. All I want is the burn of another bourbon.

Flic eyes me warily as I take my seat, but she silently tops me up.

I swirl the bourbon in my glass and take a deep gulp as someone fills the stool beside me. I glance over to find a weathered old cowboy settling in, wide-brimmed hat shadowing his face. It takes a moment, but I recognize him. Bill was a good friend of my dad's back in the day. They both bred rodeo horses and would often swap stallions for strong bloodlines, back when the ranch was alive with the smell of hay and the thunder of hooves. When Dad died and Mama had to sell the horses, it was

Bill who bought them. She couldn't run a ranch and raise three boys on her own.

"I'll take a beer, please, Felicity," he says, his voice as rough as his calloused hands.

I raise my empty glass. "And another bourbon for me. Put them both on my tab."

A moment later the fresh drinks are in front of us and Bill takes a long sip, the foam of beer lying thick on his upper lip before he wipes it away.

"This was supposed to be my first beer as a retired rancher," he says, dropping his hat down between us.

"What happened?" I ask. Either the last bourbon has loosened my lips or I'm seeking distraction from my own troubles. I'm too far gone to care which.

"Doc told me to retire, or..." He shrugs. "Breaks my heart to say goodbye to those horses. I love them like family, but I'll be no good to them dead. So I'm selling up and going to see if this world is all it's cracked up to be. Or I was supposed to. I had a deal lined up with a ranch out by Dallas. They were taking everything. Horses, equipment. All my stores. All of it gone in one go." Bill sighs, a broken man I can relate to. "But the buyer never showed. Can you believe that?" He pulls out a folded document and drops it on top of the hat. "Figures, doesn't it? Had everything packed to go tomorrow. All the guy had to do was meet me and sign the contract." He taps the folded pages before concentrating on his beer.

My fingers move without thinking, brushing the rim of Bill's hat. I think of my dad and the cowboy hat that still hangs on the hook in the hall at the ranch all these years later. Dad was larger than life—a man with an easy smile and a way of making everyone feel at home. The ranch was his kingdom, the horses his passion, but he always had time to throw a ball or listen to a problem. He died too young, too suddenly. Knocked on the head by the hoof of a spooked horse in a thunderstorm. A few degrees to the left, a few seconds different, and he'd still be here.

I blink slowly, the bourbon tugging loose the edges of thoughts I usually keep tucked away, hidden. In another world, I'd have worked alongside him, breeding horses. When I was a kid, it was all I wanted.

I think of Oakwood Ranch. It's where I grew up, where Mama lives. Of all of us brothers, it's just me who lives there full time—a grown-ass man who had to give up the sweet loft apartment a few blocks from the Stormhawks training facility because I could barely hobble from one room to another, let alone face the five flights of stairs to my apartment.

The room tilts. Oakwood Ranch is my home. Those rich green paddocks that stretch over the land, split by weathered wooden fences. The sprawling white ranch house, the tall red barn. Acres of beauty framed by the craggy foothills and the distant peaks of the Rocky Mountains, snowcapped even now in the blistering July heat, with the air as dry as dirt and the sun unrelenting.

Earlier today I couldn't wait to leave, but now all I can think is that it's a ranch that hasn't seen horses or real ranch work for two decades.

I finish my drink and the warmth spreads through me, making my body feel loose, my mind stepping out of itself, drifting away. I don't even have to think as I say the next words that come into my head. "We've got space at Oakwood."

Bill laughs, a strong hand clapping my back. "You're a football player. What do you know about ranching?"

"I *was* a football player. I'm not anymore." My eyes drop down to my chest where it feels like a knife must be lodged. "And I remember some." The hell if it's true, but the weight of Bill's hand on my shoulder has reminded me of Coach Allen's pitying smile.

I don't know how much time passes, how many more drinks

we share, but the late-night drinkers have replaced the after-work crowd by the time a plan is taking shape.

"It's poetic," I say, my words slurring at the edges. "You bought our horses from Mama after Dad died. Now I can buy your horses from you."

Bill is all smiles now, talking about how much he loves his horses. How lucky he was to have the best ranch hand in Colorado helping him out. Both of us are sold on our idea. "You agree to keep my ranch hand on for a month—no, let's say six weeks—so I know the horses will be looked after while you find your feet, and they're yours. Up to you whether you keep Brooks on after that."

I nod, trying to stay sitting up straight on my stool. I scan the bar for blondie, but she's gone. It's an effort to keep my thoughts on the conversation.

"What do ya say?" Bill asks, sounding a little tipsy now, too. But he's got nothing on me. Man, I'm drunk. Room spinning, everything is fuzzy and funny and who cares about football anyway? Maybe it's the bourbon that makes me do it. Maybe it's the memories of my dad and the hole his death left behind. Maybe it's the need to escape the sting of failure. Whatever the reason, I raise my glass to Bill's and pick up the contract.

"How hard can ranching be anyway?"

FOUR

DYLAN

JAKE: *Dyl, wake up and get your ass downstairs.*

CHASE: *What happened?*

JAKE: *Dylan fucked up!*

CHASE: *What did he do?*

JAKE: *Get back to the ranch with Mama and see for yourself.*

The banging is relentless. Loud. Invasive. Like someone's taking a hammer to the inside of my skull. The pounding only gets louder. Where the hell is that noise coming from? How much did I drink last night?

I groan as I force my eyes open, squinting against the daylight spilling into the room. Relief trickles in when I recognize my bed, my dark gray walls, and the solid wood furniture of my room. Last night's clothes are tossed over a chair and an empty water glass sits on the nightstand. My eyes catch on my gym bag on the floor by my weights rack, the bright white of my new cleats sitting on top, ready for the training camp in Arizona I'm not going to.

I'm not on the team.

My stomach churns. Last night's bourbon and the bitterness of disappointment burn the back of my throat. I can't think about this right now. I pull the covers over my head, cutting out the light but doing nothing to keep out the noise. Why does it sound like the entire population of Denver is outside my window?

Then come the footsteps. Light and fast, tapping on the wood staircase. A second later, my door flies open.

"Uh... Dylan?" Harper's voice cuts through the haze. "You might want to come see this."

I pull the cover down an inch and crack open an eye, hissing softly at the light. Harper stands in a white sundress that floats around her ankles, her expression halfway between amusement and concern. My soon-to-be sister-in-law is petite but fierce, with brown hair that always looks like it's styled ready for a magazine cover. She's not one to burst into my room, though, which means something is definitely wrong.

"Whatever it is," I mutter, "it can wait."

Harper hesitates. "It's just... well—"

Heavy footsteps cut her off, and a second later Jake appears. A year younger and an inch shorter than me, with the same thick, dark hair, he's still massive as he towers over the bed. He's already dressed for the day in jeans and a fitted gray tee that stretches across his broad chest.

Before I can stop him, Jake's ripping my covers off and throwing them on the floor. "Rise and shine, sleeping beauty," he says with a grin that I know—from the number of times I've hauled his ass out of fights—spells trouble.

"What the hell?" I growl. The sound of my own voice pounds in my head. "I could've been naked. Or had a woman in here."

Jake snorts. "Please. You've spent the last two years celibate and sulking. The only thing in here is you and your pity party." I don't miss the amusement Harper is trying to hide or the wink he gives her. "You really don't remember me carrying your sorry ass home from the bar last night, do you?"

"What are you talking about?" I ask, not sure I want to know the answer.

Jake's deep chuckle echoes across the room. "Oh, Dyl," he says. "You've always been the good one. Mr. Reliable. But when you fuck up, you do it monumentally. Now, get up before I dump a bucket of water on you."

The water isn't an empty threat. It was Mama's go-to move for getting us out of bed when we overslept. But it was always Jake and Chase who got the water treatment. Never me. Jake's right—I am the good one. Jake's always been the one who lands himself in trouble, and Chase is the jokester who seems to bounce through life. They've been in more scrapes than I can count.

I pull myself up slowly, every movement causing another stab of pain from my hangover. Flashes of the night before hit me: The Hay Barn. Handing my keys to Flic. Telling her to keep the bourbon coming. The night is a blur, but I have a vague memory of kissing someone.

I look at Harper, already cringing. "I didn't try to kiss you, did I?"

Harper's laugh hits right between my pounding temples. "Do you think you'd be alive right now if you did?"

She makes a good point. As I search my fuzzy brain for more details of last night, I have a vague sense of singing my way to Jake's truck, Harper with the keys to my truck, following behind. And underneath all of it, the hollow ache of why I was drinking my ass into oblivion in the first place. Coach Allen's words rush back into my spinning head.

Your time playing for the Stormhawks is over.

Whatever emotions I tried to drown at the bar last night didn't stay down. They rush back, feeling like another kick to the balls. I thought I could come back from my injury and prove everyone wrong.

I glance at Jake from the corner of my eye. Does he know? His comment about my "pity party" rattles in my head.

"Where's Mama?" I ask, knowing I'll have to face her at some point, surprised it's not her dragging me out of bed.

It's Harper who answers. "She's at the press event for Chase. His first official event for the Stormhawks."

Shit! It must be after ten in the morning. "I was supposed to be there."

Jake steps to Harper's side, throwing an arm over her shoulders. Hard to believe they once hated each other. "That's the least of your worries right now, Dyl. I'm guessing you don't remember buying something last night?"

The first prickles of unease begin to spread through me. I blink at Jake, trying to piece it together.

"Oh, this is gonna be good." Jake laughs. "Get dressed and come downstairs. You've really fucked up this time, big brother."

Swallowing down the nausea, I throw on a pair of jeans and yesterday's shirt, ignoring the fact that it smells of bourbon and regret. Barefoot, I follow them down the stairs.

"Seriously, what did I buy?" I ask.

Jake opens the front door and I step outside, shielding my eyes to the bright morning light. Fuck, my head is killing me!

The ranch is... It's the ranch. It's my home. It's the place I grew up. As always, the land stretches before me in a patchwork of fenced paddocks. Beyond them, the foothills rise, their rugged edges cutting into the sky. Deep green spruce trees grow to the far left, hiding the lake from view. And in the distance, the ghostly peaks of the Rockies loom. It would be beautiful if it wasn't for the chaos unfolding on the driveway.

There are trucks with their engines rumbling, and horse trailers parked side by side. Men in work boots and gloves lead horses into the paddocks. A bay mare snorts as she's unloaded, her coat gleaming a rich chestnut. Her mane and tail ripple like black silk. Another horse follows. Then another and another. Each one more striking than the last.

"What the...?"

I scrunch up my eyes, realization washing over me in a crashing wave of nausea and dread.

Jake leans against the porch railing like he has all the time in the world. "You're remembering now, aren't you?"

If my head wasn't pounding with the worst hangover of my life, I'd be kicking his ass right now. But all I can do is stare at the horses filling the paddocks as the memory of the bar last night slams into me: the bourbon, Bill Brooks, a contract on the bar.

"Tell me I didn't," I say, my voice a croak as I bury my head in my hands.

"Oh, you did." Jake's laugh is low and deep.

"But I don't know the first thing about running my own ranch," I mutter. "I don't *care* about ranching."

"Clearly."

I shove past him, stumbling down the steps barefoot, squinting as the bright sun hits the back of my eyes. My jeans feel heavy, my shirt clinging to the sweat building on my back as I wave my arms toward one of the men unloading horses.

"Stop!" I shout. "There's been a mistake."

The man turns to me with a patient smile, his hands gripping the lead rope of a dapple-gray mare. He's wearing a battered cowboy hat pulled low over his brow. "Bill said you might say that. Told me to tell you a deal's a deal."

"But... you can't hold someone to a deal they made when they were drunk!" Even as the words fly out, I have a sudden memory of calling the bank and transferring the funds to Bill.

Shit!

The man adjusts his hat and shrugs. "All I know is Bill's on a plane to the Bahamas. He said to tell you he'll check in when he's back in a few months."

"A few months?" My voice cracks embarrassingly high.

Jake, of course, doubles over laughing behind me.

The man keeps going, unfazed. "He also said to remind you that you have the equipment and supplies to get you set up, and you've hired his best ranch hand for a minimum of six weeks. Brooks'll be here soon. Believe me, you'll want to keep this one."

I rub at my head, trying to keep up with the whirlwind of information, but the man has already turned back to unloading horses, whistling to the next worker to bring the tack boxes. Help from Bill's best ranch hand can't come soon enough.

"How many horses are there?" I ask.

"Eighteen," he calls over his shoulder. "Mares in those paddocks. You've got one pregnant mare with a late foaling. She's due next month." He points. "Foals with their mothers over there. Couple of seasoned rodeo geldings, and the stallions are in the far paddock. Ranch is in OK shape considering," he continues, and I think of the hours I've spent repairing fences, tending the paddock grass, keeping it looking like a real ranch, even if it was an empty one. I did it for Mama. Not for this. "But you've still got some repairs to do."

I turn, taking it all in. Eighteen horses. Eighteen living, breathing responsibilities I never wanted outside of a bourbon-fueled moment of insanity.

Jake appears beside me, clapping a hand on my back. "Looks like you're a rancher now, Dyl."

The words crash into me as I stare at the equipment being hauled into a barn I haven't set foot in for months. Last I checked, it was where we stored old football equipment and the boxes of Stormhawks merch we get sent every year. It's all too much. Too loud. Too real. This place—my home—has been my refuge during my recovery. And now it's crawling with people and noise and a future I want no part of.

My jaw tightens. My mood curdles.

I can't do this. I don't want to do this.

Hell, I *won't* do this.

~

A couple of hours later, the ranch is quiet again as the last truck kicks up a cloud of dust on the road out from the ranch and it's just me, Jake, and Harper... and eighteen rodeo horses I don't have the first clue how to look after.

I nurse my second coffee in the kitchen at the back of the house. It's a large open space with a long bench table on one side and modern kitchen units on the other. Every few seconds, I stare out the open back door. Jake's yellow Labrador retriever, Buck, is lying half in, half out, tail wagging tentatively as he watches the horses graze beyond the fences, like he isn't sure what to make of the new arrivals. *You and me both, Buck!*

Harper slides a sandwich in front of me and I nod my thanks, making quick work of the food. Between the sandwich, the second coffee, and the two Tylenols I downed earlier, the brutal edge to my hangover has dulled. But nothing touches the tightness in my chest, like a weight pressing down. All I want to do is go back to bed and wallow in my failure.

I can't give you the fullback position or any other space on the team.

Across the kitchen, Jake leans against the counter, an arm slung around Harper. Seven months into their relationship and they're still obsessed with each other. Their happy faces are the last thing I want to see right now.

"Don't you need to be heading back to the city now?" I ask, shooting Jake a glare.

Jake's smile widens and he shakes his head. "Actually, we thought we'd spend the weekend here."

I usually like that Jake divides his time between the city and the ranch. I like that we get to hang out more, throw a ball around, talk through plays, and continue to repair our relationship after I stupidly spent too many months blaming him for not being on the field the day I got my ACL tear. But right now, I could really use some space. "Could you try and look less happy about this at least?"

It's Harper who replies. "Maybe this could be a good thing." Her voice is soft, like she's trying not to spook a wild animal. It's the closest either of them has come to mentioning the giant fucking elephant in the room. The fact that the only reason I was drinking alone in The Hay Barn last night—the only reason I was drunk enough to buy Bill's horses, the reason my life's currently spiraling out of control—is because my time playing for the Stormhawks is over.

I heave in a deep breath and catch the comforting scent of fresh bread. Mama must've put a loaf in to bake this morning before leaving for Chase's press event. I can just imagine the joy on his face as he holds up his new number 10 jersey for the cameras.

Four years younger and somehow three steps ahead when it comes to charm and talent. Chase got drafted to the Kansas City Trailblazers straight out of college and made it look effortless. But I've seen behind the jokes. I've seen the hours he puts in, the way he plays like he's got something to prove.

Technically, Chase is our cousin—Mama's sister couldn't cope as a single mom, and our parents took Chase in when he was two and I was six. I still remember the shy little boy with the big Afro who barely spoke. It didn't take long for him to find his confidence on the ranch, and as far as I'm concerned, he's never been anything but my little brother.

Buck barks, leaping out the back door at the rumble of a

truck engine, followed by two car doors slamming. A second later, as though my thoughts have summoned him, Chase bursts into the kitchen like a hurricane, Buck dancing around him. My youngest brother is a fireball of energy, as usual, tall and athletic, with a smile that screams he's one second away from causing trouble. There's a new confidence to him since he came home to Denver in the spring. Like he's right where he's meant to be. And I was supposed to be right there with him.

My head spins. Too many thoughts. Too much pain. I need time to process the last twenty-four hours, but with this family, it ain't gonna happen.

"You bought horses, Dyl?" Chase's face lights up like a kid on Christmas morning. "This is awesome!"

I drop my head into my hands. "Not now, Chase."

"Come on, man." He claps a hand on my shoulder. "This is incredible. You going full cowboy?"

I bite back another groan.

"Dylan Sullivan." Mama's voice carries from the open doorway, cutting through the air like a referee's whistle. At home, she's all oversized Stormhawks jerseys and overalls, pinning her gray-blonde bob out of her face. But right now, she steps into the kitchen in loose, smart slacks, a navy blouse, and a matching blazer, looking every inch the unstoppable sports agent she is. She's never said, but I'm certain she has plans for all of us when we hang up our cleats, and drunk-buying horses isn't part of it. "What have you done?"

Her expression is a mixture of exasperation and disbelief, her steel-blue eyes narrowing as she looks from me to the paddocks and the grazing horses beyond. For a second, it's like she's seen a ghost. The last time horses stood on this land, she was newly widowed, doing everything she could to hold it together for three boys who had no idea how much she was hurting. Mama's feelings about making this place a working ranch again never crossed my mind last night. A lot of things didn't.

Suddenly, I feel like a kid again, fumbling over my words. "I... well... last night... Bill Brooks came into the bar and well... I didn't mean to—"

Mama cuts me off, her tone stern but not cruel. "You own eighteen horses. A ranch hand is arriving any minute. And you have no clue what you're doing. Does that about sum it up?"

I nod, unable to argue and not a bit surprised she knows as much as I do. Probably more.

She lets out a long, measured sigh. She never could stay mad with any of us for long. It's just usually Jake or Chase incurring that sharp look. She steps toward me and I feel her worry wash over me. Mama has been by my side every day of the last twenty-two months, making sure I've had every available resource for my recovery, even talking her way into an ACL specialist clinic in LA with a three-year waiting list. And yet, I feel myself bristle. I know what's coming.

"Coach called me yesterday after the meeting. I'm sorry, Dylan. I know it wasn't what you wanted."

I dip my head, unwilling to see the pity I know is written across her face—or worse, my brothers' faces. "You don't sound surprised," I reply.

Mama's arms wrap around me, pulling me into a hug. She's petite, her arms barely reaching around my shoulders, but her hold is strong. "I hoped I was wrong," she says quietly.

"As if that ever happens."

"There's a lot to discuss," she says, moving to the counter and reaching for the coffee pot. "This doesn't have to be the end of your life in football."

My head shoots up, the words rushing out, still edged with a bitterness I don't think will ever leave me. "If I'm not playing football for the Stormhawks, I want nothing to do with the game. Don't set me up with commentating gigs or whatever else you're thinking. I don't need it and I don't want it." I stand then. The weight of my disappointment and the silence from Jake and Chase are too much.

If Mama's surprised by my outburst, she doesn't show it. "Right now, it looks like you've got your hands full anyway," she says.

Jake and I used to talk about picking up where Dad left off someday, but it was just a pipe dream. Something we said after a few beers to feel close to him. I never really thought we would, and right now it's the last thing I want.

Mama's voice softens like she can see where my thoughts have taken me. "You might've signed the deal drunk, but you're sober now, so figure it out."

"We'll help," Chase says. "Won't we, Jake?"

I glance gratefully at Chase, even if his brand of "help" won't stretch far. Where Chase goes, chaos follows. On the football field, he shakes up plays and throws the opposing team into confusion. But off the field is a different story.

Mama shakes her head before Jake can reply. "You, Chase, are only here when you run out of food in your apartment and want feeding. Jake and Harper come and go, too. And you've both got the high-altitude training camp in Arizona coming up. Not to mention pre-season games starting in August."

The reminder is a kick to the balls.

"This is Dylan's mess," Mama says. "He needs to be the one to clear it up. And this ranch isn't going to run itself."

Clear it up. She means find a buyer, and fast. She's right, but I have no idea where to start.

Mama's words are still ringing in my ears when something outside catches my eye. A woman is standing in one of the paddocks, her jeans and white tank top dusty, a dark blonde braid swinging down her back as she rubs the nose of one of the horses.

I frown and I'm out the door in seconds, still barefoot with my coffee in my hand. The bright afternoon sun jabs at my hangover, causing a new throbbing to start behind my eyes. Already, the ranch feels different. It's in the slow amble of the horses in the paddocks and the sound of their soft whinnies. For a gut-wrenching moment, it's like I've stepped back in time twenty years. I'm a kid again, racing outside to help Dad top up the hay, hoping he'll give me that proud smile it felt like he saved just for us boys. Out of nowhere, the grief punches through. Raw in a way I haven't felt in years. It's the last thing I need right now, and so I focus on the woman standing in one of my paddocks, rubbing the neck of a chestnut mare.

"Hey!" I shout, closing the distance between us. "What the hell are you doing?"

The woman doesn't flinch. Doesn't stutter an apology like I half expect. Instead, her shoulders pull back with an easy confidence. She turns around and recognition slams into me. Those feline green eyes, all fire and challenge, lock onto mine.

It's her. The woman whose rusted compact I bumped yesterday. The one I left stranded in traffic, two hundred bucks lighter and zero apologies given.

But that memory gets knocked aside by another. The bar. That kiss. Hot and furious. The way she tore away like she was half a second from either slapping me or dragging me into a dark corner for more. And now she's on my ranch like she owns the place.

Irritation flares. "You," I bite out.

"Me," she says, like we're picking up a conversation instead of hurtling toward another fight.

"If you're after that money you threw back at me last night, you can talk to my lawyer." My voice is sharp and defensive.

She rolls her eyes. "Relax, big guy. I'm not here about my car."

"Then why are you here, blondie?"

"I'm Izzy Brooks? Bill sent me."

My brows slam together. "Sent you? For what?"

A smirk twitches on her lips, but there's steel under it. "I'm his granddaughter," she replies. "And his lead ranch hand. I was part of the deal you and Bill made at the bar last night."

Brooks... the ranch hand Bill threw into the deal. *Izzy Brooks.* Stupid of me to assume the ranch hand I'd hired would be a man...

"Six weeks," I mutter, mostly to myself. Trying to catch up. Trying not to sound like I have no clue what the hell I agreed to.

She nods. "That's what Bill told me. But I've got other offers, so if you've got this all handled, I'll be on my way." She starts to turn.

"Wait," I call out, unable to disguise the panic in my voice. "Sorry. Can we start again?" I stick out my hand. "Dylan Sullivan."

Izzy tugs off a suede work glove, steps closer, and takes my hand. Her grip is strong, her hand warm. In stark comparison, her expression is cool as she takes in my bare feet and rumpled tee.

"I know who you are," she says, releasing my hand like it burns. "Just like I know you're no rancher."

My temper flares. "My dad was a rancher, OK? I grew up raising horses. I'm not a complete idiot."

Even as the words leave my mouth, I hate them. I don't want these damn horses. So why am I pretending any different?

Izzy lets out a short, mocking laugh. "Sure. And I used to braid my doll's hair. Doesn't make me a hairdresser."

Pressure builds in my chest. "Listen—"

"No, you listen," she cuts in. "These horses, they're some of the best rodeo stock in Colorado. If you screw it up, you're not just failing yourself—you're failing them. You can't just play at being a rancher."

She turns away without waiting for a response, her words hitting harder than I'd like. I watch her go and can't help but notice the way her jeans fit like they were made for her. I curse under my breath and turn toward the house. And that's when I see the long silver trailer parked beside the barn.

"What the hell is that?" I call out.

Izzy doesn't even look up. "My home. How else did you expect me to run your ranch? From the city?"

Oh, hell no. I storm inside to an empty kitchen, the others having quickly vacated, and head straight to my room, needing time alone. Needing sleep. Needing this day to be over.

Thoughts of Izzy follow a step behind. That look in her eye, like she knows I'm full of shit. She's a smart-mouthed reminder of how much I've fucked up. My teeth grind just thinking about her and that infuriating smirk. Judging by the glare she just threw my way, the feeling is more than mutual.

You can't just play at being a rancher.

Well, fine. If I can't play football, I don't want to play at anything—especially not pretending I give a damn about ranching. Let someone else play cowboy. I'm done.

FIVE

IZZY

IZZY: Are you sure Dylan's a nice guy? All I'm seeing is a jerk who buys horse stock then disappears for a week!

FLIC: I didn't say he wasn't grumpy, but yeah, he's one of the good guys. You could do a hell of a lot worse!!

IZZY: I'm working for the guy and that's it. Grumpy assholes are not my type.

FLIC: I didn't realize dried-up spinsters had a type!

IZZY: I'm not taking dating advice from a woman who knows every word to every Disney song in existence.

A week passes, and it does nothing to soften the annoyance simmering in my blood. If anything, it's sharper. It's a feeling that started the moment I heard that a drunk pro athlete—a jerk who crashes into women's cars and drives off without an apology—bought my granddaddy's horses. And I'm thrown in as part of the deal, like an afterthought.

I could throttle Bill if I didn't love the stubborn old man so much. Deep down, I know he meant well. He was thinking of the horses. Thinking of me, too. Last week, I was out of work and heartbroken at the thought of leaving the horses I've given the last eight years of my life to. I was dreading taking the only option left—going back to the residential suburbia of my parents' house in East Denver and living under their microscope again. At least now Bill has bought me a little more time to keep doing what I love. Six weeks to figure out a next step that doesn't involve surrender.

Maybe I wouldn't be this pissed if Dylan Sullivan had actually shown up to handle the mess he made. But no. In the week I've been here, all I've caught are brief glimpses of his hulking frame ducking out the back door and heading for his truck with the speed of a man who thinks he's being chased. He's been a total no-show. *Just my type*, I think bitterly, hauling myself out of my bed in the trailer I've called home for six years. Tugging on my jeans and a tank top, and braiding my hair back with quick, practiced fingers, I pull on my boots and blow out a sigh.

I can't believe I kissed him. Or that he kissed me. Dylan is exactly the kind of man I promised myself I'd steer clear of: hot as sin but unreliable, emotionally unavailable, and absolutely wrong for me. The kind of man who never sticks around long enough to clean up his messes—just like Hooper, my first love. My first mistake.

From the moment Hooper and his parents moved down the street from us when I was sixteen, my heart was gone. He was stick-thin, long-haired, all charm and music and danger. I was lost and feeling like I didn't belong. My parents banned me from seeing him more times than I could count. I snuck out just as many. Hooper was my everything. The boy I ran away with. The man I married in a secondhand white dress at a roadside church on the outskirts of Nashville at eighteen, thinking I had it all, when really, I had nothing.

I shove the memory down where it belongs and step out of my trailer to find the air is crisp and fresh, carrying the scent of grass, earth, and just a hint of horse sweat, reminding me of why I'm out of bed so early.

Maybe I also wouldn't be so pissed at the situation I've found myself in if the ranch was in better shape. But this place hasn't been used as a working ranch in two decades, and it shows. It took me the better part of a day just to move the old football equipment cluttering the barn, piling it all into the back stall because where else was I going to put it? The wood dividing the stalls in the barn is all rotten, the feed room is a disaster, and the water lines are temperamental at best.

Everywhere I turn, there's more work to be done. Overgrown paddocks, and fence posts rotten straight through, looking just one gust of wind away from coming down. I haven't had time to breathe, let alone admire the view of the tall spruce trees and the backdrop of the foothills cutting into the horizon. It's the kind of view that begs for saddle leather and trail rides. But ranching waits for no man or woman. Especially a woman doing it all on her own...

My boots crunch across the gravel as I make my way to the barn. The early-morning birdcalls are the only sound in the still air, aside from the soft whickers of the horses waiting for breakfast.

A coolness lingers, but it won't last. Another hot July day is coming, the kind that will have me sweating before I'm done with the morning feed. I check the horses first, running my hands over their soft coats and talking softly to each in turn. I'll spend some extra time with Moonlight—our last pregnant mare of the season. Her due date is five weeks away.

Five weeks. The same length of time I have left here. Whatever happens, no way am I leaving Moonlight until I know she and her foal are in capable hands. The mare snorts softly as I approach, her dark eyes bright.

"Hey there, Moonlight," I coo, brushing my hand along her flank. The first foal for any mare is always the hardest, but the vet has been checking in regularly and everything is running smoothly. "You're gonna do great. Just hang in there."

Moonlight nudges my arm, her head bobbing in the way that tells me she's impatient.

"You wouldn't happen to be hungry, would you?" I laugh as she scrapes a hoof against the ground.

"Never get between a pregnant mare and her breakfast, hey?" I rub her nose a final time before jogging to the feed bins and hauling a bucket back to the paddock for her. The tension in my chest loosens with every familiar task. Horses don't judge. They don't care about your baggage or mistakes. They just need you to show up and do the work. If only people were as simple.

I'm halfway to the barn to grab the feed for the stallions when the back door to the house swings open and Mama appears in her overalls, holding two mugs of coffee in her hands. She came to introduce herself on my first morning, with Jake's dog, Buck, at her heels.

I'm Joanna Sullivan. Everyone calls me Mama. You strike me as someone who knows how to get things done. And if you're the same granddaughter Bill used to talk about, who spent the summers on his ranch as a kid, then you're more than capable of looking after yourself. But if there's anything you need, you come find me. I'm usually in the kitchen, and the door's always open.

Since then, Mama has brought me a coffee every morning. And no matter how furious I am with Dylan, Mama is a woman I really like. I have no idea how he came from her...

"Gonna be another hot one," she calls.

"Sure is." I smile, taking the mug. "Thank you."

I close my eyes, drawing in a long breath of roasted beans before taking my first slow sip. Some days back in Shamrock, it could be past lunchtime before I got a chance to fix a coffee, and it usually wasn't freshly ground or this delicious. "Have I mentioned how much I love this coffee?"

Mama smiles. "Every morning, but I never get tired of hearing it. No one else in the house appreciates it. They chug it like it's gas station sludge."

"Barbarians," I reply, savoring the buzz of caffeine already skipping through my veins.

"You need anything today?" she asks like she does every day.

My mind flashes to the broken washing machine in my trailer. I've been meaning to get it fixed for months, but it was so easy to use Bill's that I never got around to it. I swallow the thought. I'll figure it out, like I always do. There's bound to be a YouTube tutorial on how to fix it. "I'm all good, thanks."

Mama watches the paddocks and sadness colors her expression. "I don't think I'll ever get used to seeing horses here again," she says. "Before my husband, Harry, died, they were his life. Seeing them on the ranch again... It's..." She trails off. When she speaks again, her voice is steadier, with a forced brightness. "Jake and Chase are going to Flagstaff, Arizona, for training camp next week. I'm throwing a family dinner on Saturday night. You'll come, I hope?"

My thoughts flash to Mad and a tightness grips my chest—love and guilt and a humming anxiety that never fully goes away. I canceled our plans last weekend when it became clear I'd be running this ranch solo. Mad wasn't happy, and the disappointment is still eating me up. I feel like I'm failing. Again. I can't cancel a second weekend in a row. I won't.

"That's very kind, but... I'll have a guest with me this weekend."

"Bring them," Mama says. "Chase usually brings a friend, and Jake and Harper come as a pair. Let's say seven on Saturday."

I want to refuse again, to say thanks, but no thanks. I don't need a dinner, and I doubt Dylan will be pleased to see me at his table considering the efforts he's made in avoiding me this week. But Mama is already turning on her heels and heading back inside.

"There's always coffee in the kitchen. Come by anytime," she calls over her shoulder like she does every morning.

"Thanks," I say again, then dive back into the work. Feeding, watering, checking hooves, patching fences.

Eighteen horses for one full-time ranch hand is doable. But only just. And that would be on a ranch that hasn't been neglected for twenty years. I'm stretched thin and yet still a part of me is relieved to be here, doing what I love.

I told Dylan on that first afternoon that I had plenty of other offers for work. It was a lie, and one I thought for a moment he'd seen through. The truth is, I need this job. Even before Bill got the warning from the doctor last Christmas, he'd started scaling back, selling off horses and breeding less, shrinking our stock from thirty to eighteen. The sale to a big outfit in Dallas happened too fast. Bill fought for me to stay on, but they had their own hands. Even if they'd offered, I couldn't have left. Not with Mad.

When I first heard the horses were staying in Denver and I'd be with them, I can't deny I felt a spark of hope. I thought if I worked hard enough, proved myself, there was a chance I could stay past the six weeks Dylan agreed with Bill. But that hope has crumbled and died this week.

I'm here for five more weeks, or until Dylan bails and sells them. Which, judging by the barefoot hangover he greeted me with last week and his disappearing act, feels like it could happen any day. The man is not serious about ranching. As soon as he faces up to his mistake, he'll sell the horses and I'll be heading back to a life I barely survived the first time around.

But if he thinks I'm going to spend the next five weeks sacrificing everything, keeping this place running alone just so he can give up when he realizes he's a failure anyway, he's all kinds of wrong. The next time I see Dylan Sullivan, he won't know what hit him. It's time to set things straight.

SIX

DYLAN

I'm drifting in that place between asleep and awake, fighting to keep my thoughts out of my head for one more minute. But my bedroom door is opening with a familiar creak, followed by quick footsteps.

A second later, the curtains are pulled back and bright sunlight floods the room. I groan, pressing my face into the pillow. The taste of last night's bourbon is sour in my mouth. I stayed up too late again, like if I just drank enough, I could pretend none of this was happening.

"Rise and shine, cowboy," Mama says. A moment later she's crossing to the bed and placing a cup of coffee on the nightstand before sitting heavily on the edge of the mattress.

"Mama, seriously," I mumble, throwing an arm over my eyes.

"Do you know what time it is? It's past eleven," she continues before I can reply.

"So?" I reply, wishing I didn't sound like a surly teen.

"So I'm going to say something, Dylan. And you're going to listen."

I bite back a sigh. Whatever is coming, I already know I don't want to hear it.

"When your father died, I know it hit you hardest as the oldest. You saw my grief in a way your brothers didn't, and it shaped you. No one asked you to step up and look out for your brothers and for me, but you did it anyway. You didn't take a single day for yourself."

I close my eyes harder, not wanting to hear any more.

"Even when the doctors said your career was over, you didn't fall apart. You worked your ass off, every single day, proving them wrong."

"Turns out they were right though, weren't they?" I spit out.

"Don't do that," she says. "You played at the top of your game for one of the best teams in the NFL for nine years—"

"Seven," I reply. "I've spent the last two injured, remember?"

Mama gives me a look I haven't seen since Jake's teenage years—usually right before a blowout over unfinished homework. "Seven years playing at the top of your game before you were injured. Then you defied all the odds. You got your knee working again and your fitness back. I'm sorry it wasn't enough. And I know it's been hard. So I gave you this week. I let you sulk and drink and wallow in a way you've never done before. But you've got a ranch full of horses and a good woman running herself into the ground trying to keep things together—"

"I get it," I cut in. "I've messed up." The words sting more than I want to admit.

Mama's voice softens. "This isn't about what you did, Dylan. It's about what you're going to do. I've never known you not to show up. Don't start now. So get your ass out of bed and get your head straight."

She pats my leg then stands and walks out, her footsteps fading down the hall. I stare up at the ceiling and hate how right she is. I know I need to finder a buyer, and until then I should be helping out. But I'm not ready to face the ranch. Or the horses. Or Izzy Brooks, for that matter.

Instead, I drag myself out of bed and hit my weights rack. In seconds, the barbell is loaded, and I'm wrapping my hands around the cool metal. Sweat builds quickly, dripping down my spine as I push my body hard. Every lift and pull burns through the fog of guilt and anger. I push through the final set like the right number of reps could rewrite the last week.

Get your ass out of bed and get your head straight.

I let the barbell crash back on the rack as my chest heaves and my muscles burn. I wipe my face and glance toward the window. I catch sight of Izzy dragging a piece of wood across the dirt, a tool belt around her waist. I turn away. I'm not a football player. Not a Stormhawk. Not anything. And if I stay here much longer, I'm going to lose what little I've got left of myself. I need to get the hell off this ranch.

I shower fast, throw on some clothes, and five minutes later I'm in my truck, heading toward the city. Like every day so far this week, I don't have a destination in mind. But somehow, I always end up in the same place—Stormhawks Park. Sitting a few miles south of the stadium, the state-of-the-art training facility has three full-sized fields, an indoor gym, a rehab center with a pool, and a sauna in the basement. Every square foot of the place is designed to build champions. And this place, along with the stadium, feels like my second home.

I pull into the lot and kill the engine. For a minute, I just sit there, staring through the windshield, fingers gripping the wheel. I'm not sure why I keep coming back. Why I can't stay away.

The afternoon sun is blazing down on the green turf as I make my way to the training field. Something in the sight drags my thoughts to the ranch. I think about the paddocks—how I kept the grass from turning to weeds over the years, enough to keep the place from looking abandoned. But now? Now I'm not sure it was enough. Not for horses. Not for real work. A new kind of guilt twists in my gut, and I shut the thought down before it can take root and focus on the practice instead. This is where I belong.

Out on the fields, the team has been divided into groups, each running drills. Coach Allen is standing back, watching it all, seeing everything. All around me are the noises of bodies slamming into pads, the yells of the players, whistles, and the coaching staff shouting plays. I skirt the edge of the field and head toward the far corner by the fence. Coach Allen nods a greeting my way but leaves me alone, and I'm grateful. Talking to him will only dig deeper into a wound I don't think will ever heal.

I take up my position, leaning against the fence, and just watch, pretending my muscles aren't twitching, like I don't want to be in the middle of every play. I focus on the rookie squad. They're paired up, running blocking drills. One of the rookies is way too eager. He keeps lunging forward during the block. Every time, he's stepping too deep into the gap, allowing his teammate to shoot straight through. It's a mess, and nobody's calling him on it.

I can't help myself.

"Hey!" I call out, stalking forward, jamming a finger at the rookie. "You're overcommitting."

The kid—barely twenty-one, judging by the baby face— blinks up at me. I see the recognition in his eyes. He knows exactly who I am and is already nodding nervously. Instantly, my face softens. Maybe I'm not on this team anymore, but I still know football. "You need to keep your feet under your hips and let the defender come to you. Anchor your stance." I show him how to place his feet and he copies the gesture. "Right now, you're a revolving door."

The rookie adjusts his stance and runs the drill again. It's solid.

"Good," I call out. "Just keep your weight centered."

A whistle blows and one of the rookie coaches finally notices me. There's a brief flicker of surprise on his face, but he gives me a nod before turning back to the squad.

I spend the rest of the practice feeling like a ghost haunting my old life. When practice winds down and the team hits the locker room, I catch the shout of a familiar voice.

"Look what the bourbon dragged in."

I turn to see Jake jogging over, helmet tucked under his arm, smile wide, sweat coating his face. Chase isn't far behind, looking real good in the Stormhawks red jersey.

"Don't tell me, you couldn't stay away," Jake says, wiping his face on his sleeve.

"Just watching," I reply.

Chase's smile fades a little like he sees something Jake doesn't. "You good?"

"Peachy," I reply.

They exchange a look. The same look I saw a hundred times during those months I was injured—every time football came up at family dinners and I had to pretend it wasn't ripping me apart to hear them talking through plays I wasn't part of.

Chase shifts first. "This really sucks, Dyl. You should be out here with us."

I lift an eyebrow. "Glad we're all caught up."

Jake nudges my arm, telling me without words to stop being a dick.

I heave a sigh. "Yeah, it sucks."

Chase's gaze is still on me. "You're OK, right? I mean, you coming here and watching practice—can't be fun."

I glance away, jaw tight. "This place has been home for too long. I don't know where else to go. But I'm not looking for hugs or sympathy."

"You ever need a hug though..." Chase lifts his arms, coming at me in sweat-soaked pads.

"I can still put your ass on the ground, Chase."

Jake snorts. "Seriously though, Dylan. We've got your back. On the field and off."

I look at them both—Jake, who beneath the charm is always looking out for others, and Chase, pretending to be the jokester when sometimes I think he's the most serious of all of us. And I know they mean it. But that doesn't make the ache any less painful.

Jake nods toward the field. "Did I see you giving the rookies some coaching?"

"Just pointing out something they were doing wrong."

Chase eyes me for another moment. "You sticking around? Coach has got us doing a meet and greet with some fans. Not exactly my first choice for a Friday evening," he adds, but I can tell he doesn't mind really. The fans are the beating heart of this team and we all know it.

"Just needed to get away from the ranch for a while."

Another look passes between them.

"What?" I ask.

It's Chase who answers. "Look, not my business, but you bought those horses... You gonna—"

I groan. "Not you too. I've already had Mama on my back this morning."

Jake is quick to steer the conversation to teasing Chase about the pre-game ritual he developed playing for the Trailblazers—eating exactly four slices of toast with almond butter and listening to Taylor Swift like it's a religious experience. When they disappear into the locker room, I head for my truck and slam the door too hard as I climb in. I know I don't belong here anymore. I sure as hell don't belong at Oakwood Ranch right now, either. But I've got nowhere else to go. So I turn the key, gun the engine, and head back to the last place I want to be.

SEVEN

IZZY

The sun is still blazing over the paddocks as I step from the barn. It's late afternoon on Friday and my shirt is clinging to my back. My muscles ache from a day that started at sunrise and hasn't let up since. I haven't eaten. Haven't showered. Haven't done any of the things I needed to do for myself. On top of that, I've just taken stock of the feed bins and it's not good. We have less than a week's worth of food left.

A low rumble breaks the quiet, followed by the crunch of gravel and a cloud of dust kicking up from the road. An engine growls louder, like it's being summoned by my rage, and when Dylan's truck pulls into the driveway, I see red.

He climbs out of the cab slowly, like he's got all the time in the world. Like he hasn't spent the last week dodging every responsibility on this ranch. Judging by his bloodshot eyes and the dark beard shadowing his jaw, he's been using his time for late nights and bourbon.

"Hey!" I shout, already marching toward him.

His boots falter, and for a second, I think he might keep walking like he can keep pretending this ranch doesn't exist.

"Hey! Sullivan!" I snap again, closing the distance between us.

Finally, he turns. If I weren't so goddamn furious, I might feel sorry for him. But I'm all out of sympathy after a week running this place alone. He's wearing old jeans and a black tee that stretches over the muscles of his chest and shoulders. Muscles that look tailor-made to make women everywhere swoon. *Every woman except me*, I correct.

"What is it?" he mutters, scrubbing a hand over his face.

I laugh, the sound edged with bitterness. "Oh, I'm sorry. Am I bothering you? I wasn't sure if you even remembered there were horses on this ranch. You know, the ones *you* bought and have left me to take care of alone for the last week?"

"I'm working on something." He momentarily looks like a deer caught in headlights, betraying his lie.

"What, exactly?" I reply. "Your next disappearing act?"

"If you can't handle the ranch, Bill shouldn't have made me take you on."

"Excuse me?" I take a step closer, my voice low and deadly. "My job is caring for these horses—and maybe you haven't pulled your head out of your ass long enough to notice, but I'm doing my job. What *isn't* my job is running your finances and trying to figure out what the hell kind of ranch you think you're running here."

He looks like he might argue, but I don't give him the chance.

"We've got less than a week's worth of feed. I tried calling in an order, but guess what? Oakwood Ranch doesn't have an account with Triple Ridge Feed Supply and I don't have the authority to open one. So come Tuesday, we're going to have some very unhappy horses."

"So if I set up an account with Triple Ridge..."

"And tell them I have the authority to buy whatever I need," I add.

"Then you'll get off my back?" he asks.

I sigh. "If that's the only way I get anything out of you, then yeah."

He turns to walk away as though this conversation is over, but I haven't even scratched the surface of all the things I want to yell at him.

I shout after him, "I guess bare minimum is still asking too much from you, Sullivan."

Dylan spins back, eyes blazing. "Don't act like you know a damn thing about me, Brooks." His words are fierce, but there's something raw in his gaze that stops me short.

I hesitate, forcing the next words I speak to sound softer. "What I know is horses. These are living creatures, not footballs. They need care and attention and respect. You can't just toss them around and hope for the best."

He lets out a loud, exasperated sigh. "You think I—"

Before he can finish, a horn blasts from the driveway. A familiar blue pickup swings into view, and my irritation is instantly replaced with an anxiety I know all too well. *Of course* they arrive right when I'm in the middle of a fight with my new boss. But then I see the figure waving from the passenger seat, and all that tension evaporates. A wide smile breaks across my face.

"What now? This place is a circus," Dylan mutters.

The truck has barely stopped when the passenger door flies open and a ball of energy launches toward me. I'm already laughing as she barrels into my arms, dark blonde curls bouncing, little arms squeezing tight. Emotion wells in my chest, tightening my throat, but I draw in a steadying breath.

"Dylan," I say, lifting my chin to meet his eyes, "this is my daughter, Madison."

She scrambles from my arms and steps toward him, her hand outstretched. "Mad for short," she says with a bright smile and a confidence that never fails to take my breath away. "I'm eight years old, but I'm nearly nine. I'm allergic to kiwis and I love horses." She squints up at him, all curiosity and confidence. "You don't look like a rancher."

A flicker of surprise crosses Dylan's face and I brace myself for more of his outrage. I should have told him about Madison sooner—for his sake and hers. Guilt and regret wash over me, like sliding on a pair of old jeans. The crippling fear that I'm failing my daughter. She might love horses, but this life is hardly a stable upbringing for a child. Living in a trailer on a fold-out bed with a mom who works every day from dawn until dusk. The knowledge that we'd be moving on from Bill's has hung over us for months—a dark storm cloud. And now we're at Oakwood for a matter of weeks.

With a musician for a dad who barely remembers his daughter from one tour to the next, I'm all too aware that any stability in her life has to come from me, which is something my parents remind me of frequently. It's why they want us to live with them. They want Mad to have the same structured upbringing they gave me. I just wish I knew what was the right thing to do for my daughter.

But then I remind myself that not having mentioned Mad to Dylan yet is on him, not me. If he'd shown up even once in the past week, I would've told him about her.

To my surprise, he nods a greeting, his big hand engulfing hers. "Nice to meet you, Mad. And you're probably right." He looks down at his sneakers and shrugs. "I guess we could use the help," he adds, glancing at me.

We. The word throws me. I clamp my mouth shut around the caustic reply that rises up, choosing to focus on the way he gently shakes Mad's hand.

"I'll say goodbye to Grandpa Joe," she says, tearing off toward the truck.

I watch her wrap her arms around Joe's middle. He hugs her tight before handing over her weekend bag. My chest squeezes.

If only her father could show her even half the love his parents do. Mad is lucky to have them.

Dylan looks from Madison to me and I meet it head-on.

"Before you say anything, Madison knows her way around a ranch, and she's only here on weekends," I say, voice tight. "Her grandparents run a summer camp a few hours away near Granite Lake. In the summer, she stays at the camp during the week, but she loves ranching, so she comes back for weekends."

He seems to think that over for a moment. "Where was she last weekend?"

"I asked her to stay at camp. It didn't seem fair for her to come when I'd be working twenty-four-seven trying to get this place into some kind of working order."

The dig lands and Dylan shifts on his feet as something like guilt flickers across his face.

"But if you've got a problem with Mad being here," I continue, "I can take her somewhere else and leave you to ranch this place solo on weekends."

He huffs. "My only problem is the giant stick up your ass."

"Really? That's your comeback?" I snap. "You haven't lifted a finger in a week, and now you're throwing attitude?"

He steps close, dropping his voice to a low rumble. "Are you sure you're not the one with the problem, blondie?"

His nearness seems to buzz in my veins, tightening something low in my belly. For half a second, I forget how to breathe. Then without a word, I walk away to greet Mad's grandpa Joe. No way am I giving Dylan the satisfaction of seeing he's gotten under my skin.

I'm already one week into my six weeks here. It's all the time I've got doing the one job I love. It's not just Dylan's complete lack of interest in ranching that's convinced me I'm on a countdown. It's him. The man barely looks at me unless it's to argue or sigh or roll his eyes. Even if he decided not to sell, even if a miracle happened and he wanted to keep the horses and run this place as a working ranch, I'd still be the last person he'd want hanging around.

Five weeks to find another ranch, another paycheck, and another shot at stability for Mad. Because if I don't, it's back to my parents' house. Their life. Their rules. I might as well try to enjoy my time here. If that means biting my tongue and putting up with a man who is consumed by misery, sulking from his bruised ego, and who doesn't give a damn who he takes with him on his way down to rock bottom, then so be it.

But something's gotta give. Because this? This isn't working. Not for me. Not for the horses. And sure as hell not for Dylan.

EIGHT

DYLAN

JAKE: *Family dinner 7 p.m.! Chase, you bringing dessert? Nothing wacky this time!*

CHASE: *Sure am. Sweet potato pecan pie with chili chocolate drizzle wacky enough for you?*

JAKE: *Gross!*

DYLAN: *I'm busy.*

JAKE: *If you're throwing another pity party, Dyl, maybe invite us next time!*

CHASE: *Before you buy a fleet of antique tractors?*

JAKE: *Or a herd of llamas. Ranch diversification, right?*

DYLAN: *Dicks!*

JAKE: *Yeah, but you're gonna miss us next week.*

DYLAN: *Not even a little bit.*

The sound of laughter drifts through the open window of my bedroom and I can't stop myself from glancing out to where Izzy and Madison are striding out from the barn, deep in conversation. Guilt gnaws at my insides. They're already halfway through the morning feed. Madison laughs at something Izzy says, the little girl's face lighting up like waking early on a Saturday to work the ranch is the best thing in the world.

I watch them slip through the gate of the first paddock and force myself to look at the horses. Their coats gleam in the morning sunlight. They look like they belong—Izzy, Mad, the horses. They all belong on this ranch in a way I don't anymore.

I head to my weights corner, grab a dumbbell, and launch into a shoulder set. This room has always been my safe zone. The place I came when I was a kid and struggling with the grief of losing my dad and not wanting to show it. The refuge I needed when I was recovering from my injury. Now, though? It feels like I'm hiding. Like I'm a coward, and everyone knows it.

Get your ass out of bed and get your head straight.

These are living creatures, not footballs.

Even Chase—the guy who only remembers appointments when Mama calls him twice—asked me what my plan was. I drop the dumbbell on the rack. I set up the damn feed account, didn't I? Doesn't that count for something? But Izzy's voice echoes in my head like a barb: *Bare minimum is still asking too much.*

Shit, I don't want to be here. I don't want to do this. But this mess is mine and hiding sure as hell isn't getting me anywhere.

I yank on jeans and a clean tee, lace up the work boots I haven't worn in months, grab a cup of coffee and stalk into the morning sun. Madison is still in the paddock with the foals. If I didn't know better, I'd think she was deep in conversation, holding a team meeting, like she's the coach and they're the players.

So it's just Izzy who greets me by the barn. "Hey, you found some appropriate work boots," Izzy calls, nodding at my boots, reminding us both of my barefoot, sorry-assed state the day she arrived here and the sneakers I've been wearing every day since.

"Shame you couldn't find any manners," I bite back before I can stop myself. All my resolve to help disappears under her harsh glare.

She raises one eyebrow before she replies, "What are you doing here?"

"What am I doing on my ranch, you mean?"

"A ranch you haven't shown up to for over a week, you mean?"

I stop myself from vocalizing the expletives running through my head. "I'm here now, aren't I?"

"Well, you're late." She gestures toward the paddocks. "Feeding's done. Water's topped. Moonlight's checked."

Suddenly, my pulse is racing. Who the hell does this woman think she is? Izzy's glare is ice cold, but when our eyes lock, something flitters through the back of my mind, something that feels a lot more dangerous than anger.

"If you're looking to help," she continues, "you can start by getting the stalls up and running. The horses are fine outside for now, but they'll need cover if it rains and the barn is in no state to hold them. And Moonlight's gonna need somewhere to foal. She's due on the twentieth of August. Less than five weeks."

"Got it," I mutter, heading for the barn without another word.

My boots hit the ground, every step feeling heavier than the last, like they're encased in cement. I thought I'd be packing for training camp today like Jake and Chase, relishing the buzz of a new season. Not here, not doing this.

~

Hours later, I'm slumped on a stool in the shade of the barn door, a bridle in my lap and sweat dripping down my back. Every joint, every muscle aches like I've run four quarters straight, no timeouts, and no crowd to cheer me on.

My hands throb with blisters from the repairs to the stalls earlier. Why didn't I search out a pair of work gloves? I'm sure Dad's old ones are still in the boot room somewhere. Something tells me he'd be laughing his head off at my pathetic attempts at ranching today.

At least the stalls inside the barn are halfway to being fixed and Moonlight will have a safe place to foal. A few more days and they'll be safe to house the horses when we need to. The work is nothing flashy—pulling out the rotten slats of wood that divide the stalls, adding new slats, replacing nails, sanding down splinters. It should've been done a week ago. I know better than anyone how fast storms roll off the mountains. If we'd hit bad weather last week, the horses would've had nowhere to go, and that's on me.

I'm here now, I remind myself, even if I don't want to be.

My thoughts pull back to this morning and Izzy's biting question.

What are you doing here?

The truth is, I don't know. My time would be better spent calling Dad's old friends, putting the word out I'm looking for a buyer, and yet I'm hammering wood and polishing bridles. I curse under my breath and scrub a hand over my face. I glance toward the far paddock, where Izzy and Madison are grooming one of the stallions. I've kept my distance from the horses today. Even just looking at them stirs something raw in me. They remind me of Dad—of how much this ranch meant to him. They remind me of my failure.

Looking at Izzy does the same damn thing. She belongs out

here, and she knows I don't. She sees all the ways I've fucked up and it's a kick in the guts I can't outrun. And then there's her smart mouth, always ready with a comeback, always so sure of herself. Sharp-tongued and whip-smart, and that only makes it worse—makes *me* feel worse.

But there's something softer about Izzy when she's with Madison. The sharp edges of her sarcasm and judgment have smoothed out today. Her face lights up, her cheeks catching the golden light of the setting sun. For a second, she looks... approachable. More than approachable. I think of our fight yesterday, how I stepped in to give her a piece of my mind, and instead caught the scent of her perfume—a fresh sea breeze and something sweet. Subtle in a way that had me wanting to move closer.

I shake the thought away, remembering the woman who's spent all day telling me how I'm doing everything wrong.

Movement on the porch catches my attention and Mama appears, hollering across the ranch like she used to when she wanted to call us in as kids. "Wash up! Dinner's ready in twenty!"

Izzy leans down, saying something to Madison, who nods before they both start walking back toward their trailer. I heave a sigh. Of course Mama invited them to dinner. The realization comes with another tug of guilt. Izzy's new here and working for me. It's a dick move that I didn't do it myself. But tonight's dinner isn't about Izzy or the ranch. It's a goodbye dinner for Jake and Chase. Tomorrow they leave for their week-long training camp in Flagstaff ahead of their three pre-season games next month.

I want to be happy for my brothers, but this dinner is a reminder of everything I've lost. Even as I start up the polish again, I know I'll suck it up for Mama and for Jake and Chase. I showed up today on the ranch. I can show up for them tonight even if it feels like I'm being sucker-punched again and again.

The blisters on my hands throb as I carry the polished bridles into the barn. I'm halfway through hanging them on the hooks in the newly organized tack room when I feel a presence behind me. Little feet, little eyes.

"You're doing it wrong," Madison says, voice matter-of-fact.

"Excuse me?" I raise my brows at this miniature version of Izzy. Although this version is half my height and a lot nicer.

"The straps shouldn't twist like that." She steps closer, taking a bridle from me and showing me how to hang it. "See? It keeps them neat. It'll make it easier to slip over their heads."

"Thanks," I reply, rehanging the bridles. "Your mom wasn't kidding about you knowing your way around a ranch."

She beams at the compliment. "Mom says she likes horses better than people."

"That sounds about right."

"Except me. I'm her favorite human." Madison grins as she skips out of the barn.

"So I guess that means I'm her second favorite, right?" I joke, following her out, knowing I'm bottom of Izzy's list.

Madison laughs and shakes her head. "Mom says you don't know the difference between a mustang and a mare." Suddenly Madison's body is attacked by a fit of giggles.

Her laughter is almost enough to break through my mood. Almost.

"She said you think a mustang is a car," she gasps out. With that, she skips toward the trailer, and I crack a smile despite myself. But it fades fast, and five minutes later, I'm kicking off my boots and padding into a kitchen that smells of roast chicken, herbs, and Mama's gravy. She's at the stove, humming softly to herself, wearing her usual oversized red Stormhawks jersey. Harper is setting the table, laughing with Mama over something I don't catch.

Buck jumps out of his bed in the corner to greet me, pushing his head into my hands, tail thumping as I stroke him.

"Hey, Buck." I crouch and run my hands over his yellow fur. "It's good to see you, too." Buck might be Jake's dog, but he spent plenty of nights keeping me company when the Stormhawks were playing and I was stuck at home with an ice pack on my knee. "You staying here next week?"

Harper replies for him. "You don't mind? I can keep him with me in the city, but we both know he'd rather be here."

I scratch Buck's ear and he tilts his head, leaning into my touch. "Be good to have the company."

"So... you been working today?" Harper asks with a little hesitation. I don't miss the way Mama pauses her stirring from across the kitchen to listen.

I nod. "Had to show up sometime," I say, heading for the door before another question comes my way.

In the shower, I let the hot water beat down on my aching body, cleaning off the dirt and sweat of the day and wishing it was as easy to wash away the failure that feels like it's clinging to my skin. I shove my head under the spray of water and my thoughts pull back to Izzy, to the fire in her eyes this morning during our fight. How the tension felt like it could snap at any moment.

My thoughts drag to the kiss in The Hay Barn. The press of her body against mine. Her tongue exploring my mouth. Her hands on my body. Heat coils low in my gut, and suddenly my dick is hardening. I grab it in my hand, letting images of Izzy play through my head. My release comes fast, leaving me breathing heavily against the shower wall as the water beats down on me. *What was that about?*

I turn off the shower, dry fast, and throw on fresh jeans and a clean tee, willing thoughts of Izzy away as I head downstairs. But when I walk into the kitchen, she's the first thing I see. She and Madison are standing at the counter with Mama, who's showing Madison how to stir a pot of gravy. Madison is wearing a pink tee with a horse on the front, but it's Izzy my eyes are drawn to. She's wearing a simple black sundress that stops mid-thigh, showing her tanned legs and sandaled feet. Her hair is loose like the first time I saw her, falling in waves down her back. Something about the look, after seeing her in work boots and denim for the past week, catches me off guard.

She sees me staring and there's the same spark of defiance and challenge in her expression she's had since we met, like maybe she knows exactly what I was thinking about in the shower. I glance away, adding *perv* to the growing list of reasons I'm failing at life right now.

At least this look is better than the one where she knows I'm in way over my head with this ranch. That one makes me want to walk right out the back door, climb in my truck, and drive the hell out of here for good.

NINE

IZZY

"If you get tired of the grumpiness, I've got a spare room in the city with your name on it," Chase says with a wink so exaggerated it feels like it should come with a health warning. The man's magnetic, with that shaved head and the mischievous spark in his dark brown eyes. I can already see he's the kind of person who lights up a room just by walking into it. Just as I can see his outrageous flirting is more about annoying Dylan than it is about me.

I laugh, happy to play along. "I'll keep that in mind."

"Is that the spare room where you and JT store your football equipment?" Jake asks from across the table, mentioning the Stormhawks kicker Chase moved in with when he came back to Denver. "That room is a biohazard." Jake has one arm slung casually around Harper's shoulders, the pair of them practically glowing. His dark hair is longer than Dylan's, curling slightly at the ends and pushed away from his face, and his smile is broad and easy, which I guess has a lot to do with the rock sparkling on Harper's delicate finger.

"And yet it's still nicer than being around Dylan's grumpy ass." Chase laughs.

Dylan barely grunts in response as he takes a sip of water. He's like a storm cloud in the middle of all this sunshine. And yeah, I think Dylan is a massive jerk with a serious attitude problem, but even I can see it can't be easy having your brothers still playing NFL football when you're not.

Across the table, Dylan shifts in his seat and reaches for the bowl of potatoes. He looks around the table, pausing when he sees Madison's near-empty plate. Without a word, he spoons the last two onto her plate.

"Thank you, Dylan," she says, stabbing one of the potatoes with her fork and popping it straight into her mouth.

It's a small gesture, but I'm surprised he noticed or cares enough to make sure Mad has enough to eat. I force my eyes away before he catches me staring. Dylan is as closed off with his family as he's been with me. If there's anything else beneath that scowl, it's buried deep.

Madison's fork clinks against her plate as she sets it down and leans back, rubbing her belly with both hands. "Why are you all so big?" she asks, staring from one Sullivan brother to the next.

"Mad," I hiss as the table erupts in laughter, the kind that's impossible not to join in with.

"What?" Madison asks, her face the picture of innocence. "I really wanna know."

Mama reaches to pat Madison's hand with a conspiratorial smile. "You ask whatever questions you like at this table, Miss Madison. The answer might have something to do with my boys always eating a second helping of vegetables," she says with a wink to me before pushing the bowl of roasted carrots and green beans toward my daughter.

With a gleeful smile usually reserved for ice cream, Mad scoops two heaping spoonfuls of vegetables onto her plate and starts eating.

I shake my head in disbelief, hiding my own laughter as well as the yawn threatening. Caring for the horses while making sure Madison has my full attention has been exhausting, and I still have a pile of clothes to handwash in the sink of the trailer after dinner. I really need to get my washing machine fixed.

The conversation flows easily around the table as Mad munches on her vegetables. Harper lights up as she talks about dividing her time between working on features at *Sports Magazine* and writing a book about vampires that's being published next year, her voice animated as she describes the process. Jake looks like he's about to burst with pride as she speaks, and I like them both already.

We zigzag from one topic to another, and as Chase and Jake descend into fits of giggles with Madison over a story about their dad falling in a puddle of mud they'd made with the hose as kids, I can't help but compare it to the dinners at my parents' house. Polite conversations that always loop back to the hospital and their patients. My family never means to exclude me—it's just that their world is so different from mine. At least once during those dinners, someone—usually my brother, David— will steer the conversation toward my work on Bill's ranch. But their eyes will glaze over fast.

Whatever wildness lives in Bill's blood, the thing that made him save every spare cent he had to buy a patch of land near Shamrock and build a horse ranch from scratch, it skipped a generation. His son—my dad—chose hospitals and air conditioning over open land and dirt. Dad always talks about growing up in a tiny apartment above a bakery in Northglenn, only moving to the ranch when his parents finally had the money saved when my dad was seven. Dad's ranch stories are of the hard years—when the bills piled up, and the bank kept circling like vultures. That struggle pushed him into med school, and into a life of white coats and neat routines. I respect it. But I never wanted it.

I grew up in a house where everything had its place,

including me. My parents' love felt like it came wrapped in expectations. Straight As. College. Med school. But summers spent on Bill's ranch while my brother and sister went to camp—that was freedom. I'd brush down the horses for hours, throw myself into every job, and fall asleep with a smile on my face. It was the only time I ever felt like myself growing up.

Working for Bill for the last eight years felt as easy as those summers. We never needed small talk. We'd pile sandwiches high with whatever we had, head out to the porch steps, and talk through the work still ahead. I love my family, but they understand my world about as well as I understand theirs. And when those summers ended as a kid and I went back to the city, it felt like a part of me was being locked away. This right here— the Sullivans with their noise and laughter and teasing—is a different kind of family.

I'm pulled back to the table by Madison tugging at Dylan's tee, where the material stretches over his bicep. "Do you have a girlfriend?" she asks, her tone casual, like she's asking him if he wants dessert.

For some reason, the question causes a wave of heat to creep up my neck and my thoughts to flash to our kiss. I take a slow sip of water, grateful for the distraction of Chase's laughter. "That would require Dylan to talk to women," he says, his grin wicked.

"That Sullivan charm is in there somewhere, Dyl," Jake throws out.

"Buried under a mountain of grump," Chase finishes.

Dylan's glare sweeps the table, and they bite back their laughter, shoulders shaking silently as Dylan turns to Mad. He isn't laughing, but he isn't angry either. "Ignore them," he says.

Madison doesn't miss a beat. "My daddy has lots of girl-friends," she says in the matter-of-fact way she does that never fails to make me both insanely proud and also want to bury my head in my hands. "I can ask him if he can give one to you, if you want."

"I'll be fine, but thank you, Mad," Dylan replies, and just for a second I think I catch the ghost of a smile. Our eyes lock and something else passes between us.

"That's probably best." Madison nods earnestly, completely oblivious to how the air is suddenly charged in a way I didn't expect and sure as hell don't want. "Unless you can sing. My daddy's girlfriends like him because he's a country singer."

"Anyone we know?" Harper asks.

Pride shines in Madison's bright eyes. A well-worn pain surfaces, the kind that twists like a knife. I hope she never realizes what a lousy excuse for a dad Hooper is.

"He's Hooper Greene," Madison announces.

My ex-husband's name causes a collective gasp around the table. Of all the promises Hooper made when he dropped to one knee when I was eighteen and pregnant, him becoming a star was the only one he kept—and the least important, it turned out.

"He travels all around the country. He said he'll take me with him one day," Madison explains, her small hands gesturing animatedly as she talks.

I stay quiet, keeping my expression neutral. Hooper gets to flit in and out of her life whenever it's convenient for him, leaving me to pick up the pieces of broken promises.

Sometimes I wonder if I'm messing this whole parenting thing up. Madison says she loves our trailer—calls it a cozy space just for us. And I try to believe that's enough. It gave us our own place at Bill's ranch once Mad started walking, and it meant we weren't imposing every time he wanted to watch his war documentaries instead of the tenth rerun of whatever Disney movie Mad was currently obsessed with. But still, I worry that a tiny trailer, no matter how filled with love and laughter, isn't the kind of stable home she deserves, especially when we've spent this past year so unsure of what the future holds.

I watch Madison now, stroking Buck's head beneath the table. She skipped through every task today like she belongs on a ranch as much as I do. I silently will her not to fall in love with this ranch or these people. Because in five weeks we'll be gone.

Assuming Dylan doesn't pull his head out of his ass and sell the horses before then.

I miss Mad like crazy during the week when she's off at Hooper's parents' summer camp—spending the days swimming and playing with friends. I know she's safe and happy, but the quiet of the summer weeks eats at a part of my soul. It's easier during the school year. I count the hours until she jumps off that yellow school bus, and Mad tells me about her day as we cook dinner together.

"I don't get to see him much," Mad adds, still talking about Hooper. A sadness creeps into her voice that cracks open my heart.

"Well, that sounds a lot like he's missing out," Dylan says, the sincerity in his voice throwing me off balance.

Mama nods, her warm smile spreading across her face as she looks down the table at her boys. "Families aren't just the people you're born into. They're who you choose. Who you show up for. And who shows up for you."

"I don't know, Mama," Chase says, voice teasing. "If Dylan keeps up his terrible excuse for ranching skills, we might need to audition for a replacement brother before he brings down the Sullivan name."

Across the table, Jake cracks up, and maybe it's the kind words Dylan had for Madison just now—or a temporary lapse in judgment—but before I can stop myself, I'm stepping in. Not to defend Dylan exactly. He's still a grumpy, unreliable pain in my ass.

I flash my sweetest smile. "Sounds a lot like you boys think you could do better. Why don't you both join me at five tomorrow morning and we'll see how long you last? I mean, unless you're scared of getting your hands dirty and seeing what a real day's work looks like?"

The table falls quiet. I catch Dylan's head jerk up, his eyes flicking to mine with something like disbelief in their dark depths—maybe even gratitude.

Jake's laugh breaks the silence. He shakes his head, raising his hands in surrender. "Fair point, Izzy. And thanks, but I'll leave the ranching to the two of you."

"Three," Madison throws in.

"I'll leave ranching to the *three* of you," Jake corrects with an apologetic smile so sincere, I'm certain it's got him out of a lot of trouble over the years.

Later, when Jake and Harper take Buck for a walk around a lake I didn't even know existed at the back of the ranch, and Chase leaves to drive back to the city, Dylan, Mad, and I help Mama tidy the dishes. My arms feel heavy with exhaustion as I lift the last plate from the rack to dry. I can't fight back the long yawn that escapes me.

Mama doesn't miss it. "When my Harry was alive—that's my late husband and Dylan, Jake, and Chase's father," she explains to Madison. "He died when the boys were not much older than you. He used to be asleep on his feet by this time most nights," she says with a knowing smile. "You girlies need to get some sleep, too."

"Thank you," I say, tucking my hair behind my ears. "This has been a very fun evening." One I didn't expect to enjoy as much as I did.

"It has," Mama agrees. "And a lot of that fun came from this one," she says, wrapping her arms around Madison and kissing the top of her head. "You come for dinner anytime," she says. "Now, have you girls got all you need?"

"Yes, thanks, Ma—" I start to say, but Mad is already speaking up.

"Can we use your washing machine tomorrow, please, Mama?" she asks. "Ours is broken, and Mom's been washing all our clothes in the sink."

Heat floods my face as a mortified "Mad!" escapes. My voice is soft, but the warning is clear. "It's fine, honestly," I tell Mama. "We're managing just fine."

Mama's gaze on me is firm and assessing. It's the same look she's given her boys all evening when their teasing goes too far, the one that says she knows exactly what's what, no matter what you try to tell her. I don't need to look at Dylan to know he's finding this exchange amusing.

Jerk!

Mama takes Madison's hand. "This way, sweetheart." She leads Madison to a utility room by the back door. "We've got a washing machine and a dryer right here by the boot room. When we had the kitchen built, I made Harry install a shower room too, so he could wash off the smell of horses before trailing through the house."

She shoots Dylan a pointed look and he rolls his eyes. "Message received," he says. "From now on, I'll shower there before coming in."

Mama smiles back and I get the impression she's a woman who always gets her way. It makes me like her more, even if the embarrassment is still burning on my face.

"You two use this shower or the washing machine anytime you like. The back door is always open," she continues, opening the door to a neat utility room. "There are two machines in here. If I show you now, then you can show your mom when she's ready to admit that asking for help is a sign of strength, not weakness."

I bite down hard on my bottom lip, willing the words to roll right off me. I know she's right, but it doesn't make it easier to hear. Not when I've spent years rebuilding myself brick by brick after my marriage crumbled. I think back to those early days when Madison was just a baby and I'd had no choice but to crawl back to Denver at the age of nineteen, to my parents' house and accept help. When Bill took us in and hired me as a ranch hand, I swore to myself that I'd never ask for help again. Never rely on anyone but myself. I don't need anyone's help now. Except maybe for a washing machine until I can get mine fixed...

TEN

DYLAN

JAKE: *How's cowboy life going, Dyl? Training camp isn't the same without you.*

CHASE: *Yeah. It sucks you're not here!*

JAKE: *Try not to buy anything else while we're gone!*

CHASE: *Something tells me Izzy will keep him in line.*

JAKE: *If she doesn't kill him first.*

CHASE: *True! See you this weekend, Dyl (if you're still alive)!*

The unrelenting beep of my alarm cuts through my sleep. I groan into my pillow, wanting to block out the noise and the world it's dragging me into. For a second, I forget why I even set the damn thing. It's Wednesday. Jake and Chase are in Flagstaff with the Stormhawks while I'm stuck here with a bunch of horses I don't want and don't know what the hell to do with, and yet I've done nothing to find a buyer either.

My hand reaches for the alarm and I silence it. Not because I have a plan. Or even because I want to. But because of Izzy. The way she defended me against Chase's ribbing on Saturday night while still looking like she wanted to throat-punch me has been lodged in my head like a thorn ever since. It's the only thing that's dragged me out of bed these past few mornings, working down a list of ranch jobs I barely understand.

Not that it's stopped Izzy from correcting my every move. I swear she has the mouth of someone who gets up in the morning just to pick a fight.

All those muscles don't mean a thing when you're knee-deep in hay and horse shit, she said yesterday. *Now use the shovel like this.*

Watching her earn herself a sharp look from Mama on Saturday after dinner was the first time I've seen her slip. Who doesn't ask to use a washing machine on a ranch like this when there's nothing but land and foothills for miles? Izzy, that's who.

But my feelings stem from more than just that. Izzy challenges me. Every look. Every word. She pushes back. And that's... new. I haven't had the best track record with women, and sure it's been a while, but the women I dated never pushed. Kate always let my gruff moods slide and never complained when I skipped dates because of football. She didn't expect anything deeper.

Izzy, though—she expects so damn much from me. She doesn't care I was a pro athlete at the top of my game two years ago, or how much I'm hurting right now. All she cares about is the horses and keeping my ass in check, and that infuriates me. So why is it so hard to stop thinking about her?

I groan and turn onto my back, staring at the ceiling. Outside, the sun is already creeping up over the foothills, promising another scorching day. I still don't know what I'm doing or what I want. Only that it isn't this. But hell... I might as well do something while the team is in Arizona.

Then what?

The question needles. Am I going to spend the rest of my life lurking on the sidelines, watching a life that isn't mine? I shove the question aside, throw back the covers, and head for the shower, bracing myself for another day of trying not to screw everything up. Even working with Izzy is easier than trying to answer questions about my future.

Ten minutes later, I'm heading downstairs, catching the scent of fresh coffee and Mama's lavender laundry detergent. The stairs creak beneath my weight, old wood and familiarity. The white walls are lined with framed photos of our childhoods. I've passed them so many times they barely register, but something makes me look today. I stare at a photo of me and Dad, standing side by side with a new black foal, born that morning and legs like sticks. I'm wearing Dad's old cowboy hat and looking on top of the world. Mama used to call me Dad's shadow around the ranch. I loved watching him work the horses, making every task look effortless.

I take another step, and two photos along, it's me, Jake, and Chase—all three of us wearing our football jerseys and padding. Dad no longer in any of the photos. I see the way our smiles don't quite reach our eyes, and even though it's been nearly two decades without Dad, a strange lump of emotion lodges in my throat. I swallow it down and keep moving. I wonder if he'd think ranching was a mistake, too.

Downstairs, I pass the living room. Plump cushions on the old leather couches slouch like they've seen one too many family movie nights. The stone fireplace stands cold and empty, but I can still picture Chase sitting in front of it last Christmas, tossing popcorn into Buck's eager mouth with Jake beside him, lovesick and pining for Harper when they hadn't figured out what they were yet.

Buck greets me in the hall, eyes bright and tail wagging.

"Ready for another day of annoying the hell out of me?" I

say, running a hand over Buck's back and not meaning it for a second. Buck has taken to staying by my side on the ranch, following me from the barn to the paddocks while I do the repairs Izzy asks for. Both of us keep our distance from the horses.

Mama is pouring coffee when I step into the kitchen. The air smells like baking bread and I don't need to open the oven to know Mama is making my favorite sourdough. A flood of emotions hits. It's love for this woman, who is always one step ahead, who has always had our backs and shown us love in more ways than most people would think possible. But even this is laced with resentment and the knowledge that I'm not where I'm supposed to be in my life. I know Mama's love is unconditional, but there's still a small part of me that feels like I've let her down.

"Morning, baby," Mama says, handing me a cup of steaming black coffee.

I mumble a thanks, pretending not to notice those blue eyes assessing me.

"You OK?" she asks.

"Yep," I reply, hiding behind my mug and taking a sip that's way too hot. I recognize the set of Mama's face. She's got something to say and I'm not gonna like it.

Mama leans against the counter. "What's your plan, Dylan?"

I shrug and stay quiet. She knows I don't have one.

"I know you don't want to hear it, but there's plenty of other ways for you to keep doing what you love with football."

"Mama," I warn, already knowing where this is going.

"Let me say my piece, please," she says. "It's OK to admit you made a mistake buying these horses. Find a buyer and move on. You always loved coaching kids in the outreach program. If that's what you love, any high school in Denver would kill to have you as their coach. There's still a future for you in football.

I've been getting calls all week from TV and radio asking if you'll become a guest expert."

I shake my head. "No." It's an effort to keep the frustration from my voice. No matter what, I won't lash out at Mama. "I love you, Mama," I say, "and I know you're trying to help, but if I can't be part of the Stormhawks, then I want nothing to do with football. And I don't need you trying to fix this."

Her eyes narrow, her voice firm. "Stop being so stubborn and take some time to think about this—"

"Are you sure it's me being stubborn?" I cut in. "No offense, Mama, but I don't need an agent anymore. You need to focus on Jake and Chase. I'm fine."

"But, Dylan—"

"No." I cut her off again. "You're fired." My words land in the silence. I hadn't meant to say it like that, but now it's out, it feels right. I swallow down the sting of failure threatening to take over, and I soften my voice. "Just be Mama now. OK?"

I take her hand in mine. It's tiny and warm. For the first time I see the exhaustion in her face, the lines that weren't there a few years ago.

"You've been the best sports agent I could've asked for. I played for my dream team. I earned a lot of money doing what I love for a long time, and the only reason I'm not going to spend the rest of my life walking with a limp is because of everything you did to help me recover from my ACL tear. I know you're going to try and fight this, but please don't. My life in football is over. I'm struggling to accept it, but you need to do the same."

Mama straightens, lifting her chin, and for a second I think she's going to argue. But then she lets out a slow breath. "OK," she says softly. "If that's what you want. Just as long as you know I'll always be here for you."

"I do," I say. "Now quit hanging around the ranch. Haven't you got meetings with the management staff and with sponsors to be having?"

She hesitates.

"Go. I'll be fine," I say, not sure if I mean it, but knowing it's the only way to get Mama to accept I don't need her as an agent anymore.

She reaches a hand to my cheek like she used to do when I was a kid. "I just want you to be happy, Dylan."

"I know." I walk out the back door before she can see the pain in my eyes and the knowledge that without football, without my team, happiness doesn't feel possible.

ELEVEN

IZZY

"You're early." I don't mask my surprise as Dylan steps across the driveway to the barn, Buck trotting happily at his heels. I reach down to greet the dog, scratching behind his ear the way he likes.

"Good morning to you too," Dylan says with that edge to his voice like he's all kinds of pissed. At me. At the world. Himself. I'm never sure.

He's wearing a red Stormhawks baseball cap pulled low, shielding his eyes from the bright morning sun. With a black branded sports tee stretching across his chest, he still looks more like a pro athlete than a rancher, but the work boots and the gloves sticking out of the back pocket of his jeans are a start. The fresh beard covering his jaw helps, too. I prefer it to the clean shave, not that I'd ever admit it.

"Since you're here, we're going to make a start on replacing the fence posts in the top paddock. Repairs aren't going to cut it, and the new posts I ordered arrived yesterday. I've already roped off the paddock to keep the stallions secure until it's done."

Dylan rolls his eyes. "Would a few pleasantries kill you,

Brooks? You could try saying 'thank you'. Believe it or not, I'm here to help."

I let out a short laugh, shaking my head. "Help? You've been making more work for me this week, Sullivan. This is your ranch. I'm your ranch hand. I'm here to help you. If anyone should be saying thank you, it's you. But bring me coffee tomorrow morning and you'll get a thanks."

His eyes narrow as they lock with mine. "You've got a real attitude, you know that?" he says, but his tone lands somewhere between annoyed and something else, like maybe my attitude is something he doesn't hate as much as he makes out.

I can't stop my lips from lifting at the edges. "And you've got a real ego. Now grab the tool belt and let's get to work."

We head toward the top paddock, Buck weaving between us like he wants to help. At least someone does. Dylan might be showing up, but everything about that damn scowl screams he'd rather be anywhere else.

The sky is a perfect stretch of blue above us, and the ranch hums with the sound of life—the soft thud of hooves on grass, the occasional whicker as the foals scamper around their mothers. The day is only just heating up, and I pull in a deep breath of fresh air as my gaze moves to the foothills. Dylan might not be much of a rancher, but this sure is one hell of a ranch, even if it's falling apart in places.

The back paddock is in worse shape than the others. The fence is rotten and leaning. It's going to be backbreaking work to get the posts out of the ground and set the new ones. We fall into a rhythm—Dylan loosening the packed earth around each post while I brace and shove from the other side. The wood groans as we rock it back and forth, until finally it gives way, and we haul the old post to the side.

We work in silence. The quiet is broken only by the occasional command from me or a clipped question from Dylan. It's only when the last of the old posts is out and we're striding back to the barn to start loading the new posts into the back of the truck that I finally let myself ask the questions burning a hole in my thoughts.

"There's a rodeo auction coming up a week from Monday," I tell Dylan. "If Bill hadn't been selling all his stock, he'd have sold Logan and Willow's foal there. Do you want to do that? Or would you rather keep the colt a while?"

"Bill would've sold now?" he asks, readjusting his cap.

I nod. "But Bill's been selling them young for a few years. Less work in breaking them in. So it depends on what kind of breeder you want to be. Whether you're planning to keep the ranch small like it is now, work with the foals for longer to get a higher sale price at auction, or expand the herd, breed more to sell young."

"I haven't thought about it," is the only reply I get.

Of course he hasn't.

"Because if we're not selling him, I need to know so I can start building more work into his training. Right now, it's just about getting him to walk confidently on a lead rein. The longer we keep him, the more we need to do. The rodeo is in their genes, but that's only half of what makes them the strong rodeo stock."

"I said I don't know yet," he replies, voice practically a growl, reminding me what a jerk Dylan can be. I don't know why I'm bothering to ask about the future of this ranch. Even if he keeps the horses, no way he keeps around someone he seems to barely tolerate. Which means my time here is nearly done.

Four weeks left.

I swallow my irritation. I've been checking job boards and messaging old contacts, looking for openings in ranch work, but there's nothing available. I stride ahead, grabbing the first post. It's heavy, but I've lifted worse and I hoist it up so it's resting lengthways in my arms, then I take a determined step toward the truck.

"I've got it," Dylan says, appearing at my side like I'm about to collapse. Like I'm not capable.

"I'm fine," I reply.

I shift slightly, trying to balance the awkward weight.

"Jesus, would you just—" Dylan reaches out, grabbing the other end.

I jerk to the side. The movement causes my foot to sink into the dry earth, the post slipping a fraction in my arms. "Let go!"

"You let go!" he fires back, showing no signs of listening to me.

Then Buck barks—loud and excited—darting between us. His solid body hits the back of my knee and everything goes to hell. My leg buckles, the post lurching sideways. Dylan tries to catch the weight, but it's happening too fast. The next thing I know, we're both going down hard—a tangle of limbs and timber.

The post lands across our shins, the pain sharp and searing, but it's the way my shoulder knocks into the solid muscle of Dylan's chest that has me gasping out in surprise, trying to pull back as Buck dances in a circle like he's laughing at us.

Dylan's shoulders shake and I realize he's laughing too. Or trying not to. A second later his laugh rings out, a deep, full-bodied sound that rumbles through his chest.

"This isn't funny," I say, but even before the words leave my mouth, a reluctant laugh escapes me and soon we're both giddy and breathless, the kind of laughter that loosens something inside.

Then the laughter fades and we're lying side by side, my body against his, our legs tangled, the post forgotten. I lift my face and find he's looking down at me, his lips inches from mine. Our eyes lock, and suddenly nothing feels funny anymore.

I force myself to shift away, break the moment. I groan as I blink up at the blue stretch of sky.

"You OK?" Dylan asks, pushing onto an elbow, gaining more distance from me too.

My braid has come loose in the fall and I tuck a stray strand of hair away from my face and nod as I sit up. "Nothing bruised but my pride. Wouldn't have happened if you'd let me carry the post on my own."

"Wouldn't have happened if you'd let me help."

We wrangle the post off our legs, then he stands, pulling off his glove and reaching down. I hesitate—but only for a second—before I remove my glove and take his hand.

The second our palms touch, a snap of heat shoots through me. Of awareness. A pull that makes the world go a little quieter around the edges, yanking my thoughts right back to the moment just now where we almost kissed and wishing I'd let it happen.

His grip is strong and steady, and he hauls me up, and then we're both stepping back, brushing off the dirt.

"Next time, listen when I say I've got it," I say.

One side of his mouth shifts into a smirk. "Next time, let me help." Buck gives a low, sheepish woof. Dylan's tone softens as he speaks to the dog. "Yeah, you should be sorry, Buckie. Stay out from under our feet next time."

I huff a laugh and finish brushing the dust from my jeans. I grab one side of the post and Dylan takes the other, and we start loading the truck. The tension between us is still there, and there's no way I'll ever admit it, but it's easier with the help. Maybe there's a rancher buried somewhere deep inside Dylan after all.

If he wants it.

And that's one big if.

TWELVE

DYLAN

CHASE: *Yo Dyl, I'm at the ranch. Where are you?*

JAKE: *Izzy probably had enough of the grump and buried him in one of the paddocks.*

CHASE: *Who would blame her?!*

DYLAN: *I'm on the field.*

CHASE: *Got time to help me with my timing on out routes?*

DYLAN: *Sure.*

The football field sits at the back of the ranch, out of sight from the house and the paddocks. It's quiet here, away from the sounds of the horses and Buck's occasional barks. It's been a while since I've been up here and the field is rougher than I remember—grass long, lines faded—but the goalposts still loom, and the space still feels sacred, like our own home turf.

As kids we were out here every day we weren't in school—

me, Jake, and Chase. Playing until we couldn't see the ball. It was on this field where football stopped being just a game and became a language it felt like only the three of us understood.

I've got cones set up in a drill I've run a thousand times before. Today, I'm testing footwork, timing, trying to work around a known gap in the Stormhawks defense. I might not be on the team anymore, but the habit hasn't left me. It feels good to do something I'm good at.

I throw the ball into the air, watching it spin before I catch it again, trying to ignore the ache in my knee. It's been sore since the post landed on it three days ago—thanks to Izzy being too stubborn to let me help.

My body moves on autopilot, leaving my mind to spin out. I know I should be helping with the ranch, but it's Saturday and Izzy is spending the day working with the horses with Madison. I've made myself scarce, telling myself it's to give them some mother–daughter time. The truth is, I'm hiding. Jake and Chase arrived back from training camp first thing this morning, their energy electric, and being around them is like pressing on a bruise. But when Chase asks for help, I'm always gonna say yes, no matter how much football feels like a wound that won't heal.

I hear footsteps behind me and call out without turning around. "First pre-season game next weekend. You ready?"

"First game playing as one of the Stormhawks." Chase jogs up, scooping the ball into his hands. "Yeah, I'm ready, but I'm nervous. I don't want to let the fans down. They're expecting more Sullivan magic."

"You know you're the best out of the three of us, right?" I shoot him a look, meaning every word and feeling nothing but pride. "Always have been."

He shrugs, but his smile is wide. We fall into the rhythm of the routine. Chase lines up as quarterback and I run out routes —short, sharp sprints where I break hard to the sideline, reaching out as Chase sends the ball spiraling perfectly into my hands.

We do it again. And again. Until sweat is dripping down my back and I feel more alive than I have done in weeks. When we break for water, I glance over at Chase. I haven't exactly been around for him much lately, I think with a tug of guilt. "You thought any more about contacting your mom?"

Chase doesn't answer right away. I'm the only one he's told about this and I tread carefully. He mentioned a few months back he was thinking of tracking her down. He said it as a throwaway comment and I was careful not to react, just accept. Support.

We line up again, tossing the ball back and forth before Chase answers. "Still thinking."

"You know Mama and Jake would be fine with it, right? It's not us holding you back."

He nods, looking off toward the tree line. "It's not that. I just don't know if it's what I want. Life's good. Really good. It's only that sports psychologist I saw last year—she said I'm carrying too much from my past. Says I'm holding back. I don't know if it's true, but sometimes it feels like I have more to give."

He pauses before adding, "And after what happened with my dad..." Chase shrugs, like it's nothing, but the tension in his jaw says otherwise.

Everyone knows the story by now. Jamel Bishop played one season with the Stormhawks when he met Chase's mom, Leanna. A one-night stand. Nine months later, Chase was born. Jamel gave her a wad of cash and vanished. His career nose-dived soon after, and he stayed out of the picture—until Chase lit up the league with the Trailblazers.

Then Jamel reappeared all over socials, bragging about how proud he was of "his boy," and angling for a reunion. He pushed for their first meeting to happen on a morning talk show. When Chase refused and said he'd only do it if it stayed private, it quickly became clear it wasn't Chase that Jamel wanted—it was airtime and a shot at a commentating career. The whole thing fell apart and Jamel disappeared again, but it rattled Chase for a while.

"What if it's the same thing again?" he says quietly. "What if I reach out to my mom and she only wants a relationship with me because of who I am?"

"She hasn't reached out, though, has she?" I ask, already knowing the answer.

He shakes his head. "No. And that's what I keep thinking. Jamel never wanted me. That part was clear. But my mom... she did. She just couldn't cope. And a part of me wants to find her. To tell her that leaving me here—on Mama's doorstep—was the best thing she could've done. And that I'm OK. Better than OK. That I'm grateful."

I nod but keep quiet. Moments when Chase drops the jokes are rare. He's like a horse I don't want to spook. I almost groan at the thought. Using horse analogies when I'm still too much of a coward to go near them on my own ranch. Dad always said horses can sense emotions. What if they see through the bull- shit, see me for what I really am?

Chase drops back, lining up for another drill, telling me he's done talking. I know he'll open up again when he's ready. I promise myself I'll make more time for him. I've been way too focused on my own problems lately and it hasn't exactly done me any good.

He's about to throw me the ball when there's a shout from the far end of the field. We turn to see a little hand in the air, dark blonde curls, and Madison's skipping run. "Will you teach me to play, Dylan? Please. If I keep eating my vegetables, I'll be as big as you," she says, lifting her stick-thin arms and flexing. "And then I'll be a great football player too."

I can't stop the laugh bubbling up. Like when the fence post landed on me and Izzy and our fight suddenly felt ridiculous. The moment—a pinprick of light in a pitch-black night.

I drop to a crouch so we're face to face. "Let's see what you've got."

Chase jogs over and high-fives Mad. "Here you go," he says, placing the ball in her hands. "I'd better get back to the city. You coming to watch the game next week, Dyl?"

I hesitate, insides tightening. For most of my recovery, I avoided watching the Stormhawks games. It was too damn painful watching from the skybox, knowing I should've been on the field. But this is Chase's first game with the team, and there's no way I'd miss it. "You know it," I reply, catching the way his smile widens and knowing it's the right thing to do.

When it's just me and Mad, I set up some simple drills like I've done with the kids in the Stormhawks outreach program. Run to the cone, spin, throw. She fumbles the ball a few times, but she's a quick study and she keeps practicing, talking the whole time, asking questions, sharing details of her life—campfires and roasting marshmallows and friends.

"Did you used to play every day?" Madison asks as I'm helping her readjust her grip on the ball.

"Pretty much," I say. "Mama used to say we only came inside to eat and sleep."

Madison grins. "Like me and Mom with the horses."

"Exactly."

"Mom said we might not find another ranch when our time here is up," Madison says. "I don't want to live with Grandma and Granddad in the city and be away from ranching, but Mom says we might have to."

For the first time, reality hits. I've been seeing the ranch as my problem. My mistake. There's four weeks left on the six-week clock Bill set when I agreed to hire Izzy, and I haven't lifted a finger to find a buyer or figure out what I'm gonna do. I've buried my head in the sand like a coward. But this ranch isn't just about me. It's not just the symbol of my failures or whatever future I'm supposed to be figuring out. It's about the horses. It's about Izzy, and about Mad, too. I think back to the look in Izzy's eyes when I didn't answer her questions this week. Didn't want to think about the answers.

I wouldn't blame her if she walked when the six weeks are up. Why would she stay when I'm the one wasting time, ignoring my problems, not making the decision I need to make? And seeing it through the eyes of an eight-year-old who just wants to keep doing what she loves makes me want to do better. Whatever that means.

"Do you miss playing football?" Mad asks.

"Yeah," I say, surprised how even that admission causes emotion to lodge in my throat. "For a long time, football was all I wanted. Playing for the Stormhawks was my dream. Being told I couldn't do that anymore broke something inside me." It's the closest I've come to admitting how I feel to anyone. Somehow, it's easier with Mad than with Mama or my brothers.

"Which is why you bought the horses," Madison says. "For a new dream."

"Maybe." That and a lot of bourbon, but I can't tell Mad that. "Right, we need to work on your throw some more if you're going to be a star quarterback like Chase."

Madison beams and we get back to the drills. It's easy, it's fun, and the more we play, the more something eases in me. Madison's laughter ringing out every time she fumbles and her whoops of joy when the throw is good.

When my hands next wrap around the football, it doesn't feel like a reminder of what I lost. It just feels fun.

And for a little while, I let myself believe it could be as simple as Mad has made it seem—a new dream taking shape. But that means letting go of the old one, and I'm still gripping hold of that with both hands.

THIRTEEN

IZZY

FLIC: *Dylan made an appearance yet or is he still hiding behind a hay bale somewhere?*

IZZY: *Reluctantly, but yes.*

FLIC: *He's going through a tough time, but I knew he'd get his head out of his ass eventually.*

IZZY: *His head is still firmly up his ass! And he's still a jerk!*

FLIC: *Didn't stop you from kissing him in the back of my bar!*

IZZY: *Really wish I hadn't told you that. And he kissed me.*

FLIC: *Seriously though, you OK?*

IZZY: *Aside from the fact I can't find any ranch work anywhere and only have four weeks left in this job, I'm great. Mad loves it here.*

FLIC: *All I can offer is bar work, but it's yours anytime you want it. Come see me soon!*

I take the path that snakes away from the back paddock, following the sound of excited yells that can only be Mad. I knew she'd spotted Dylan heading out beyond the paddocks earlier and was eager to explore what was up there after we'd finished the grooming. I remember that feeling of wanting to explore and escape, and Mad knows to be sensible, so I didn't stop her. I turn the corner, expecting to find a stretch of open pasture or dry scrubland. But instead, I come face to face with a huge football field with goal posts and faded white lines.

Of course Dylan has a football field on his ranch.

I shake my head as I spot Madison, standing in the middle of the field, legs apart, a ball in her hand. She swings her shoulder back then forward, putting her whole body into the movement as she releases the ball into the air. It wobbles a little but arcs close enough to Dylan for him to catch it. Mad whoops like it's the winning touchdown and Dylan shouts some praise, his face lit up.

This isn't the same man who's been grumbling through every task I've thrown at him this week. Maybe I'm being unfair. Things have been different since the fall with the fence post. He hasn't complained once when I've corrected his work. He's up earlier too, stepping out the back door with two cups of coffee, passing me one with an exaggerated show and even cracking a smile when I give him my promised "thanks."

He's been avoiding the horses, though. I'm not sure why, but he always finds something else to do, somewhere else to be when the training starts or there's grooming to do. I know he rode as a kid. You don't grow up on a horse ranch without getting thrown in the saddle by the time you can walk. So it can't be that he doesn't know how to handle them.

With an idea in mind, I push off the fence and head toward

the barn, boots hitting the dry earth. We've made progress this week. The last stall in the barn is finally cleared of boxes and clutter, swept clean and bedded down, ready for the horses. The tack room has fresh nails lining the wall where bridles and reins now hang in neat rows. The feed stores are full and it's finally starting to feel like a real working ranch. Inside the barn, the air is thick with the scent of hay and oiled leather as I gather what I need before stepping back into the afternoon sun. It's slipping toward the horizon, but the heat still clings to the day. By the time I've led the three horses to the fence line for saddling, my shirt is too hot on my back. I strip it off and finish tacking up in my tank top, the warm air brushing against my shoulders.

Ten minutes later, three horses are saddled and waiting for their riders. Rusty is the biggest. A tall bay gelding with a reddish coat the color of the foothills in summer, he's Bill's old ride. Steady and patient. I run a hand down his flank and he huffs, nudging me with his nose like he knows he's being called up.

"You're going to be on babysitting duty today, handsome," I whisper as I tighten the girth. "For the record, I still think he's a jerk, but we'll give him a try, OK?"

Next is Rosie, the dapple-gray mare Madison loves to sneak treats to. I move around to each side, adjusting the stirrups. She's one of the smallest mares and comes with a little sass, but she adores Mad, and I trust her. Last is Bramble, my favorite gelding to ride. Midnight-black and sturdy. A horse who'll ride forever.

I hear them before I see them. The excited, babbling chatter of my daughter followed by the lower, shorter replies from Dylan. I turn in time to see Mad break into a run, a football still tucked under her arm. Her cheeks are flushed and her hair is wild.

"Dylan's been teaching me how to play football," Mad says,

a little breathless and a whole lot of happy. "I'm going to be a quarterback like Chase. Dylan said we can go with him and Mama to watch the Stormhawks play next weekend. Can we go, Mom? Please! We're watching from the sky."

"Only if Dylan is sure," I reply.

I shoot him a questioning look as he adjusts his baseball cap and says, "We watch from the skybox, Mad. Not the sky. It's where friends and family get to watch the game."

"Skybox, that's what I meant." Then Mad's eyes widen like she's only just clocking the three horses. "Are we going riding?"

I smile. "Helmet's on the hook."

She gives another whoop and shoots off as I turn to Dylan.

"Three horses?" He eyes Rusty like the horse just challenged him to a fight. "What's going on?" he asks. It's a dumb question, and by the way he winces, he knows it.

"Well, seeing as I only just discovered you have a football field, I thought it was time you gave us an actual tour of the ranch."

"But I—"

"You've been avoiding the horses," I cut in.

His shoulders tense, but it's Madison who speaks next.

"A rancher who doesn't like horses?" Her mouth pops open. She looks halfway between laughing and being utterly scandalized.

Dylan rubs at the stubble on his jaw. "I like horses fine. I'm just not sure they like me."

"Mom says horses don't like jerks," Mad says. "Are you a jerk?"

I huff a laugh, and he glares at me, but there's a flicker of amusement in his eyes, too. Either way, I'm enjoying his discomfort way too much.

"I hope not," he mutters, placing the football equipment on the ground. "Better get my boots." He nods down at his cleats, still looking less than thrilled at the prospect of riding as he jogs toward the house. A minute later he's back and taking the reins I'm holding out.

"This is Rusty. He's grumpy, so you'll get along fine."

Rusty snorts like he agrees, his ears flicking back.

"I haven't ridden in twenty years. Don't you have a starter pony or something?"

I swing onto Bramble with ease, feeling the joy that always spreads through me when I'm on horseback, before looking down at him. "You're six foot five and all muscle. A pony ain't gonna cut it."

"Been checking out my muscles, Brooks?" he shoots back, voice still a grumble.

"Shut up and get on your horse," I reply.

Dylan plants one boot in the stirrup and hauls himself up. He's halfway there, leg about to swing around into the saddle, when Rusty shifts position, sidestepping to the left, leaving Dylan nothing but air, and a split second later he's landing flat on his ass in the dirt, a grunt and expletive hissed under his breath.

I know I shouldn't laugh. This was supposed to be about helping Dylan—getting him past whatever's had him avoiding the horses all week. But the second his ass hits the dirt and that stunned expression flashes across his face, the laughter bubbles up and spills out before I can stop it. Madison's already doubled over on Rosie, clutching the horn, her shoulders shaking with giggles—and that only makes it worse.

"That was... majestic," I say, not even pretending to keep a straight face. "Seriously, are you OK?"

"Never better," he growls.

"OK then. Time to try again!"

He shoots me a murderous look but moves back to the stirrup, more cautious this time. Rusty shifts again, testing him, and this time, Dylan gets stuck hopping alongside the horse with one foot in and one on the ground as Rusty wanders toward Bramble.

"You've gotta talk to him!" Madison calls when Dylan gets his foot free. "Tell him he's doing a good job!"

Dylan gives her a look like she's lost her mind.

"Just try it," I say.

He leans toward Rusty's ear. "Look, big guy, I... don't know what I'm doing here, but if you don't throw me, I promise you a treat when we get back."

Rusty flicks an ear back, and this time, he stands still long enough for Dylan to mount. He looks about as comfortable as I'd probably be on a football field on game day, but when I nudge Bramble forward and we start to move, his shoulders drop and he settles into the sway of Rusty's walk.

We ride around the fenced paddocks; the sun is warm on my shoulders. The horses move steadily beneath us, and Madison's constant chatter keeps me smiling, even if that worry is still clawing at the back of my mind.

"What's through those trees?" Mad asks.

"I'll show you," Dylan replies, walking Rusty through the spruce trees, looking like he's remembering how to ride and liking it. We follow him through the shade of the trees, the smell of earth, and the fresh piney scent from the spruce needles, and when we step out into the sunlight again, I draw in a breath.

"Oh! You have a lake," Madison shouts.

"It's beautiful," I say at the same time.

"We used to swim here a lot as kids." There's that almost smile again on Dylan's face as we move around a sandy shoreline. "But I mostly use it now for my knee exercises. The water helps take the weight off my body. It's real safe. I'll take you for a swim next weekend if you like?"

Madison whoops with delight as we skirt the edge of the lake.

I bite down on my bottom lip, forcing out the words I don't want to speak. "Just remember we're only here for a short time, Mad. Don't get too settled."

I hate how her face falls at my warning and the silence that follows, but I need her to be prepared. Even Dylan's expression tightens at my comment, and I wonder again if he'll sell before then.

We guide the horses into the foothills. The land turns wilder—scrubby brush and tall grass alongside clusters of trees. The breeze picks up, smelling like wild sage and cooling the sweat at the back of my neck. Bramble's hooves crunch over loose rock as we follow a narrow trail that winds between two boulders.

Dylan reins Rusty to a stop and nods toward a rocky rise off the path. Something about the way he sits in the saddle—broad shoulders, those muscular arms and tight jeans, one hand loose on the reins, like he was made for this—makes my mouth go dry. It's infuriating how damn hot he is.

"Up there," he says. "There's a cave tucked into the side of that slope. I used to run away there anytime I got in trouble."

Madison leans forward in her saddle, eyes wide. "A cave? That's cool."

"I'd last an hour before my snacks ran out, then sneak back to the ranch hoping Mama wasn't still mad."

"Mom ran away too," Mad says as we take a path that turns us back toward the ranch. "She was going to be a doctor, but then she found out she was pregnant with me and ran away from medical school." She says it so matter of fact. Typical Mad.

"Easiest decision I ever made. And you're not the reason I'm not a doctor, Mad," I remind her gently.

The truth is, I knew long before I saw that double line on the pregnancy test that medicine wasn't for me. Maybe I'd always known but was too chicken to do anything about it. I'd spent my life on a conveyor belt—honor roll, AP classes, extracurriculars. Schedules that left me no time to breathe. I would've quit eventually—Madison just gave me the push I needed. She didn't derail my life. She gave me the chance to build a new one.

"White coats and hospitals—doesn't feel like you," Dylan says, and something in his voice makes me glance over.

Our eyes meet. Something warm curls in the pit of my belly. There's no scowl, no sharp retort, no wall up between us. Just him seeing me. And for a moment too long, I let him.

I force myself to look away, but the pull is still there, thrumming like a live wire just under my skin. I'm grateful when Madison breaks the moment. "Did you always want to play football, Dylan?"

He shakes his head. "You know what? I didn't. I was just like you at your age. Obsessed with horses and ranching. I spent every second I could out on the ranch with my dad, doing any job he'd let me. I always dreamed of taking over the ranch one day, making it my own. Dad used to take us to the rodeo, and I'd sit up in the stands, watching the horses he bred take the ring. I remember looking at my dad's face and the pride he had and thinking it must be the best feeling in the world."

I watch Dylan swallow, the column of his throat shifting like he's pushing the memories down.

When he speaks again, his voice is quieter. "But then he died, and football was loud and demanding and didn't give me time to think. It became everything."

Mad looks thoughtful, staying quiet now. The only sound is the creak of the saddles and the hooves hitting the dry ground. I stare at Dylan, something catching in my chest. The way the last rays of sunlight hit his face makes him look younger, less guarded. And the way he's looking out over the land, lost to his thoughts and his past, I swear in that one moment I've never seen anyone look more like they belong on a horse.

And when I follow his gaze to the paddocks and the horses grazing in the light of the setting sun, it's not Madison I need to remind that there's less than four weeks before I'm out of a job and we're out of a place to live. It's me.

FOURTEEN

DYLAN

Saturday night games are my favorite. Biggest crowds. Loudest cheers. Electricity buzzes through the stadium, making your skin prickle and your pulse race. They're rare. When the season starts, games are Thursdays, Sundays, or Mondays. And maybe because they're rare, Saturday night games always feel like they have that extra drop of magic.

No. Saturday night games *were* my favorite.

My shoulders stiffen and I pull my baseball cap lower as I follow Harper, Mama, Madison, and Izzy to the skybox at the top of the Stormhawks stadium. I'm not on the field tonight. I'm stuck watching like a goddamn spectator with a weight in my gut, and a dark mood that's been clinging to me all day, heavy and unshakable. I should be down there. I should be in pads and cleats, lining up with the team. And as if to taunt me further, my knee throbs with every step—a reminder of another week of hauling hay and mending fences.

The skybox is crowded—management staff, friends, family, sponsors. People I know. No one I want to talk to. The mood is buoyant. Laughter and handshakes, flutes of champagne clinking. Harper makes a beeline for her best friend, Mia, dressed in a floaty skirt and tight top, standing beside Chase's best friend, Serena: tall, blonde, and wearing her old Stormhawks cheer team top with a denim skirt and cowboy boots. Harper motions for Izzy and Mad to join her, but I don't follow. Instead, I give a nod of greeting their way before dipping my head and making my way to the glass.

The view overlooking the field nearly punches the breath out of me. Every single one of the 70,000 stadium seats is full. The roar of noise as the Stormhawks take the field in their red jerseys and white helmets feels like another throat punch. Across from them, the Arizona Scorchers pour out of their tunnel in black and yellow. I imagine Coach Allen is already on the sideline, headset on, clipboard clutched tight, barking last-minute plays.

This was my world. I don't know who I am without it. The thought threatens to drag me further into the darkness, but it's cut short by Mama appearing at my side. I turn to find her watching me like I'm made of glass. I sigh, throwing an arm around her and hugging her to my side. "I'm fine, Mama."

She squeezes my side. "You sure?"

Pain cuts through my chest. "Yeah."

She nods and steps away to greet one of Chase's sponsors.

Mama's been different these past few weeks. Now that I'm not lying in bed all day, hiding from the world, she's backed off. She checks in each morning, bright and breezy. Just being Mama, not my agent. Then she disappears into meetings and takes her calls, but there's always fresh coffee brewed, always food in the oven by dinner. The quiet ways she tells me she cares.

Tonight's game doesn't count for the standings; it's just pre-season. But it means something to the team. It's a message to the fans: We're ready. After winning the conference last year and making it to the playoffs, hopes are high that they'll push all the way to the Super Bowl this time.

I've been watching the rookies give it their all this week in practice. Despite throwing myself into the ranch work, I've still found myself driving to Stormhawks Park in the afternoons. Watching practice by the fence. Answering the occasional question from a rookie on footwork or game prep while trying to ignore the way my stomach knots thinking of all the jobs I should be doing back at the ranch. I don't know where I belong anymore. Not at Stormhawks Park. Not entirely at Oakwood Ranch either.

"Dylan!" Now it's Madison who cuts through my spiral. She skips up to the glass, holding a soda can like it's a trophy. "A man gave this to me." She lowers her voice conspiratorially. "He said it was free."

I look over and see Don Hubert lift his hand in greeting. Don is in his eighties and the son of Larry Hubert, who founded the Stormhawks. We're one of the last family-owned teams left in the NFL—something that means a lot to the fans and the family. Don's children and grandchildren now run the club day-to-day.

I nod a greeting before turning to focus on Mad. That big smile of hers is sunshine to the storm in my head. It was the same earlier when we were on the field at home, practicing her throw as she told me about her camp's raft-building competition, talking for ten minutes straight about strategy and flotation and how her team was going to win, thanks to Grandpa Joe sneaking her extra rope and empty containers.

"Oh, they're about to start!" she says, throwing herself into one of the wide leather seats in the front row. "What happens now?"

I drop down beside her, gesturing toward the middle of the field. "Scorchers won the toss. They've chosen to kick off."

She leans forward and I talk her through the plays—coverage schemes, offensive sets, what the quarterback's looking for—and it's just the distraction I need as the Stormhawks take an easy lead.

Halfway through the second quarter, Izzy comes to sit on the other side of Madison. She's in ripped jeans and a fitted V-neck tee, dark blonde hair loose down her back, and wearing minimal makeup, seeming completely oblivious to the appreciative glances she draws from every man in the box.

At least she's not wearing those damn cutoffs from yesterday. I nearly nailed my thumb to the barn wall when she bent over to grab a bale of hay and my eyes dragged to her rounded ass, dick stirring like a perv.

And suddenly I'm not thinking of the game; I'm thinking of the moment last week when I fell off Rusty, sending Izzy and Madison into hysterics. I'm thinking of how familiar it felt sitting in that saddle, even after twenty years. As natural as lacing up my cleats. The steady sway of a horse, the creak of leather, the freedom of it. The way my mood lifted.

"Hey," Izzy says, settling into the seat. "What's the score?"

I let Madison answer. "Stormhawks are crushing it, 17-10." She holds out her hand to fist bump and damn if it doesn't make me smile as I tap my knuckles gently to hers.

Izzy shoots me a look. It's the same one she gives me anytime Mad asks me to play football. The same look I get when they're video-calling on Madison's grandpa's phone and Mad shouts out as I'm walking past, wanting Izzy to pass the phone to me, always with the same opening question. *Do the horses like you yet?*

Always the same reply. *I'm getting there.*

I get it. Izzy is protective of Mad. And she wants to make sure I'm OK having her around and teaching her football. If Izzy got over that stubborn streak of hers and just asked, I'd tell her hanging out with Madison on the football field is one of the best moments of my week. But she doesn't, and so I just nod.

Things have been... easier between us this week. There's

still moments of tension—her sharp mouth that gets under my skin. My gritted replies. But we've found a rhythm.

Whether our truce will hold while we're stuck in the truck together for the three-hour drive to the rodeo auction on Monday is anyone's guess. One of us might not make it back, especially if we get talking about the future of the ranch and what I'm gonna do—questions I'm still ignoring.

And then there are the times when Izzy isn't laughing at my expense, when she's calm, focused, kind. When she talks to the horses or smiles because I've done something right for once. In those moments, the spark between us turns into something electric and my thoughts flit to that moment in the back of The Hay Barn when I hauled her to me and kissed her like it was our last moment on earth.

I don't know what those moments mean, if anything. But I can't stop thinking about them. I can't stop thinking about Izzy, either.

FIFTEEN

IZZY

Monday dawns like every other day since I've been on the ranch —clear sky, bright sun, a promise of heat. It's still early. That strange place where the sun is rising but a crescent moon and a scattering of stars are still clinging to the sky. But the crispness of the early-morning air is doing nothing to cool my mood. I glance toward the back door, expecting to see Dylan striding out with two cups of coffee in hand.

Where the hell is he? I check the time on my phone before I shove it into the pocket of my jeans and focus on attaching the horse trailer to Dylan's truck, tightening the bolts until my hands ache. I told him last night we had to leave early for the rodeo auction if we want to get Willow and Logan's foal registered in time for a good slot on the docket. The paperwork is time-stamped. Late arrivals get put to the bottom of the list.

Irritation circles my thoughts. Sure, he's been great with Madison—really great—and he's been showing up more on the ranch, taking control more. But he's still unreliable. Still no closer to making an actual decision. About the horses. About the ranch. About anything. I shouldn't be surprised he's a no-show.

The days are slipping away so fast. Broken only by Madison's weekend visits and the laughter and fun she brings. Football on the field. Swimming in the lake. I had to bite my tongue every time she jumped with joy. Because now there's only three weeks left and only two more weekends with Mad here. Then camp will be over and Mad will be back at school and I'm still no closer to finding more ranch work or a solution that isn't moving to my parents'.

I've been trying to focus on the good with Dylan. On the way he's started interacting with the horses—showing himself to be steady and intuitive. I don't need to watch over him anymore. But I find myself watching for a whole other reason. The way his broad shoulders fill out those faded tees. The way he brushes down the geldings, strong and sure in a way that has me thinking about those hands on me. I lie awake every night, thinking of that one kiss—that moment of madness. The way it felt like something I haven't let myself want in a long time, leaving me aching for more. For him. For that damn kiss and what it promised.

But then I watch him climb into his truck every afternoon and drive away. I know exactly where he's going. I overheard him tell Mad. He's watching the team practice. Can't stay away. It's a reminder that he's kidding himself if he thinks the ranch is anything more than a distraction. And the truth is, anytime I soften toward him, I'm kidding myself too. Dylan Sullivan is still the pro athlete with the big ego who doesn't give a damn about anything but himself.

I'd be a fool to forget that. A fool to think I have a place here even if he does keep the ranch.

I test the bolts on the horse trailer a final time before stepping back. The sun is climbing steadily, the temperature with it. Already I long to swap my black plaid shirt for one of my cooler tank tops, but it's taken years of hard work to earn respect in this industry. To be known as a good ranch hand—one who's skilled and reliable. I'm not about to undo that by wearing something revealing. It's not unheard of for women to work on ranches, but it's not exactly the norm either. Besides, word will have spread that Bill sold his horse stock to a pro athlete. My reputation and that of the horses is more important than ever.

A reputation that will mean shit if Dylan doesn't actually join me for this auction. If he was even remotely serious about running this place, he would've joined me an hour ago when I checked the horses and fixed their feed. And now it's already six thirty, and if we don't leave for The Rocky Plains Foal and Yearling Sale soon, we won't make it in time to put the foal into auction at all, let alone get a good place on the docket.

I stride across the drive and open the back door to the kitchen, half expecting to find him by the counter fixing coffee, but it's Mama I find. She's at the kitchen table with a laptop and an appointment book open beside it. I wonder if she ever sleeps.

She lifts her head and smiles a greeting. Despite her standing offer to help myself to coffee and anything I need, it's never felt right to stroll in. I've only been using the washing machine on the weekends, because Madison insists.

"Morning, Izzy," Mama says. "Finally taken up my offer of coffee, I hope."

"Thanks, Mama. I was actually looking for Dylan. We're supposed to be heading out to an auction."

Her smile is replaced with worry, like she knows as well as I do that Dylan is lost between two worlds and the only one who can save him is himself. "You'd better go on up. Third door on the left."

I slip off my boots and pad through the house. It feels awkward, like I'm intruding on Dylan's space, but if he'd bothered to get up this morning, I wouldn't have to be doing this. I step into the hall, passing a cozy-looking living room filled with mismatched furniture. There's a pair of armchairs near a large fireplace, and a coffee table scattered with magazines and books. The dining room beyond is simpler: a sturdy oak table and high-backed chairs. Binders of paperwork are stacked in one corner. A room that looks like it's used more as an office than a place to eat. Everything about this house feels lived-in and homey—the kind of ranch house I've always dreamed of owning one day. As if I'll ever be able to afford it.

I pause at the bottom of the stairs, my eyes dragging to the wall of family photos. I see Dylan as a boy around Madison's age, his gap-toothed grin half-hidden beneath a cowboy hat so oversized it practically swallows his head. The photo is almost enough to soften my irritation.

"Dylan?" I call his name as I take the stairs.

No reply.

I head straight for the third door on the left and give three confident knocks. "Dylan," I call again.

There's a muffled grunt that sounds like the audio version of his scowl. There's nothing else for it. I push the door open. The first thing that hits me is the scent of rich leather, cedar, and something deeper, more distinctly male. It's a scent I remember from the night at the bar, Dylan's hands running over my body, my back against the wall. Heat creeps up my neck before pooling low in my belly, and it's a fight to shove the memory aside.

The curtains are drawn. In the gloom there's just enough light to see Dylan sprawled across the bed, lying on his back with the covers twisted low around a muscled torso that draws my attention like a magnet.

Shit. Does he have to be so damn hot?

"Dylan," I say again, louder this time.

He groans, one hand reaching blindly to the nightstand where his phone is sitting.

"Dylan," I snap. "If you don't get up, we're going to miss the auction."

Finally, he opens his eyes, hair mussed from sleep. "What time is it?" he asks, voice like gravel.

"Time to move." Despite the traitorous way my eyes linger on his body, annoyance pulses through my veins. Before I can think about what I'm doing, I yank the covers away from him—only realizing a second too late that he might be naked.

He isn't.

But any relief is short-lived because my eyes go straight to the obvious: morning wood. Bold. Impressive. And straining against the fabric of his underwear. *Begging to be—*

I cut the thought dead, heat rising up my neck.

"You like what you see, Brooks?" Dylan's voice is thick with sleep, but the smirk is wide awake. He knows exactly where my gaze is fixed.

My eyes snap up to his face, cheeks on fire. I cross my arms and snort, trying to look unaffected. "Relax. I've seen bigger."

"Now you're just lying to both of us," he says with a low chuckle, grabbing a pillow and casually dropping it to his lap as he swings his legs around into a sitting position, one hand scrubbing through his hair, the other anchoring the pillow in place. "You always wake people up with full body scans and sarcasm, or am I just special?"

"The only thing you are is late." I turn away, needing to look anywhere but at Dylan's body. "You've got five minutes. And if you're not outside by then, I'm leaving without you."

"Promise?" he calls after me.

I don't give him the satisfaction of a reply as I head down to the kitchen to take Mama up on her offer of coffee—when really, what I need right now is an ice bath after whatever the hell *that* was between us.

Unreliable. I cling to the word, hoping it'll cool the heat still pulsing through my body.

It doesn't help. Not when my mind's replaying Dylan, practically naked in his bed, that damn smirk pulling at the corners of his mouth. Not when my body is still humming with the heat of something I have no business wanting.

~

Ten minutes later, Dylan and I do a good job of pretending everything is normal, like he didn't oversleep and we didn't just exchange words that felt a whole lot more like flirting than fighting.

We lead the foal into the trailer. The five-month-old colt has a midnight-black coat, long legs, and a personality more curious than skittish. His ears flick at every sound, nostrils flaring as he takes in the world with wide brown eyes. With parents like Logan and Willow, he's got all the right instincts—quick on his feet, smart, responsive. A future cutting horse with real potential.

The excitement of auction day is always laced with something heavier. Saying goodbye never gets easier. These horses are family. And for one awful moment, I wonder, *What if this is my last auction?* The thought hits like a hoof to the ribs.

"I'm driving," I say, stepping around to the driver's side before Dylan can argue.

But he just tosses me the keys. "Works for me."

I blink. "Huh."

"What?" he asks, the teasing tone he used in his bedroom gone.

"I figured you'd be the type of man to insist on driving."

He shrugs. "I've never driven with a trailer before. I want to practice around the ranch before I take it out on the road. Assuming you're not planning any sudden braking today?"

My grip tightens on the keys, but I let the jab slide and climb in.

We drive in silence. It's awkward. In that way that feels like we're both one breath away from fighting some more. Awkward in a way that makes me want to saddle up and ride hard into the hills until the noise in my head quiets down. The only thing that's ever worked.

Then Dylan pulls a thermos from the bag at his feet and places two cups in the holders, pouring coffee into both.

"Figured we could use the boost."

I glance over, surprised. "Thanks."

"So," Dylan starts. "Tell me everything I need to know about this auction."

"It's all about knowing when to sell and who to sell to," I explain. "Some trainers prefer foals young so they can break them in themselves and tailor their training from the start. Others want them older, with groundwork already done—haltered, saddled, and used to commands. Timing's a big factor, too. Buyers are always thinking ahead to the next rodeo season or their breeding schedules. The bidding can get heated—especially if it's a foal like ours with good bloodlines in events like cutting or barrel racing."

"So we're not buying today?" Dylan asks.

I laugh softly, shaking my head. "You've already got your hands full, remember? Later down the line, if you decide to keep the horses, you'll need to think about expanding—new mares for breeding or maybe a stud stallion to bring in fresh bloodlines. For now, though, we're here to sell."

I try not to think about the "if" in my comment and how it seems to hang between us like an unanswered question.

He nods, staring into the distance for a while before speaking again. "Madison would've loved today."

I smile at the thought. "Yeah. She would." But there's hesitation in my voice I can't quite swallow, and I know Dylan picks up on it.

"What?" he asks.

I take a quick sip of my coffee. Keep my eyes on the road. A whole minute passes and Dylan doesn't try to fill the silence.

"I just don't know if ranching is what's best for her."

His brow furrows. "You don't think she's happy?"

"No, she is. She loves ranch life. But sometimes I wonder if

I'm being selfish. Ranching is my dream, not hers, and it's not exactly stable." My hands tighten on the wheel. "My parents want us to live with them. It'd mean security. Madison would have her own room in an actual home, not a pull-down bed in a trailer. Plus, she could do any extracurriculars she wants. Choices I can't give her while ranching."

"But..." Dylan prompts.

"But I felt so trapped in that life. Like I didn't belong. Everything I did, I felt like I was a disappointment."

"So why consider it for Mad?"

I bite my lip. "Because she already has one unreliable parent. Hooper flits in and out of her life, forever breaking his promises. I can't protect her from that. But I can be the one to give her structure and stability."

"And you don't think she has that with you right now?"

I sigh. "If I could split myself in two, live both lives, see which one makes her happiest... God, I would. But I don't get that luxury. I just have to guess and hope I'm not screwing it all up."

"For what it's worth, Mad is a great kid," Dylan says. "She's happy and smart and confident as hell. So whatever you're doing, Brooks, it's working."

The hum of the tires on asphalt fills the silence. I focus on that, fighting a lump in my throat. Being a single parent means never having anyone to tell you that you're doing a good job. Hearing these words from Dylan means more than it should.

"Thank you," I reply. "And maybe you're not a total jerk."

He huffs a laugh. "High praise." Dylan is quiet for a moment before he speaks again. "I'm trying, Iz. I'm really trying to get my head around my football career ending and what my future looks like." He hesitates, like he might say more, and my heart thumps harder in the pause. "There's less than three weeks left on your contract. I know that. I haven't forgotten. I just... I promise I'll do better. I'll figure it out."

I glance over, expecting the usual brooding grump—that edge to his dark eyes telling me to back off—but there's only honesty and a flicker of raw vulnerability I've never seen in him before.

And damn it if it doesn't hit me square in the chest. We both have a decision to make. Dylan about the ranch and football. Me about my future and Mad's. The weight of it sits heavy in my stomach. Dylan made a deal with Bill to keep me on for six weeks. But just for a second, I want to ask him, what will happen when my time is up? Is he just waiting for the time to pass so he can sell the horses without feeling guilty? Or is there a chance...?

I can't bring myself to think about the question trying to break into my thoughts, let alone voice it. In the last few hours, I've swung from being furious at Dylan for oversleeping to practically drooling over his body to flirting—if that's what it was. I can't trust my own feelings toward him. And I sure as hell can't trust him.

But when I glance over at him again, I find myself wondering if there's more to this man than I've let myself believe. And maybe... just maybe... I don't actually hate Dylan as much as I've been trying to tell myself.

SIXTEEN

DYLAN

By the time we reach the arena, the sun is beating down, glinting off row after row of trucks and trailers. Even though Izzy doesn't say a word as we park, I know she's thinking we should've left earlier, and it's my fault we didn't.

I almost say something. I want to. I want to tell her how I'd meant to be up and helping her first thing, but I'd lain awake half the night thinking about the ranch and what kind of future I want, no closer to finding an answer when I finally drifted off somewhere close to dawn, sleeping straight through my alarm. It's a lame-ass excuse and one there's no point voicing. We're here now.

I glance her way as she cuts the engine, thinking of the moment she stormed into my bedroom this morning, bringing with her the smell of that sweet sea breeze perfume. All fire and wrath, hauling the covers off me like she had a point to prove. The flash of want in her eyes when she caught sight of me—all of me, considering my underwear wasn't doing much to hide what was underneath. Did I imagine that flicker of desire crossing her face?

The truth is, it wasn't just the ranch keeping me awake last night. It was her, and how the sharp edges between us have started to wear down over the past week or so. The way we move around each other now—like maybe we're actually becoming something more than extremely reluctant co-workers.

Every time she opens up about Mad and her life, about who she is beneath all that stubbornness, it has me wanting to know more. Then there's the way she looks at me sometimes, staying quiet at the right moments, pushing in others, that has me opening up too, telling her things about my childhood and my life I've never shared with anyone. And when she smiles—not the sarcastic smirk, but the rare, soft smile she tries to hide—I find myself wondering what it would be like to reach for her hand, tug her toward me, and press my lips to hers.

Izzy cuts the engine and jumps out, snapping me back to reality. I step out of the truck to air heavy with the scent of horses and dust, mingling with the smell of grease and fried food wafting from the food trucks. By the time I'm joining her beside the horse trailer, she's got the doors open and she's speaking to the colt in low, soothing tones as she unhooks his tether. A shiver runs over the foal's back, rippling his black coat and mane, but he stands steady, ears pricked, eyes curious.

"I need to register him for the auction," she says, handing me the lead rein and pointing me to a block of metal pens to one side of the arena.

A dozen other foals are already there, some grazing, some skittish, others standing close to their handlers. There are year-lings and a few older stallions and mares too. Izzy leads the way and I follow with the colt, the little guy stepping lightly at my side, his hooves clicking softly against the ground.

Once he's inside the pen, Izzy pats his flank as she assesses the other horses. "Stay here. I'll go do the paperwork."

Before I can reply, she's striding in the direction of the regis-tration tent, head high, braid swinging. I watch her make her way through the growing crowd. Cowboys in wide-brimmed hats and women in denim skirts and tight Levi's move between pens. Most of them look like they've lived this life forever. I catch a few sideways glances and wonder if they recognize me from my time playing for the Stormhawks—or is it because word has spread that I got drunk, bought some horses, and decided to play rancher? I squash the thought and focus on Izzy as she reappears from the registration tent.

Two men in sun-faded jeans and work gloves pause in the crowd to greet her. Even from this distance, it's clear they respect her—the way they stand, the easy way they smile when she speaks. And I get it. For all her smart-mouthed jabs and the way she manages to push every one of my buttons, Izzy Brooks is one of the most capable people I've ever met. She laughs at something one of the men says, the sound bright and easy, reminding me of the weekends and how much I've started to look forward to them, and to Mad's and Izzy's laughter ringing across the ranch.

I notice the way one of the men lets his eyes linger on where the buttons of Izzy's shirt pull across her chest. My gut tightens and I fight the desire to walk over there and plant myself between them like a warning. Like a linebacker protecting his quarterback.

What the hell?

Just for a second I let my mind go back to the question that's been churning my thoughts up night after night. What if it isn't just the ranch work that's getting under my skin—the steady rhythm and that sense of building something? What if it's Izzy getting under my skin, too? But acting on the pull I feel toward her would be reckless. Another crazy mistake that would make my decision that bit harder. Because no matter how much I try, deep down, I'm no rancher. And at some point, I need to face that thought head on.

In minutes, Izzy is slipping into the pen, and the colt steps into her touch. His trust in her is absolute. It's a reminder that there's a lot more I need to get to grips with than just feeding horses and mending fences.

"Go on." Izzy beckons to me, opening the gate to the pen and motioning for me to step out.

I hesitate. "What do I do?" The words slip out before I can stop them, and for a moment I feel just as clueless as the morning I woke up with a hangover and a ranch full of horses I didn't know the first thing about.

Izzy flashes me a smile, and for once it's more amused than mocking. "The foal auction is up first," she says. "I need to lead him into the ring and show him off. Go watch. It should be exciting. If all goes well, we'll get a decent sum for him and head home happy."

I step from the pen and walk toward the arena. It's nothing fancy. An oval-shaped, metal-fenced ring packed with dirt, and tiers of wooden benches. It's a space I remember from years ago, coming here with Dad and my brothers to watch a rodeo competition. Back then, the stands were full, the crowd cheering. I can almost feel the sticky sweetness of the soda in my hand and the awe that came from watching the cowboys ride like their lives depended on it.

Today, the crowd is smaller and bunched around the fence. The seating empty. As I approach the ring, I feel a flare of excitement. Unexpected but not unwelcome.

The first foal is led into the ring. It's timid with a coat the color of storm clouds. His handler struggles to keep him steady as he trembles at every noise. No one bids and the foal exits after only one circuit.

More foals follow. Some skittish, others bold and sparking a flurry of hands.

The announcer's voice crackles from the speakers. "Next is lot number seventeen from Oakwood Ranch. Presented by handler Izzy Brooks. A five-month-old colt, sired by Logan's Legacy, National Cutting Horse Champion three years running, and out of Willow, a mare celebrated for her exceptional temperament, agility, and consistent performance in reining competitions."

The anticipation tightens in my chest. Nerves and excitement—like the adrenaline before a game. Izzy walks into the ring with her head high. The colt doesn't trot at her side like the others. Instead, she loosens the rein, allowing him to move around the edge of the ring, his black coat gleaming under the lights. He looks like he belongs and the crowd notices.

Something flickers to life inside me as I watch Izzy and the foal. It's been a while, but I know the feeling. It's pride. I can't take credit for Logan and Willow's colt. That's all Izzy. But damn if I'm not proud anyway to see him in that ring representing Oakwood Ranch.

The bidding starts in a flurry, the number climbing steadily as hands rise one after another. My pulse kicks up, a steady thrum in my chest that builds with every new number.

Izzy continues moving around the ring, her face calm and professional, but I can see the gleam of triumph in her eyes. The announcer's gavel strikes down on the podium. "Sold!" The announcer points toward a man near the back of the crowd. The buyer is dressed in straight-leg denim and a white shirt. The buzz of victory humming in my veins feels like a touchdown as I watch a young ranch hand lead the colt away.

As I make my way to Izzy, people glance my way, but this time I don't feel the weight of my past in their stares. Maybe they're curious about something else—about what comes next. And for the first time, the thought of that doesn't feel quite so scary.

My eyes find Izzy as she steps out of the arena, her shoulders relaxed. The faintest smile pulls at the corners of her mouth.

"I'm going to assume that went—" My phone vibrates in my pocket, cutting short the rest of my words. I reach for it, glancing at the screen and seeing Coach Allen's name. My next inhale is sharp. My pulse kicks up. Why is he calling me? Hope sparks. A hope I thought was dead. I wave the phone at Izzy, gesturing I need to take it, and turn away without waiting for her reaction. In seconds, I've pushed through the crowd and I'm out the gates, standing in the shade of the arena, away from the noise.

"Coach?" I say, keeping my tone casual, trying to hide the desperation I feel pounding through me. Is he having second thoughts? Does he want me back on the team?

"Dylan, how are you?" Coach Allen's voice is deep and gruff and painfully familiar, carrying echoes of a lifetime of team talks.

"I'm great," I say quickly. "I'm still working hard and my knee's feeling strong."

The silence on the other end is a sinking weight. "That's... good, Dylan. Keeping busy is good. I was just calling to check in, see how you're doing. I know you've been coming by practice and watching the rookies a lot."

"Yeah, can't stay away," I joke, wondering where this is going as that spark of hope turns to something darker.

"And it's always good to see you, you know that. It's just, some of the rookies are finding it a bit confusing, coming to you with questions instead of the coaching staff, and well—"

"Oh, sure," I cut in, saving Coach from having to finish. Hurt slices through me. I don't belong. That's what he's dancing around. "Say no more, Coach. I'll stay out the way from now on."

"Hang on, Dylan—"

"Sorry, Coach. I'm in the middle of something. I need to go."

I end the call before I have to listen to whatever pitying words of consolation he's about to offer. I shove the phone back in my pocket and scrub a hand over my face, trying to breathe as if it doesn't feel like I've been kicked in the balls by a fifteen-hand stallion. The excitement of the auction, the thrill of watching our colt take the ring—all of it is gone, sucked away by the weight of crushed hope.

I move back into the arena, my steps heavier than before, scanning the crowd for Izzy. She's standing near the trainer in the white shirt who bought our colt. He's smiling wide and I straighten my shoulders as I approach, ready to do my part—be polite, say thanks, and pull Izzy away so we can get out of here.

Her back is to me as I close the distance. I don't cut in on their conversation but wait for an opening. That is until I catch the words leaving her mouth. "He might be able to catch a ball, but ranching? Let's just say we're still working on that one."

The trainer laughs, a hearty sound that makes my fists clench. Her words burn through me. The air is suddenly hot and suffocating, but what really gets me is how my irritation twists with something sharper. It's not like Izzy is saying something she hasn't said to my face. Or something that isn't true. But to hear her say it to someone else, to make a joke at my expense, stings more than I'm willing to admit.

Izzy turns, and her eyes widen like she knows damn well I just heard her. She opens her mouth to say something, but I'm already whirling around before I can retaliate with something I'll regret. I shove my hands deep into my pockets and disappear into the crowd.

For a moment there, I thought maybe there was something in this life for me. The pride of our colt as he took to the ring. I was enjoying the way it felt almost like winning again. But Coach Allen's call has pulled me back to reality. I don't belong with the Stormhawks. I'm an embarrassment. A washed-up has-been who couldn't let go, coming to every practice. But I don't belong here either.

Football. Ranching. My whole damn life. I don't belong anywhere.

I don't know how much time has passed before I find myself leaning against the railing of the arena, watching the final run of auctions. The crowd has thinned to the die-hards and the curious. My head is still somewhere else, my mood dark, and I'm only half watching as the next handler enters the ring. The stallion with him is huge and strong, muscles rippling under a dark coat that gleams like polished obsidian. But it's obvious from the first step that something is wrong. The stallion is straining against the lead rein, head tossing left and right, ears pinned flat. His hooves scrape the ground, kicking up dust like the only thing on his mind is escape.

His entire body sways one way then the other, and a second later, his hind slams into the arena's frame with a clanging crash. There's a yell of surprise from the crowd and the shuffle of people stepping back. Even the handler looks nervous, giving the stallion a wide berth as he tries to guide him around the circle.

The announcer's voice carries from the speaker, his tone lacking his earlier enthusiasm. "Shadow's Fury is a six-year-old stallion with strong lineage from champion reining horse Midnight Mirage. Shadow's Fury showed exceptional promise last year in barrel racing until an accident during transport left him injured and unable to compete. While his injuries have healed, he's since developed a nervous temperament and hasn't taken a rider since." He pauses, his next words already carrying defeat. "Let's open the bidding."

No hands rise as Shadow's Fury continues his uneasy circuit around the ring, his every step coiled with tension. They're halfway around when a crash of a railing nearby spooks the stallion. The handler stumbles back, losing his grip on the lead rein and landing hard in the dirt. Gasps ripple through the crowd as Shadow's Fury rears up, powerful hooves slicing through the air, muscles rippling. His front hooves hit the ground with a resounding thud, and for a split second, his wild eyes lock with mine and it's like I'm staring straight into his fear. It's wild and raw and unsettlingly recognizable. The moment is gone in an instant. A second handler runs into the ring, helping the first to his feet, and between them they manage to stop the rearing stallion.

Beside me, a woman murmurs to her companion, "That horse will never take a rider again. Poor thing should've been destroyed already."

"He will be after today," comes the reply.

The words sink, but I can't tear my eyes away from Shadow's Fury. He's skittish and unpredictable, but there's a fight still burning inside him.

"Any bids?" the announcer calls again.

Before I can stop myself, before I can think, my hand shoots up, and I'm calling out, accepting the bid.

Heads turn my way. "Got money to burn, Sullivan?" someone shouts, causing a wave of laughter among the crowd.

And maybe it's the sting of their laughter. Or maybe my head has caught up with what I've just done. Either way, dawning horror hits. I've just made another huge mistake, and this time, I don't even have bourbon to blame.

My eyes dart around the crowd, willing someone else to bid. Silence.

The announcer's voice rings out loud and clear: "Sold to Oakwood Ranch."

Shit!

I barely know what I'm doing with the horses I have, and I've just gone and bought another one. I remember Jake's and Chase's messages about llamas and hide my groan. No way am I giving this crowd the satisfaction of seeing my panic. I square my shoulders, lift my chin as I follow the handler to the back of the arena.

By the time I meet Izzy at the trailer, her expression is thunderous and she looks as pissed at me as I am at her. It takes her and three other handlers fifteen minutes, and a lot of cursing, to coax Shadow's Fury into the trailer. He resists every step, nostrils flaring and hooves scraping the pavement. Every single minute of sweat and fight hammers home what I've done. I've just bought a rodeo stallion who doesn't trust, doesn't listen, and can't take a rider. Izzy's right—I'm nothing but a washed-up pro athlete playing at being a rancher. But I'm done hiding from my mistakes.

SEVENTEEN

IZZY

I draw in a deep breath as we take the final turn for Oakwood Ranch, letting the air out slowly as the smooth asphalt gives way to the dirt track. The drive home has felt endless, stretched out by a spiky silence I didn't try to fill. Fighting with Dylan while towing a spooked horse wasn't an option, no matter how many times I thought of something else I wanted to shout at him. The way he's sat with his arms folded, face stormy, I'm guessing he's just as pissed as I am. But what the hell does he have to be angry about?

Beneath my frustration, I know the answer. He heard the comment I made to the trainer. It wasn't my finest moment—a throwaway remark made without thinking after the way Dylan rushed off to take that call I know was from his coach. Do I regret it? Sure, but regret isn't a luxury I can afford right now. Not when I'm the one who's left picking up the pieces of Dylan's impulse buy. Again.

We round the turn and the ranch house comes into view. Not even the beauty of the horses grazing in the afternoon sun can calm my anger. I throw the truck into park, and before I've cut the engine, there's a clang of hoof on metal from the trailer. I jump down from the truck, and a second later, I hear the thud of Dylan's boots hitting the dirt. And of course, he makes straight for the back door of the ranch. Of course he's going to hide from yet another mistake he's made. To hell with thinking there might be more to Dylan.

"Hey!" The one word is bitten out, loud and sharp. "You planning to help me get your latest stroke of genius out of the trailer?"

He turns back, his expression calm except for the storm raging in his eyes. "I just thought I'd grab us some water first. We've been on the road for hours, and I thought we'd need a drink." He disappears into the house, and I curse under my breath, already expecting him to take his sweet time. But he's back in seconds, striding toward me with two full glasses of water.

"Here," he says, holding one out.

I glare at him for a moment but take the glass and grumble a thanks, annoyed that he's right. I am thirsty. But what really pisses me off is the jolt of electricity that shoots up my arm when our fingers brush—like my body hasn't gotten the memo that I'm furious.

"You didn't happen to impulsively buy five skilled ranch hands while you were in the kitchen, did you? Because it's going to take at least that to care for this horse alone."

Dylan's expression is hard as he replies. "Shadow's Fury has a hell of a lot of promise. I saw something in him in that arena."

My laugh is short and laced with bitterness. I can't remember ever feeling as angry as I do right now, which is saying something considering I followed a man I thought I was madly in love with halfway across the country only to find him tangled in our sheets with another woman when Madison was three months old. Oh, I was mad then, but it was a slow, festering burn. This—this rage feels wild and alive.

"Right," I say. "You, with your years of ranch experience,

saw potential in a horse that everyone else in that arena today knew couldn't be saved."

"Yeah, I did, as it happens." He shoves his hands on his hips, making his massive shoulders appear even broader. "Despite what you clearly think of me, I'm allowed to have an opinion on my ranch. And by the way, I'd appreciate it if my ranch hands didn't mouth off about me to our clients."

"Ranch hands?" I repeat, my voice rising despite the way I'm cringing inside. Half of me wants to blurt an apology for my stupid comment earlier; the other half wants to tell him to go to hell. "It's just me. And your recklessness affects me."

His eyes narrow. "You get that this is my ranch, right? And if I want to buy a horse, I will."

"And you get that my six weeks are almost up, right?" I fire back. "In just over two weeks, your deal with Bill is done and I'm gone. What are you going to do then, Dylan? Are you keeping this place as a working ranch or not? Are you keeping the horses?"

"I don't know," he replies, and damn, it still hurts to hear that uncertainty in his voice.

I shake my head, keeping my voice like steel. "Well, just so you know, whatever you decide, I'll be leaving. Keep the horses. Don't keep them. I don't care anymore. I've got plenty of other ranch offers." The words fly out before I can stop them, the lie about other options feeling sour in my mouth. Self-preservation.

I've known since day one that I was only here for six weeks, but the hope has crept up on me, so slowly I hadn't even realized it was there. Every time he's shown up, done a decent day's work alongside me, it's made me hope just a little bit that there was a chance this could be more. But I've been kidding myself. This job, this land, these horses—they're not just a paycheck. They're my whole damn life. And yet to Dylan, they're still a mistake he won't admit to and won't try to fix.

Then a pang of worry grips me. Who will care for Moonlight if she hasn't foaled before I leave? What does Dylan know about delivering a foal? About managing the stress of a first-time mare? He barely knows how to saddle his own damn horse. How can I trust him to hire someone halfway decent to help if he does keep the horses?

I open my mouth to say something—what, I'm not sure, but Dylan gets there first.

"Good," he says, and the word lands like a slap.

"Fine. Then let me give you some home truths before I go." I wave a hand in the direction of the paddocks. "This? Breeding and training and selling horses? It's a business, Dylan. And you just spent a huge chunk of profit on a stallion who can't be ridden, doesn't trust people, and sure as hell won't be breeding."

"You don't know that," he snaps, but there's a flicker of doubt in his eyes.

I step in close, so close I can feel the heat rolling off him. "What I know is that you never think before you act. Ever. Has it always been like this for you? Taking what you want, when you want it, and letting the rest of us clean up the mess?"

His eyes flick to my lips for half a breath before locking on mine again. "Are we still talking about horses? Or are we talking about the kiss in the bar?" His voice so low it's barely a rumble.

I freeze, breath stalling. Even furious, I can't stop staring at his mouth, at the rise and fall of his chest, at the way he looks like he's barely holding himself back. How even though I should be running in the opposite direction from this man, a part of me wants to lean in, wants him to stop holding back.

Then a loud clang from the trailer shatters the moment.

"This is about Shadow's Fury," I say. "And the burden you just dumped on me—or whoever's here when I'm gone. Like everything else, I'll be the one stuck dealing with the fallout until then."

"You're not alone," Dylan growls. "I'm here. These are my

horses. This is my ranch. You're just too obsessed with control to let anyone help."

"Oh, that's rich," I shoot back, sarcasm clinging to every word. "You think this is about control? You have no idea what you're doing. Your heart's not in this. And your head isn't either. I saw the way you reacted when that call came in. Coach Allen is the Stormhawks coach, right? Tell me, Dylan, if he offered you your old position, would you take it?"

"Damn right I would."

The air leaves my lungs in a sharp exhale, taking my annoyance with it. He didn't even pause. "And that," I say, "is your problem."

Dylan's shoulders sag under the weight of the truth hanging between us. For once, he doesn't try to argue. Doesn't throw it back. Just sighs.

"I know." He glances toward the trailer. "But standing here fighting isn't helping either of us. And the longer we leave Shadow's Fury in there, the worse he's gonna get. So let's put a pin in this, and you tell me what you need."

Damn him for being right!

"The top paddock is the most secure with the new fencing and it's the quietest. We need to move the other stallions first. Fury doesn't look like he's going to be willing to share with the other horses, and we don't want to put them or him in danger."

Dylan nods and we get to work. And even though the silence between us is sharp, I throw myself into the work and let it steady me. The ache of leaving this place doesn't vanish, but it settles. Because I've survived worse. I've made harder choices. Even if it means starting over again. Because if there's one thing I've learned the hard way, it's that I don't need saving, especially not by a man who doesn't know what he wants.

EIGHTEEN

IZZY

FLIC: *How's it going with Dylan this week?*

IZZY: *Confusing.*

FLIC: *Spill!*

IZZY: *He's so infuriating. He still hasn't said if he's keeping the horses, but he bought that spooked stallion at the auction last week and has been working with him more hours than I've been out there. He even skipped the second Stormhawks game on Thursday night because Fury let him approach for the first time without bolting to the other side of the paddock.*

FLIC: *Sounds pretty committed to me.*

IZZY: *So why hasn't he said anything? I have less than two weeks left. What's his plan?*

FLIC: *Have you spoken to him?*

IZZY: *I can't. Things have been pretty tense since he bought the stallion. Long story.*

FLIC: *Is Mad doing OK?*

IZZY: *Loving Oakwood. Loving Dylan teaching her to play football and swimming in the lake. He promised to build her a rope swing this week.*

FLIC: *What a jerk.*

IZZY: *We've got one weekend left. It's going to be hard enough for her as it is.*

FLIC: *Just her?*

IZZY: *Shut up.*

My eyes fly open in the darkness. I'm wide awake in a heartbeat, unsure what's woken me. I reach for my phone to check the time and gather myself. I groan. It's 1 a.m. I have four and a half hours until my day starts. Instantly I'm thinking about the jobs I've got planned, the supplies order I need to make. I've got eleven days at Oakwood Ranch and I want to make sure whatever happens, there's enough feed and hay to last for a while.

I flick on the side light, its warm glow lighting the trailer's interior. It's bigger than it looks from the outside—a little oasis Madison and I have carved out for ourselves. The bed against the far wall is neatly folded away, pulling down like a shelf when she's here. Just seeing it tucked out of sight makes my chest ache with longing for my daughter's chatter. Camp will be over soon and I'll have her back at my side every afternoon after school.

The kitchenette is small, but it has a small table tucked into the corner and a bench to sit on. It's not the ranch house I always dreamed of, but it's ours. Even if I did buy it cheap at a police auction after the previous owner went to jail for tax fraud.

Cooking isn't exactly a priority in the trailer—I stick to simple things like pasta, grilled cheese sandwiches, and vegetable soups I can make in big batches and reheat. Or baked potatoes with all the toppings. Most nights, I'm so tired by dinnertime, I eat on the couch at the other end of the trailer, staring at the TV but barely watching. It's where Madison and Flic usually gather when my friend visits, the three of us curled up with popcorn and sodas and a Disney movie.

The thought of Flic has the muscles in my shoulders tightening. Her messages replay on a loop in my mind. I need to ask Dylan if he's made a decision yet. Because Flic is right. He's acting like a rancher who plans to stick around. And if there's even a chance, then I need to tell him I didn't mean what I said in my anger after the horse auction. I need to ask him if he's keeping the horses, and if there's a place here for me and Madison if he is.

It's been a week since the rodeo auction. Our fight has cooled to an uneasy simmer of annoyance. I know Dylan is avoiding me as best he can. He's thrown himself into the ranch, taking on more every day without being asked. He's not disappearing into the city anymore. No afternoons lost to watching the Stormhawks practice. Instead, he's spent hours in the paddocks with Fury, talking to the stallion like he expects him to answer, that quiet smile he doesn't even realize he wears growing with every small step of progress.

And despite the tension between us, Dylan still made time for working with Mad on her football over the weekend. Jake's joined in too—he and Harper came to stay for a few nights, bringing that loved-up glow with them. Buck barely left Mad's side for the entire two days, trailing after her like her new best friend, his ears perking up every time she called his name.

The Sullivan family is loud and loving and warm in a way that has sucked Mad in. Sucked me in too, I think. But every moment of kindness they've shown only makes the thought of leaving harder.

I sigh, realizing I'm awake now and I might as well check on Moonlight. She seemed restless earlier, and I put her in her stall tonight instead of leaving her in the paddock. She's still got a week until she's due to foal but there was just something in the way she moved today that gave me pause, and no way will I sleep until I've checked on her. I dress fast and grab my flashlight from the hook by the door before stepping outside. The cool of the night air prickles my skin. It's a welcome contrast to the heat of the day and I breathe in deeply as I switch on my light and make my way toward the barn.

The second I open the door, I know something is wrong. Moonlight lets out a sharp whinny. It's a sound I've heard many times before and it's unmistakable. Moonlight is having her foal a week early. I rush forward and flick on the barn light.

In the sudden brightness, Moonlight's stall comes into view and my breath catches. The mare stands near the back wall, her head low and her body tense. Her gray coat glistens with sweat. She shifts uneasily, her hind legs trembling a little. Then she lets out another low, keening noise that makes my gut twist.

"Easy, girl," I say, keeping my voice calm. The air is heavy with the smell of damp hay, horse sweat, and fear, and I can't stop my hands from shaking as I unlatch the stall door and step inside. "We'll get through this together." They're the same words the nurse said to me the night Madison was born, and for a moment I'm back in the tiny apartment Hooper rented for us in Nashville, feeling more alone than I'd ever felt in my entire life.

Hooper was out so much of the day and night—trying to get

the country music scene to take him seriously, taking whatever gigs he was offered. I was barely nineteen and terrified out of my mind at the growing swell of my belly. I was too young to be a mom. Too scared. Too worried I'd mess up a child's life like I'd screwed up my own. But then Madison arrived, and the nurse placed her in my arms, and it felt like I'd been given a piece of myself I hadn't realized was missing until that moment.

The memory fades and I focus on Moonlight. I've handled plenty of foalings alone before, but a mare's first can be challenging, and every instinct in my body tells me this one isn't going to be easy. Where is Bill when I need him? My granddaddy's experience and calm are exactly what I need right now. But he's not here. I'm alone. And the only person who can save Moonlight and her foal is me.

I crouch beside the mare, running my hands carefully over her belly and down her flank. I press gently, searching for the foal's position inside the womb. I feel something, but it's all wrong. The foal's legs are tucked back, the head nowhere near the birth canal.

"Shit," I whisper, pulling my phone from my pocket and opening my contacts. Camila Martinez is the best ranch vet in Colorado and we've worked together for years. She's the one person I trust with these horses' lives.

It rings three times before she answers, her voice tired. "Izzy?"

"Moonlight's in labor," I say by way of hello.

"That's a week earlier than we expected."

"The foal's malpositioned," I say, unable to keep the panic from creeping into my voice.

There's a pause before Camila replies, her voice apologetic but firm. "Izzy, I'm sorry, but I'm tied up with a colic case on a yearling. I'll get to you as soon as I can, but it's going to be a few hours."

"She can't wait that long," I cry.

"I know," she says. "But you've helped me turn a foal before, Izzy. You know what to do. Keep her calm, lubricate your hands, and work gently but firmly."

"I can't do it," I reply. I'm not a vet.

Camila's voice cuts through my thoughts. "If you do nothing, you'll lose the foal and possibly Moonlight, too. You can do this, Izzy. I know you can."

I close my eyes, steeling myself for what's ahead. "Please get here as soon as you can."

"I will," she says, and we end the call just as Moonlight unleashes a strained groan, her entire body trembling. My pulse thunders in my ears, but I force myself to take a steadying breath.

"I got you, girl," I whisper, not sure who I'm talking to—Moonlight or myself. All I know is that I won't let this mare die because I wasn't thinking clearly. "Looks like it's just you and me."

But even as I say the words, I know they're not true. I'm not alone. I have Dylan.

"I'll be right back." I sprint out of the barn. Dylan can avoid the decision about his future all he wants, but tonight, I need him. Moonlight needs him.

NINETEEN

DYLAN

I'm dragged from sleep by hands shaking me, bright light in my eyes. For a moment, I think it's Jake or Chase, needing my help with some dumb stunt they've pulled—sneaking a girl into the ranch they now need me to help sneak back out before Mama gets wind. But the hands are small and cold, and I'm not a teenage boy anymore, hauling my brothers out of trouble. My eyes snap open and it's Izzy I see. Even as I'm registering the urgency flashing in her eyes, my first thought is how much I want to reach for her.

"Moonlight's having her foal," Izzy says, breathless. Scared. "You need to get up."

It takes my head a second to catch up as I blurt out the first thing that comes to mind. "I thought she wasn't due for another week."

"Yeah, good point, I'll just go explain that to her." Her sarcasm cuts through the last of my sleep.

I'm already scrambling for my clothes as she keeps talking, voice laced with panic. "I wouldn't have woken you, but the vet's stuck dealing with a colic case. She's not going to make it in time."

"Wouldn't have woken me?" I reply, irritation flaring. I tug my tee over my head. "These are my horses, Izzy. You wake me for this kind of thing!"

"Well I am, aren't I? Can we just go?" She spins on her heels and heads for the stairs, her boots pounding each step like a countdown ticking in my head.

I grab my socks, my heart hammering against my ribs like it's kickoff in the playoffs and I'm about to take the field. Moonlight is having her foal and I have no idea what I'm doing. The thought hits hard as I shove my feet into my boots and run after Izzy. The barn comes into view, its light spilling into darkness. My chest tightens as I sprint toward the barn. But nothing can prepare me for what I find inside.

I slow as I approach the stall, not wanting to spook Moonlight. She's lying on the hay, gray coat darkened with sweat. Izzy is kneeling in the damp hay, murmuring softly to the mare.

Reality smacks into me. This isn't a playoff game, a last-minute drive with the weight of my team's season on my shoulders. This is about the lives of two horses. Moonlight is here because of a drunken decision I made in a bar. And now her life and the life of her foal are in my hands. Panic surges as images of my dad flood my mind. The way he always seemed to know what to do when a horse was sick. But even he couldn't save every horse. I remember the foal that didn't make it, the quiet grief in his eyes as he walked into the kitchen and gave the smallest shake of his head in answer to a look Mama gave him. He was a skilled rancher.

What chance do I have?

Moonlight whinnies, the sound piercing in the quiet barn. Her body trembles and her eyes look wild with fear.

"Dylan." The urgency in Izzy's voice cuts through my thoughts.

My eyes shoot to her face. Her expression is expectant. She believes I can help, and somehow her faith in me is harder to swallow than all the times she's told me to get out the way. I shake my head, taking a step back. "I... I'm sorry. I don't know what to do."

Izzy doesn't break eye contact, her voice unwavering. "Every rancher has a first time they do anything, Dylan. Tonight is your first night birthing a foal. And we're going to save them both. But for that to happen, I need to reposition the foal. It's stuck. I've never done this before either. But I need you to keep her calm. Hold her head; keep her steady so she doesn't make this harder for herself or me."

I nod, gritting my teeth. I might be way out of my depth here, but right now, I have to help Izzy. "OK. Tell me if I'm doing it wrong."

"You won't," she says simply, like it's a fact.

I step into the stall, sinking to my knees beside Moonlight's head. I reach a cautious hand to her neck, stroking gently. "Easy, girl. We've got you."

Izzy pulls on a pair of long gloves, rolling them up to her elbows. "She's going to want to stand when I start turning the foal. We need her to stay down, no matter what."

I nod, my throat dry. My hands grip Moonlight's halter firmly.

Izzy kneels at Moonlight's rear, her hands already working with a confidence that seems unshakable. "I can feel the foal," she says. "I need to rotate it." She glances at me, fear in her eyes. Her mouth is a tight line of determination. "This is going to hurt her. Keep her down."

Her hands push further into Moonlight's body and the mare shifts beneath me, her legs moving like she wants to stand. I tighten my grip on her halter, keeping my weight on her. "You're in the best hands, Moonlight," I whisper.

There's a flicker of surprise in Izzy's eyes as she glances my way. "Flattery won't save this foal, Sullivan. Keep holding her."

I nod. "Yes, ma'am."

"Dammit," Izzy hisses a second later. "I can't get the foal to turn. It just won't—" Izzy's face creases with concentration. She shakes her head. "Come on."

"Breathe, Iz. You can do this." The words neither of us say hang in the muggy air between us. There's no choice. There's no vet. No one but us. If Izzy can't do it, we lose the foal and maybe Moonlight too.

Then, finally, Izzy shifts and her shoulders sag in relief. "Got it," she whispers. "Get ready."

Her hands emerge, quickly followed by a nose and a slick head. The foal slides free in a rush, bundling into the straw. For a heartbeat, everything stills. Izzy's breathing is fast as she crouches over Moonlight, checking the mare with practiced hands. But my eyes are locked on the foal. Its coat is silvery gray with a black mane and tail. But it's not moving. Not breathing. Panic chokes me. I move fast. Somewhere in the back of my mind, I remember how my dad worked a newborn foal, and I grab a handful of clean straw and rub it over the foal's body.

"Come on, little guy." My voice comes in a rushed whisper. "Breathe." An instinct I didn't think I had takes over. I push my fingers into the foal's mouth, clearing a thick globule of mucus. Nothing happens.

Come on!

Please!

I keep rubbing the foal with the hay, a little harder now.

"Dylan..." Izzy whispers, the emotion breaking in her voice just as the foal jerks, its body twitching as it sucks in its first breath. Relief floods through me, a wave so strong my arms tremble.

"He's OK," I rasp through the lump of emotion blocking my throat.

Izzy's mouth curves into a tired smile. "Good work, rancher."

And damn if those words don't feel like the best compliment I've ever had.

It takes another hour for us to settle Moonlight and her foal. Izzy delivers the placenta while I replenish the hay and water, adding fresh straw to the stall, making sure both mom and foal are as comfortable as possible. By the time we step out of the barn, the first streaks of dawn are painting the sky in brushstrokes of pink, replacing the pitch black with a dusky gray. The fences are no longer just lines in the gloom—they're clear now, solid. Like the shape of something real is finally coming into view.

My gaze falls on Izzy. Watching her tonight—focused, fierce, unfaltering—it was magnetic. She saved Moonlight and her foal with her bare hands. She never flinched. And all I could think the whole time I watched her work was how badly I want her to stay. The truth is, I can't imagine this place without her—without that fire in her voice, that grit in her step.

I'll be leaving whether you keep the horses or not.

How can I ask her to stay when I still haven't decided if I'm keeping these horses? Still don't know what I'm doing, period. With these horses, with my life, my future.

And that's the real problem. Because a part of me I'm not ready to face does know. That part of me sees that the more time I spend working this ranch, the more I want this life. The rhythm of it, the purpose. Football is fast, furious, and electric. It's about winning the game, winning the division, winning the playoffs. Ranch life is different. Every fence mended, every horse cared for, every foal born—it's more tangible. More real than anything I've ever known, and it terrifies me. Because if I admit I want this life, then I have to risk failing at it. There's no team at my back. It's just me. If I screw this up, there's no next season. No second chance.

But if I let this go without trying, then I'm not just walking away from ranching. I'm walking away from the only thing aside from football I've felt connected to. These whispers of realization are hard to keep hold of, hard to face up to. So, like a coward, I've been ignoring them. Burying myself in the ranch work and Fury, making sure I'm too tired to think by the time I fall into bed every night.

Beside me, Izzy reties her hair into a ponytail, a few strands escaping around her face as she stares out across the ranch.

"What now?" I ask, my voice rough with fatigue but laced with something I can't name and don't want to end.

"Now we try and catch an hour of sleep before the day begins."

She steps to leave, but I can't let her go. I reach out, and when my hand grabs hers, the touch causes a tingle of electricity to race up my arm.

"Hey," I say, tugging her gently toward me. "You were amazing in there."

For a moment, Izzy looks like she might argue, but instead, she lets me pull her into a hug. My arms wrap around her, holding her close. Izzy's body is tense in my arms, like she's not used to being held, but then she relaxes, a shuddering sob breaking free that has me tightening my hold.

"Sorry," she whispers, pulling back and looking up at me, her eyes shining with unshed tears. "I'm just tired. Tonight was a lot."

I brush my thumb over the soft skin of her cheek. "Don't be sorry. If I wasn't more tired than I've ever been in my life, I'd be crying my eyes out."

She huffs a laugh. "You were good in there," she says, pulling a face.

I don't fight the smile spreading across my face. "And how hard is it for you to admit that?"

She laughs again, this time lighter. "Very."

"Well, flattery will get you everywhere," I tease. "But seriously, you saved two lives tonight."

"*We* saved two lives."

"Nope. It was all you. I was just along for the ride."

She laughs again and the sound undoes something in me. This woman in my arms drives me crazy. She pushes me to be better. And maybe that isn't the worst thing, because when the green of her eyes locks onto mine, filled with fierce determination, all I want to do is be a better man. And that's when I realize—my frustration isn't with Izzy; it never has been. It's with myself. Because I haven't been that man.

Izzy's face is inches from mine, her body warm in my arms. I feel something slip, like a wall is coming down between us or inside me—the hell if I know.

I move slowly, giving her the chance to pull back. Instead, her fingers slide up the back of my neck, drawing me closer. The world narrows. The ranch, the sky breaking open above us, everything fades until it's just us. All I see is her—lips parted, lashes low, her breath mingling with mine in the fragile space between us.

She tilts her chin, and I swear I feel the pull in my bones. The one I've felt like I've been fighting since the moment we met. I draw her closer until our lips are a breath apart—just one heartbeat away...

And then the noise of an engine cuts through the moment. Izzy moves out of my arms, her laugh shaky as we both turn to see a red truck speeding up the dirt track.

"That's Camila," she says. "The vet."

Whatever that moment was between us, it's gone, but it's left behind an ache that burns inside me.

I focus my attention on Camila as she climbs out of the

truck. She's in her fifties with short dark hair, and, like Izzy, she moves with confidence, her presence commanding. From the dark circles around her eyes, I'm guessing her night was as long as ours.

"Camila, this is Dylan—the new rancher," Izzy says.

The new rancher. Damn if my lips don't pull into a smile I've got no control over.

I shake Camila's hand. "Good to meet you."

"Well done on your first foaling," she says.

I nod toward Izzy. "I can't take any credit. It was all Izzy."

"Well, I'm here now." Camila smiles. "Might as well give them both a quick check."

"Anyone want a coffee?" I ask.

I receive two enthusiastic nods that leave me grinning as I stride toward the ranch house. I glance back over my shoulder, watching Izzy as she leads Camila into the barn. Even now, exhausted and covered in sweat and hay, I can't drag my eyes away. I know I've been a jerk. I've disappeared, been indecisive. And Izzy has called me out on it more than once. I know she wants to leave at the end of next week. She's made that clear. There are other ranches that can offer her a lot more stability than I've shown her. I can't blame her for wanting that. I won't ask her to stay, but if she would only choose the ranch. Choose me...

In the kitchen, the coffee machine is already humming and the air is filled with the scent of roasted coffee beans. Mama is by the counter, already dressed in overalls. She turns to greet me, face a patchwork of worry, reminding me that before she was Mama, before she was a sports agent with a life of meetings and schedules, she was a rancher's wife. She knows better than most how close we came to heartbreak tonight. "Moonlight's foal?"

"They're both OK." My voice cracks. I cough, trying to get hold of my emotions.

Mama sighs with relief. "Thank goodness for that. I'll take these first coffees out to the barn. You take a minute." She pours two cups, sets them on a tray, then pats my shoulder as she passes. Her voice is quieter when she adds, "Your dad would've been so proud of you, Dylan."

And then I'm alone in the kitchen, sweat and dirt still clinging to my skin, a lump in my throat and moisture in my eyes. I think of my dad and the way he'd walk out of the back door to the ranch every morning, always ready for whatever the day would bring.

I think of Moonlight and her foal. Of Izzy's confidence easing my own panic. That moment on the driveway when it felt as though we finally stopped fighting the pull—a tether drawing us closer.

When I stare out the window at the dawn breaking over the paddocks, I feel proud, too. But more than that—I finally feel like I belong.

The late-afternoon sun beats down on my shoulders as I lean against the top rail of the fence, watching Dylan in the upper paddock with Fury. Buck is sitting by my feet, panting in the heat, and I reach down to rub his silky ears, not taking my eyes off of where Dylan is approaching Fury with a saddle. Each step slow and deliberate. The stallion's coat is as black as ink, his muscles taut. Every inch of him says, *Don't trust*, and yet he hasn't bolted. He's watching Dylan, ears flicked forward, alert. Ready.

It's been three days since we saved Moonlight and her foal. Since I stood on the driveway with Dylan, the adrenaline still high and the world too still, and felt something shift between us. We haven't talked about it, haven't talked about anything beyond the day-to-day ranch work, but the tension between us is different now—charged and expectant. Our eyes meet and linger longer than they should. Our fingers brush when passing tools, and neither of us moves away.

Madison has been calling every day, begging for updates on Moonlight and her foal, already naming him Quicksilver, despite my repeated reminders that we don't name foals destined for auction. Naming them just makes saying goodbye that much harder. But Mad being Mad, she's decided, and now every time I look at the little foal, the name feels like it fits.

Quicksilver is brave and cheeky, already darting out from under his mother's legs before bounding back to her side. His coat is a beautiful shade of gray and black, like smoke and shadows stitched together, and every time I watch him, a wave of pride swells in my chest. He's already carrying himself with a confidence that will make him a star. The thought of how close we came to losing him sends a chill up my spine, but I shake it off and carry on watching Fury.

It's impossible not to notice the continual change in Dylan. How he's not just more focused, but calmer. Like whatever silent battle he's been having with himself since buying these horses, it's over.

And when Jake and Harper came by to drop Buck at the ranch and collect Mama for the final Thursday night pre-season game, away to the Dallas Outlaws, Dylan didn't grumble or retreat. He just clapped Jake on the back, hugged Mama tight, and turned back to grooming Rusty.

I should be happy. This is what I've wanted—proof that he cares about making this work. But instead, there's a knot twisting in my stomach that won't go away. Because the days are ticking down and he still hasn't said a damn thing about what happens next. He still hasn't asked me to stay.

Eight days. That's all I have left.

The last time we spoke about me working here, it was after the auction when I said I was leaving when the six weeks were up. All Dylan said was, *Good.* Mad will be back from camp tomorrow. It's our final weekend at Oakwood. All my warnings that our stay here is temporary suddenly don't feel enough. I know the first thing she's going to ask about after Quicksilver is the rope swing Dylan promised her he'd build. With Fury and then Moonlight's foaling, he's forgotten. I can't bring myself to remind him, even if I know Madison will be disappointed.

In the paddock, Fury shifts, hooves pawing at the ground, dragging my attention back to Dylan.

"Go steady," I call softly.

Dylan glances my way and flashes the briefest smile before focusing again. Fury's ears flick back; his body seems tense—coiled like a spring. But to my surprise, he doesn't move away. Not yet.

Two more steps.

One more step.

Then Dylan is lifting the saddle slowly, positioning it over Fury's back. For a heartbeat, Fury is still. Then, like a flipped switch, he bolts—exploding into motion, streaking across the paddock and only stopping when he's in the far corner with his head high, eyes fierce.

The force of Fury's sudden movement has thrown Dylan off balance, and he stumbles forward, landing hard in the dirt. Before I can stop it, a laugh bubbles up, bursts out. I clap a hand over my mouth, shoulders shaking.

"Are you OK?" I call out.

"Kinda ruins the question when you ask it while laughing, Brooks," Dylan grumbles, picking himself up. The scowl on his face only makes me laugh harder. All those muscles—that hulking frame of his—doing nothing to help.

"You think this is funny?" he calls, brushing himself off as he stands.

I wipe a tear from my face. "I do, actually."

He stares at me for a long moment before his mouth quirks into a smile. "You want to give it a try?"

"Not a chance. I'm not the one who bought him."

"Come on, Brooks," Dylan says, picking up the saddle and moving toward me. "Admit it, you're dying to step in and show me how it's done."

"Dying to watch you fall on your face again."

He's only half right about me wanting to step in. I'd love to work with Fury, but he's Dylan's horse and something about the stallion has brought out the best in him. I'd never admit this to Dylan, but I don't think anyone could've made more progress than he has.

Dylan chuckles as he looks back to the stallion. "Is it just me or is he looking pretty pleased with himself?"

I laugh again. "It's not just you. That's one smug horse."

Dylan places the saddle on the fence and leans against one of the posts. Even with a fence between us, the space suddenly feels tight. "Putting aside just now—" he starts.

"You mean falling face-first into the dirt?"

"You're not going to let me forget that, are you?"

"Not a chance."

Dylan rolls his eyes. "Seriously, I think he's starting to thaw. He let me get the saddle up there this time—mostly."

"If he likes you, he's got a funny way of showing it."

"Story of my life," he says.

Our eyes lock, the weight of everything unspoken between us hanging in the air again. I drink him in. Can't look away. His hair is growing out beneath the cowboy hat he's taken to wearing. There's a blade of grass stuck in his beard, and before I can stop myself, I reach forward and pluck it out. The second my fingertips touch warm skin, I'm thinking of all the other places on his body I want to touch.

Dylan's dark eyes are on me, like he knows exactly what I'm thinking. Like he's daring me to carry on.

"You had some grass," I murmur, holding up the single blade like it's proof.

"Thanks," he replies as his eyes dip to my lips, gaze lingering in a way that causes an aching heat to pulse between my thighs. I draw in a breath, catching the scent of leather and forest. Dylan draws his eyes back to mine, his gaze burning with the same feelings scorching through me. My lips part and I narrow the gap between us by another fraction. His hand moves like he's about to reach behind my neck, draw me to him—

The thud of hooves pounding against the ground shatters the moment. *Dammit, not again!* We jolt back at the same time and turn to see Fury trotting along the back fence, his head high as if to say, *Get a room.*

"Looks like he's ready for round two," I say with a laugh that sounds more nervous than anything.

Dylan smiles before he looks out to the horizon and the dark clouds looming over the mountains. The kind of clouds that promise rain.

"We should get the horses into the barn," he says. "Can you start on the others while I see to Fury?"

I open my mouth to argue, to tell him I've been checking my weather app every hour and the storm is due to pass us, but Dylan cuts me off.

"Don't fight me on this, Brooks." A raw sadness sweeps over his expression, his entire body. "My dad..." His voice trails off and I remember Bill explaining to me when I wasn't much older than Madison why he'd bought twenty-five horses he could barely afford. Because a good friend of his had died, leaving a wife and three boys with no way to support themselves.

"Your dad died in a storm," I say quietly, my mouth suddenly dry as I say the words Dylan can't.

Silence stretches out from one second to the next and then whatever vulnerability was showing on Dylan's face is gone—locked up tight—and he's nodding. "Yeah."

I glance at the sky again. The clouds are thicker now. Dylan's right. The horses need to be moved.

I grab the saddle from the fence, the smooth leather heavy in my arms. "I'll start on the lower paddock."

When I look back at Dylan, he's moving toward Fury with quick, determined strides. I can't deny how good his thighs look filling out those jeans or the way he's starting to get under my skin. I turn away and head to the lower paddock before my thoughts can drag me to the gutter.

The rain is loud as it hits the metal roof of the trailer and I throw a pillow over my head in a useless attempt to block out the noise. Who am I kidding? Even without the rain, I wouldn't be sleeping right now. My mind is spinning with thoughts of Dylan. The need in his eyes when he looked at me across the fence in Fury's paddock earlier. How much I wanted to climb that fence, step into his arms, and press my body against his.

The thought causes heat to burn in my core. I close my eyes, my hand straying down to the waistband of my panties, fingers brushing over the fabric as I let those thoughts flood my mind.

I stroke my finger over the flimsy fabric covering my center, imagining it's Dylan's hand, his touch setting me on fire. I can almost feel his lips on my skin, the rough scrape of his beard. I imagine his hand sliding beneath the loose tee I'm wearing, reaching up—

Cold water smacks my face, and my mind jolts back to reality. I gasp, and it has nothing to do with the images playing in my mind and everything to do with the second drop of water hitting my forehead.

"Are you kidding me?" I sit up, flicking on the light. My eyes adjust and I see the problem—my skylight has sprung a leak. The seal must have worn thin and now rainwater is forming tiny rivulets that drip onto my bed.

"Shit." I throw the cover off and grab a bowl from the kitchenette. A second later, the sound of the rain hitting the bowl is even louder than the rain hitting the roof, each drop grating my nerves with every *plink-plink-plink*. There's no way I can sleep like this. Even if I could squeeze myself into Madison's smaller fold-out bed, that dripping is already driving me insane.

I drag my hands through my hair, blowing an exhale through my lips. For a fleeting moment, I consider grabbing a blanket and trekking over to the ranch house. The back door will be unlocked like always, and I could crash on the couch. Mama is away in Dallas for the final pre-season Stormhawks game. I could be up early and out before Dylan even knows I was there. But I can almost hear Flic's mocking voice in my head. *Or you could, you know, actually talk to Dylan.*

I roll my eyes at the thought. Sure, he's been pulling his weight this week. But relying on him for the ranch work is one thing. Relying on him for me, that's different. I don't do that. I don't need that. I can fix this problem myself.

I open the cupboard beneath the sink and pull out a trash bag and a roll of tape. If I'm going to have any hope of sleeping tonight, I need to stop the leak. I tug on my boots and throw a raincoat over my loose tee and panties. The thing barely covers the tops of my thighs, but it'll do. I grab my flashlight and shove open the door.

The rain is colder than I expected, sharp needles that prick my bare legs as a gust of wind whips at the edges of my raincoat. I grab the ladder by the barn and lean it up against the trailer. With the trash bag in one hand and tape in the other, I ignore the nagging voice in the back of my mind telling me that climbing onto the roof in the middle of a rainstorm isn't one of my finest ideas, and I start to climb.

This is fine. I've got this.

TWENTY-ONE

DYLAN

I never sleep when the rain comes down in sheets like this. The sound like a broken faucet, gushing like it'll never stop. I think of Fury pacing his stall, hating the confinement. Just rain, I tell myself. No storm like there was the night Dad died. Still, the sound stirs memories I hate to think of and wish I could forget.

Eleven years old—I'd felt so grown up as I'd raced into the storm after my dad. The weather had turned in a heartbeat and the horses were still in the paddocks and needed to be brought into the barn. I charged into the rain with Jake, a year younger and a step behind me. We were soaked through in seconds, clothes clinging to our bodies. I was ice cold but determined as Dad led the first two horses through the barn doors. Then a streak of lightning lit the sky and I caught sight of the horses in the paddocks. They were spooked, galloping in circles, chasing each other. Jake and I were side by side as we reached the gate.

Now, my covers are off and I'm out of bed in seconds, needing to stop the next memory from replaying. The decision I made that night. The chain reaction it caused. Mama widowed. My brothers and I without the father we worshipped.

If only I'd—

No!

I won't go there.

I throw on a tee over my shorts and I'm down the stairs in seconds, heading to the kitchen for a glass of water and a bowl of cereal. I keep the lights off. No need to turn them on when I know every creak and dip of this ranch. So many nights I've tiptoed through the house, unable to sleep as a boy with the weight of grief and responsibility on my shoulders. Maybe no one gave me that responsibility—the feeling like I had to take care of my brothers, be a rock of support for Mama. But it was there nonetheless. Still is.

They're the same silent steps I made after my ACL tear too, when I was right back in my childhood bedroom, the pain of my injury and the fear of my future keeping me from sleep.

Across the kitchen, Buck stirs from his bed, padding over to greet me. I bend down to pet him. "You enjoyed watching me fall on my ass today, didn't you?"

I think of my brothers and the win they'll be celebrating against the Dallas Outlaws tonight: 34-17, with Jake scoring two touchdowns. It's their third and final pre-season game. Their third win. With Jake playing his best football and Chase as their quarterback, they're heading into the season stronger than ever. The pain that I'm not with them is no longer a sharp sting. More like a dull ache—something I'm finding easier to ignore most days.

It makes me realize I need to talk to Izzy about my plans. But the last time we spoke about the future, Izzy told me she was leaving. She had another ranch offer. If I tell her I'm keeping the horses, giving the ranch a real chance, will she feel compelled to stay? It's not just that I want her to stay. It's that I want her to want it. And that's the thought that has my head spinning and I go right on avoiding talking to her.

Coward!

I'm grabbing a glass and heading for the fridge when a flash of light at the window snags my attention. Lightning? No. If this were anything more than rain, Buck would be whimpering. He's always hated storms. I step to the back door and peer into the night. The rain is still coming down in sheets. The barn is in darkness. Except there's the flash of light again. Not lightning, but a flashlight. And Izzy.

"What the fuck?" I hiss, leaving my glass on the counter and throwing open the back door. My boots are on and I'm outside in seconds, wishing I'd grabbed a raincoat as cold raindrops pelt my body.

I call her name, but my voice is lost to the roar of the rain as I stride toward her trailer. The door is banging in the wind and there's a ladder lying on its side in a puddle of mud. I stare up at her, still struggling to believe what I'm seeing—Izzy, standing on the roof of her trailer, rain beating down around her, the flimsy raincoat she's wearing clinging to her body, soaked through and doing nothing to keep her dry or decent either, considering how much of her thighs and ass I see with every flicker of flashlight.

"Izzy." I bark out her name, louder this time.

She lets out a startled yelp. "You almost made me fall." She glares at me through the rain like this is my fault.

Sure, I'm the problem here. I bite back the retort. This is not the time for bickering. I force a calm into my voice. "Get down. Whatever it is, it can wait until morning."

"I've almost got it," she shouts, wrestling with a trash bag—the black plastic flapping wildly in the wind. As she moves, one of her boots slips on the wet roof and I swear my heart stops dead. Then a second later, she rights herself.

I step back, craning my neck for a better look. Rain drips down my face. I'm cold and soaked through, but it's nothing compared to the state Izzy is in. "What are you doing?"

"My skylight started leaking."

"For God's sake, Izzy," I holler. "You need to get down before you kill yourself."

Her response is so exasperatingly typical of her that I almost laugh. "I have nowhere to sleep."

"Like there isn't a ranch house with four empty beds just across the driveway," I yell at her. "Are you seriously telling me that you'd rather risk death than knock on my door?"

She pauses, and even in the flickering light of the flashlight, her face streaming with rain, I can see the realization dawn. "Yes?" The single word is a question as much as an answer. She frowns and I breathe a little easier as she stops her fight with the trash bag and steadies herself. She's still on a slippery metal roof in the middle of the night in the pouring rain, but at least she's no longer moving.

"How were you planning on getting down, genius?" I shout up.

She glances toward the edge of the roof, her eyes widening with another bolt of realization. "The ladder—"

"Is in the mud," I finish for her.

Her mouth drops open, and I can't decide if I want to keep shouting at her or charge up that ladder, throw her over my shoulder, and carry her down myself.

"It's too late, and I'm too wet and too tired to keep arguing with you," I growl before moving to grab the ladder. "I'm putting this back and you're climbing down. Then you're sleeping in the house tonight. End of story."

"I'll come down," she says, shuffling toward the edge of the roof, "but I can sleep—"

"Just get your ass down here, Brooks."

"Talking of asses, don't stare at mine while I'm climbing down, Sullivan," she calls out.

"Because you decided clothes were optional for roof repair?" Probably not the time to question her clothing choices, but I can't help it, just like I can't help my eyes snagging on the strip of black lace barely covering her ass.

"I'm wearing clothes!" she replies as her hands grip the wet rungs. "Just... not many."

I hold the ladder, trying not to be a giant perv as I watch her climb down, telling myself it's so I can be ready to catch her if she slips. When she finally makes it to the ground, I heave out a breath. Izzy is soaked through and might as well be naked for all the good her clothes are doing. Her raincoat clings to the swell of her breasts, her nipples showing through the fabric. Her hair is loose and dripping down her face and back, and damn if she still isn't infuriatingly sexy. She's also shivering. Before she can argue, I grab her hand, threading my fingers through hers, and give a gentle tug.

"You're coming inside," I say.

I ignore Izzy's protests as I lead her through the house, up the stairs, and to the bathroom, never letting go of her hand as I turn the knobs in the shower to hot. "Don't move," I say as warm steam starts to fill the room.

A moment later I'm shoving two fluffy clean towels and some clothes at her. "Get in that shower and get warm."

Izzy looks like she might argue some more, but then something else entirely dances in those green eyes of hers. "You're kind of cute when you're bossy, Sullivan."

It's the last thing I expected her to say and I can't help but laugh. "You get struck by lightning on that roof?"

"Maybe." She laughs too, the sound wrapping around my chest like it does every time I hear it. "What about you? Don't you need to get warm?"

My brain short circuits at the implication in her voice, and my dick twitches, growing hard in seconds. It's on my lips to ask if there's an invitation in that question, but I hold it in and mentally shake myself. I'm not the kind of man who takes advantage of a woman with nowhere else to go. Even if all I can think about is peeling off her wet clothes and stepping into that shower with her.

"I'll shower downstairs." I turn for the door before I can change my mind.

I'm in the kitchen with two steaming mugs of cocoa when Izzy pads barefoot into the room. I glance up, ignoring the way my breath catches in my lungs at the sight of her. Her face is glowing, clean, and fresh. Her hair is damp, scooped behind her ears. She looks softer somehow. Younger, I think. The oversized tee and shorts I dug out for her are too big, but of course she still manages to make them look good. Or maybe that's because my mind can't stop wandering to what's underneath—nothing but smooth skin and her perfect ass.

"Here." I push a mug of cocoa toward her, trying to keep my eyes on her face and not on those long legs of hers.

She comes to lean against the counter beside me and takes the mug. "Thanks." She hesitates, like she's weighing her words, and then adds, "You were right. I was an idiot."

I can't stop the half-smile tugging at my lips. "Sorry, what did you say?"

She glares at me over the rim of her mug. "Shut up."

"No, no." I chuckle. "I just want to make sure I heard you. Izzy Brooks admitting she was wrong about something. This could be national news."

"Very funny. And for your information, I'm wrong plenty."

"Yeah, but how often do you admit it?"

Izzy makes a face. "About as often as you do."

She's got me there. I take a long sip of sugary warm cocoa. From his bed, Buck heaves out a sigh like he's wondering why we're still awake. It's late, but I'm enjoying this softer version of Izzy. The one who can admit she's wrong sometimes, the one wearing my clothes and nothing else. I gesture toward the table and Izzy nods, slipping onto the bench and tucking her legs under her, wrapping her hands around the mug like she's soaking up every bit of warmth.

I rub my hand over my beard as I take the bench opposite. "I have to ask," I say carefully, searching for the right tone. One that won't immediately have Izzy throwing her walls back up. "What were you doing out there? And don't just say you were fixing a leak. I mean, what possessed you to climb onto a roof in the middle of the night, in the rain?"

"I can look after myself." Izzy's tone hardens, but I swear I catch a flicker of vulnerability in her face. Enough to make me swallow my own retort.

"No one's saying you can't," I reply carefully. "But there's a difference between looking after yourself and being so stubborn you put your life in danger."

She looks away. The tension in her shoulders eases. I can't tell if she's about to shut me down or open up. "Wow, this is really good cocoa," she says, taking another long sip.

"Making cocoa is one of my superpowers," I reply.

"How many superpowers have you got?" she teases, her brows arching.

"Don't change the subject, Brooks."

She drops the smile and sets the mug down, her fingers

tracing the rim. "I fucked up," she says, hesitating. "When I was sixteen, Hooper moved into our neighborhood and I fell madly in love with him. By eighteen, he was trying to make it as a country singer, and I was pregnant and dropping out of med school. I ignored every single one of the warnings my parents gave me. Turned out, Hooper wasn't the man I thought he was. I was nineteen when Madison was born, still a kid myself."

Her voice cracks a fraction, and I can see the rawness of what she's telling me, how hard it must have been. Every part of me wants to reach out and take her hand or get up and scoop her into my arms, but I don't want to interrupt her.

"I was completely alone with a newborn baby," she continues. "It was terrifying. Hooper was... out a lot. Trying to make it as a singer, and avoiding us too, I think. Every second of every day I was solely responsible for this beautiful, innocent little girl. If I didn't feed her or hug her or love her, then no one else would. I realized I had to do it. And I had to do the same for myself too."

My chest tightens as I watch her. She's so composed, but the weight of what she's saying feels like it could crush me. Losing my dad was hell. Feeling responsible for my brothers. Being a rock for Mama. Watching her sell Dad's horses. Then finding purpose in football. Every bad game. Every loss. And my injury, when it felt like my world ended. Through all of it—for my entire life—I've never been alone. I've always had Jake and Chase. They might not take much seriously, but I know I can count on them. And Mama too, who wouldn't hesitate to drop everything and walk through fire to get to me if I needed her.

I can't imagine raising a child alone now, let alone at nineteen. Being abandoned by the one person who should've had her back and not feeling like she belonged in her own family. That's a whole different level of strength.

"Hooper and I fell apart real quick and I came back to

Denver with Madison. My parents wanted to help, but I felt like I couldn't let them. It was like... I had something to prove. I've always been the fuck-up. They weren't even surprised when I got pregnant. It was like they'd been waiting for it to happen. Then Bill offered me a job as a ranch hand. Part-time, doing what I could while Mad slept, which wasn't often to start with. Bill gave me a lifeline and I never wanted him to feel like I was a burden or make him regret the offer. So I worked hard. Did everything myself." She stops, her fingers tightening around the mug.

"I can't imagine how hard that must've been," I say. "But you've raised one hell of a kid all by yourself, while also becoming a damn good ranch hand. You have nothing to prove anymore."

Her face lights up at my encouragement, but she hesitates for a moment before murmuring, "Yeah, it's just..."

"Hard to change," I finish for her.

Izzy nods and suddenly it doesn't feel like we're talking about her past anymore.

The silence between us stretches out and I swear I can feel every unspoken thought passing between us. I've always thought I had Izzy figured out—stubborn, prickly, self-reliant— but now I see the cracks in her armor. She's fierce and vulnerable, a walking contradiction. I have so many questions I want to ask her. I want to know everything. Every badass, sharp edge she has.

Izzy lifts her face, eyes defiant as they lock with mine, like she's waiting for me to challenge her or argue, but I have nothing in that moment but sheer admiration.

"It's late. Let's go to bed," Izzy says. And suddenly the air around us is shifting again.

I can't help the slow smirk that touches my lips. "Just to be clear, I'm a gentleman and I won't be taking advantage after inviting you to spend the night."

Izzy rolls her eyes. "Just to be clear, Sullivan, that's not what I meant."

"Yeah, but I'm growing on you, aren't I?" I tease.

Her eyes narrow, but there's amusement dancing in them too. "You're barely tolerable, I suppose."

"Tolerable?" I place a hand over my chest like she's wounded me. "That's what I get for rescuing your ass from a roof? High praise."

"Don't get used to it, Sullivan." She smiles. "And for the record—I'm no damsel in distress who needs rescuing."

I stand and cross to the stove, grabbing the cocoa pot and leaning over her as I top up her mug. I'm so close I can smell the soap from the shower on her skin. I pause for a moment, feeling the heat between us before dropping my voice to a low murmur, my lips a whisper from her ear. "And I'm no knight in shining armor." I step back, and despite all my resolve, I can't stop my eyes from dragging to her lips. "You may not be a damsel in distress, but you might be trouble, Brooks."

Her smile widens. "And you might like that."

The air feels charged, like anything could happen. If we let it. "Come on," I say before I can change my mind. "I'll show you where you're sleeping."

I lead her upstairs to Chase's room. It hasn't changed much since he left for college—it's a shrine to his teen years, complete with Stormhawks flags on the walls and matching bedcovers. I flick on the light and Izzy laughs as she takes it in.

"Just be glad Chase doesn't have a life-sized cutout of himself in here," I say, leaning against the doorframe.

Izzy turns to face me and in a blink the tension is back. Her lips part, and I catch a flicker of want in her expression that lights a fire inside me.

"Quit looking at me like that, Brooks. I meant what I said. I didn't rescue you to take—"

"I know." She flashes me a teasing smile. "You don't want to take advantage. Such a gentleman," she says like I'm anything but. "What if I want to take advantage of you?"

"Not gonna happen," I reply, trying to ignore the raging hard-on growing in my shorts and the challenge in her eyes. "It's late," I remind her. "And you've been working nonstop for weeks. Take tomorrow off," I add, trying to steer the conversation back to safer territory before I lose the last shred of my willpower. "Have a rest before Mad arrives. I can handle the horses."

Izzy opens her mouth, ready to fight, but I give a warning noise in my throat. "Do you ever not argue?"

She takes a slow step closer and my mind flashes to the driveway after Quicksilver was born, and to the paddock earlier, to every near-miss and almost-touch this week that's left me feeling like we're on the edge of something dangerous and inevitable.

I shut down the voice in my head telling me this is a bad idea, and without a word, I take the mug from her hands and set it gently on the floor.

"I wasn't done with that," she says, but she doesn't stop me.

When I look into her eyes, they are dark with need. Slowly, I reach up and cup her face in my hands. I hover my lips a whisper from hers, wondering if I'm about to make the biggest mistake. Or maybe my best one yet...

TWENTY-TWO

IZZY

The moment Dylan's lips touch mine, the world disappears and it's only us. This moment. This kiss. It's slow, and filled with a quiet intensity that makes my heart hammer in my chest so loud I swear Dylan is going to pull back and check I'm OK. But he just keeps kissing me. It's no frantic collision like the moment in the bar, but I'm still completely undone, my body on fire with the want pooling in my core and between my legs.

Every nerve ending feels charged. I'm desperate for his hands to roam over my body, down into the borrowed shorts that are barely staying up. My nipples pebble against the fabric of his plain white tee, willing his mouth to drop down to them. But his hands don't move from where they cup my face and his lips stay on mine. I wrap my arms around his neck, my fingers tangling in his hair as his beard rasps against my skin and our kiss deepens. I lose myself. Lose all sense of time as my tongue meets his with every stroke.

When he finally pulls back, I'm gasping for breath and trembling for more. He stays close, brow furrowing like he's warring with himself.

"Don't stop," I whisper.

He smiles, shaking his head at me. "Get some sleep, Brooks." His thumb brushes over my cheek a final time, lingering there for a second more before he turns and disappears into the hallway.

I heave out a breath, aware of how my head is spinning and my knees are weak.

"Get some sleep?" I murmur to myself.

Not a chance.

The sun streaking in through the window is the first sign something's wrong. I sit up in bed with a jolt. Instantly I know I've overslept.

I never oversleep. Ever. I'm always up with the sun, my body so in tune with the rhythm of the ranch that I haven't needed an alarm clock in years. Horses don't sleep in. So I don't sleep in. Except today, apparently. And it's all Dylan's fault. He's the reason I was lying awake until almost dawn, my body tingling, my mind replaying that kiss over and over.

I sit up, blinking the sleep from my eyes. Chase's room really is something. Stormhawks flags and trophies, a framed college jersey. I swing my legs over the edge of the bed and head downstairs, still wearing Dylan's oversized tee and shorts.

The kitchen is empty, but there's a fresh pot of coffee on the counter, and beside it, a note:

Day off, Brooks!

Next to the note are the keys to his truck.

A day off? Yeah, right.

I take a cup of coffee with me to my trailer, shower quickly, and throw on my cutoffs and a tank top. I braid my hair, throw on my boots, and ten minutes later I'm striding into the barn to find Dylan, his arm muscles flexed as he hoists a feed bucket onto a shelf.

"You could've woken me," I blurt.

He doesn't even turn around. "Good morning to you, too."

I stalk closer, hands on my hips. The air in the barn is muggy, heavy with the scent of hay and horses. "Seriously, you should've..."

He turns, a small smile touching his lips. He brushes down his jeans, pulls off his work gloves and moves toward me. Every step makes my heart thump a little harder. "Feeding's done. Horses are all checked."

My back hits the wood of the stall as he stops in front of me, his gaze dropping to my cutoffs, lingering for a moment too long before he's shaking his head, dragging his eyes back up to my face. The heat in that look makes my cheeks flush.

Dylan closes the gap between us, standing so close I can smell that leather and wood and all-man smell that makes my heart stutter like it's forgotten how to beat.

He scoops a strand of my hair away from my face. "You're taking a day off, remember?" he murmurs, voice low.

Then he leans in, pressing his lips to mine. The kiss is the same fiery want of last night. His body presses against mine as my hands slide up his chest, around his neck, and to the back of his hair. He groans into my mouth, and I swear the sound vibrates in every corner of my body.

My back scrapes against the stall as he pushes me back, my body melting into him. Fuck, I want him so bad it hurts—an ache that coils low in my belly and makes my skin feel too tight. I could lose myself in this moment, but whatever this is between us, it's more than me wanting to rip Dylan's clothes off. And we still haven't talked about what comes next. For him, the ranch, and for me.

I tear my mouth from his, panting, heart racing. "What are you doing, Dylan?"

He blinks, eyes dark with need. "I thought I was kissing you."

It's not what I meant, but I can't find the words to ask again. "This is my last weekend," I whisper. "My six weeks are up next Friday."

Ask me to stay!

I watch his jaw tighten like he's holding something back. I just wish I knew what it was. Then he lets out a long breath that sounds a lot like regret. "I know," he says quietly.

He takes a slow step back, running a hand through his dark hair. "I've got the water to fill. I left you the keys to my truck for a reason. Take the day off, Iz. Get ready for Mad coming later."

He turns and walks out of the barn, leaving my body aching and my thoughts spiraling. I make a step to move when a sharp sting flares across my back. I twist, fingers reaching awkwardly for the source, and hiss as they graze a fresh wood splinter—right between my shoulder blades.

Only I could derail the hottest kiss of my life and the closest thing I've had to sex in more years than I care to think about to talk about our future, and end up with a damn splinter in my back. I curse under my breath before storming out of the barn. I swap my work boots for sneakers and head to the kitchen for the keys to Dylan's truck. I need a break from this place and from him.

I head into the city, grab a few supplies and two coffees, then pull into the lot at The Hay Barn. I want to see Flic and I need help getting this splinter out of my back. Besides, I'm not ready to go back to the ranch yet. Not when I can still taste Dylan on my lips.

TWENTY-THREE

IZZY

DYLAN: *Don't buy supplies for the leak. I fixed it.*

IZZY: *I didn't ask you to do that!*

DYLAN: *You spelled "thank you" wrong.*

IZZY: *I can fix my own roof!*

DYLAN: *I didn't say you couldn't. But I had time and I didn't want you to wait until a snowstorm to go back up there.*

IZZY: *Sullivan...*

DYLAN: *??*

IZZY: *Thank you.*

DYLAN: *Why does it seem like you have a gun to your head saying that?*

IZZY: *Feels like it.*

DYLAN: *You're welcome.*

IZZY: *And you sound smug!*

"Two of my favorite people in the world are banging. I can't believe it." Flic's warm hand presses against my back. She leans in, tweezers in hand, and digs the splinter from my skin.

"I don't think people still say 'banging,'" I say, wincing at the sting radiating from my back. "And we're not banging," I hiss as she digs deeper. Even with the pain, heat floods my face remembering the way my body ached from the kiss in the barn this morning. Dylan's touch... "We've kissed three times. And judging by the way Dylan walked away this morning when I tried to talk to him about what he's doing with the horses, it was a mistake."

Flic huffs. "A mistake is climbing on a trailer roof in the middle of a rainstorm," she says. I'm already regretting telling her that. "A mistake is—"

"Buying horse stock without having the first clue what you're doing."

Flic laughs. "A mistake is something you regret. A mistake is something you don't repeat."

"We haven't—"

Her reply comes in a sing-song voice, like she's so goddamn pleased with herself. "You kissed him in the bar, you kissed him last night, and then you kissed him this morning, right?"

I groan. "Should've just left the damn splinter in there if this is the abuse I'm going—"

A final sharp scratch cuts the words short, and a second later, Flic is spinning me around on the barstool, brandishing the splinter like a trophy. "Got it!"

I reposition my tank top and make a face. It's barely a thorn. "It's tiny."

Flic pulls a face. "That's what she said."

"Really?" I say in a deadpan voice. "Are we doing that now?"

"Always," she quips, tossing the splinter into the trash before settling back on the barstool. Her long, white-blonde hair falls over her shoulder as she tilts her head, her blue eyes sparkling with mischief. She's makeup-free, in sweats and a loose tee, looking like a different person from the badass bartender she'll be later tonight when the Friday crowd rolls in.

The Hay Barn feels different, too. The overhead lights are on full, and the place is empty. The smell of cleaning products lingers in the air, competing with the aroma of the take-out coffees sitting on the bar between us. It turns out Flic's "payment" for splinter removal is a double-shot oat milk latte with caramel syrup, and a sprinkle of cinnamon on top. I swear she only orders it because she knows it drives me nuts. What's wrong with black coffee?

I look up at the row of NFL team merch stapled to the wall, confiscated by Flic from anyone foolish enough to step into her bar wearing anything but Stormhawks red. Then across the room, I spot a mop and bucket leaning against the wall.

"I thought you had a cleaning team," I say, looking back at Flic.

"I did." She sighs. "Until the landlord hiked the rent up, and..." She pretends to hold a magic wand in her hand, like the fairy godmother she tells Mad she is, making a joke of her cleaning. But I see the pinch of worry beneath it.

"Why didn't you say anything?" I ask.

"Because there isn't room in this friendship for us both to be in crisis. And I'm fine. Seriously. I like cleaning, and if it means I can keep this place, I'm happy."

Flic swipes up her drink and changes the subject. "Anyway, can I just say, you look a lot less in crisis and a lot more..." She trails off like she's searching for the right word. "I can't even describe it. You look... relaxed?" She shakes her head like that wasn't quite what she wanted to say.

I roll my eyes, grabbing my coffee, but I can't stop my fingers drifting to my lips. How is it possible they're still tingling after our kiss this morning? "Relaxed? You make it sound like I've been walking around looking—"

"Like you want to kill someone?" she cuts in, her face surprisingly serious. "That's exactly what I'm saying."

I choke out a laugh, causing a splash of coffee to land on my bare thighs. "I have not."

"You have. Very I'll-stab-you-with-a-pitchfork-if-you-look-at-me-wrong. But today..." She pauses, tilting her head as she studies me again. "You're almost... glowing."

I snort. "Glowing? Are you kidding me?"

"I'm serious! If Dylan Sullivan's kiss can do this, think what—"

"Flic!" I shout, covering my face with my hands but laughing too. "I'm begging you to stop talking."

"Why?"

When I look up, she's grinning wickedly.

"Admit it," she says. "You've got the hots for Dylan."

"What are we, twelve?"

Flic narrows her eyes, leaning closer, her voice dropping to a conspiratorial whisper. "Oh my God, you do, don't you?"

"I hate you," is all the reply I give, but the flush creeping up my face betrays me. The truth is, I do have a crush on Dylan. Who wouldn't? The man is infuriatingly sexy, and when he kisses me, it's like the rest of the world stops existing. But I'm not about to dive in headfirst. I've done that before and have the failed marriage to prove it.

Underneath the electricity between us is still a man who hasn't asked me to stay. Still hasn't said a single word about the future. A man who hasn't proven he's reliable. A man I don't know if I can trust. And as of next week, I'm out of time. Back to square one. Without any other ranch work going—despite what I told Dylan—I've got one option left. I have to move into my parents' house with Madison, where everything feels tight and small and suffocating. Fuck.

So what if I want him? Want *this*? That's not enough. Wanting something doesn't make it real. Doesn't make it sustainable. Especially not with a man who can't talk about tomorrow.

"Mm-hmm. Sure you do," Flic says, picking up her coffee and taking a smug sip. "But more importantly, does Dylan know?"

"Know what?" I ask.

"That he's turned you into a human being again. All... kiss-tinted and relaxed."

"Please stop talking," I beg, but Flic just laughs harder, clearly having the time of her life at my expense.

"You're welcome, by the way," she says breezily.

"For what?"

"For being your best splinter-removing friend."

"Best friends don't tell other best friends they look like they want to murder people," I mutter, but I can't help the smile tugging at my lips.

"Just so you know—if you two start banging, spare me the details."

"Please stop saying 'banging.' Why are we friends?"

"Because I'm delightful," Flic replies. "And because no one else would dare pull a splinter out of your back while simultaneously giving you a pep talk about your love life."

She's got me there.

"So what now?" Flic asks. She peeks at me over the edge of

her cup, taking a long sip and purposefully leaving a mustache of foam on her upper lip to make me laugh.

"Now I go back to Oakwood Ranch and pretend I didn't lie awake all night thinking about one kiss," I reply.

"I meant with Dylan."

I groan. "The truth? I don't know. He's infuriating. He's stubborn and grumpy and would throw the ranch and me under the bus if a chance to play for the Stormhawks came up." I fall silent and take a long sip of my coffee. Swallowing back the thoughts I can't say to Flic.

Like how he didn't hesitate to step into the rain and coax me down from the roof of the trailer last night. How his hand felt warm and solid in mine as he pulled me gently into the ranch house.

Or how when I told him about my past, it felt like he listened—really listened. There was no judgment in his face either.

Or how he notices things about me. How I take my coffee with a splash of cold water first thing in the mornings so I can drink it fast. The way my day isn't done until I've checked over every horse, and how he's started doing it with me, shortening the time before I can rest.

If I'm honest with myself, I've noticed things about him too. The way he rubs a hand over his beard when he's lost in thought or unsure what to do. How his jaw tightens when he's holding something back. The way his smile is rare, but when it comes, it sends me spiraling. The way his hands are strong and capable but when they brushed against my skin last night, they were gentle. Somewhere in the weeks we've spent together, Dylan has stopped being the pro athlete with the ego and the chip on his shoulder. Instead, he's become a constant presence in my thoughts, in my space. And I hate how much that scares me.

I shake my head, pushing the thoughts away. I can't afford

to get caught up in this. Not when I know better than to let my guard down.

"And I've got to think about Madison," I continue. "What would bringing another unstable man into her life do to her?"

"But Mad is crazy for Dylan, right?" Flic asks.

"Yeah, she is. But he's hardly reliable, is he? He promised he'd build her a rope swing and he hasn't. Once again, a man lets my daughter down and it's up to me to pick up the pieces. Plus, we're leaving—"

"Kind of makes sense he might not build a rope swing for a kid he's never going to see again after this weekend. I still can't believe he asked you to leave when these six weeks are up. I mean, he hasn't found a buyer, has he?"

I cringe a little, sipping my coffee and wishing I could hide inside it for what's coming next.

Flic's brows shoot up. "What?"

"He didn't exactly ask me to leave... I told him, no matter what, I'd be leaving."

"Wait. You quit?"

"I didn't quit. I..." My voice trails off, and Flic rolls her eyes. "You have no idea how impossible he is. Just look at these messages he sent me an hour ago." I unlock my phone and shove the screen at Flic, expecting her outrage to mirror mine when I first got Dylan's message.

Instead, her ringing laughter fills The Hay Barn. "Yeah, I really hate it when people fix things for me, too. And hello? I spent most of my childhood weekends and into my teens at the ranch while Mom and Dad ran this place—well, Mom, anyway. Harry and Mama practically raised me. I know how impossible Dylan is. Just how I know how impossible you are too, Iz. Has it occurred to you that he hasn't talked about you staying because you've made it abundantly clear to him that you want to leave? And I bet you haven't talked to him about wanting to stay, have you? You're seriously risking leaving the ranch and the horses you love to move back in with your parents—your absolute last resort—because you won't tell him you made a mistake."

Her words hit me with the same force as the gust of rain-soaked wind on the trailer roof. For a moment I'm unbalanced and can't answer.

"He hasn't even told me he's keeping the ranch going," I say quietly. "He hasn't even looked for a new ranch hand to replace—" I stop mid-sentence as the smile slips from Flic's face.

"What?" I ask.

"He is looking," she says slowly, pulling out her phone and swiping to a message Dylan sent her. "Apparently, he's talking to Ron Winters. He wanted to know if I thought Ron was a good guy."

I tense. My mood darkening. "Ron does cattle."

"Yeah, but Ron's nephew, Travis, is looking for work on a horse ranch."

My stomach twists, my anger suddenly hot. I shove my coffee cup away, the stool scraping loudly as I stand. "So he's keeping the horses and hasn't bothered to tell me! And now he's hiring a kid with no experience who he thinks can do my job. I'm going to kill him."

Flic rolls her eyes, unbothered by my change in mood. She pulls me into a tight hug and I don't protest even with the heat scorching through my body.

Flic gives me a final squeeze before stepping back. "Try not to actually kill him. I don't want to spend my Friday night bailing you out."

"I can't promise anything." With that, I shout a thanks, which she waves away as I storm out of the bar, teeth clenched and fists balled.

I knew this was coming. I *knew*.

How dare he? How dare he kiss me like he did this morning and then line up my replacement before my coffee's even cold?

Even as I slam the truck door and gun the engine, I know

my annoyance isn't entirely fair. I told him I was leaving when my time on the ranch was up and I haven't exactly said I wanted to stay. But it doesn't dull the ache in my chest. I want him to *want* me to stay. I can't believe I've spent the morning practically swooning over that man. Dylan Sullivan is about to regret the day he became a rancher.

TWENTY-FOUR
DYLAN

DYLAN: *Tell Mama I'm cooking tonight.*

JAKE: *Who are you and what have you done with our grumpy-ass brother?*

CHASE: *Ranch life mellowed him out. Next thing we know you'll be joining a book club, Dyl.*

DYLAN: *I'll have you know I'm currently reading The Nutritional Needs of Pregnant Mares.*

DYLAN: *Mad gave it to me. Says I need to "level up" if I want to earn my rancher badge.*

CHASE: *Smart kid!*

JAKE: *You need us to pick anything up, Dyl?*

DYLAN: *I'm good. Ranch is good.*

Coach Allen's name lights up my phone for the second time in an hour. My thumb hovers over the green button. There's that pull to my old life—the ache to be part of the game, to feel the roar of the crowd and the adrenaline pumping through my blood. The same feeling I had last night, watching the game with Buck by my side.

For a second, I let myself imagine what it would be like to answer, to hear Coach Allen tell me he was wrong. The team needs me. But it doesn't. Like it or not, the Stormhawks aren't my life anymore. Answering this call is opening a wound that's barely starting to heal. He'll only be calling to check in on me and I don't want his pity. So I ignore it and shove the phone in my pocket as I cut through the spruce trees. The smell of damp earth and pine is sharp in the air. My boots crunch against the soft dirt until the trees thin out and I emerge onto the shore of the lake.

Last night's rainstorm has cleared, leaving a cloudless, blue sky that reflects in the calm water, along with the blinding midday sun. I draw in a long breath, the air seeming fresher this time as I strip off my tee, tossing it to the ground with my towel. The only sounds are the buzz of insects, the far-off call of a bird, and the gentle lap of water against the shore. This is the kind of peace that sinks into your bones. The kind of peace I've spent the last few years hating. Storming out here in snow and rain to do my knee exercises in the lake when I was injured. Ignoring the tranquility, willing away the calm in place of a roaring crowd, the slap of helmets, the rush of game day.

But everything feels different now.

I kick off my boots and socks and step forward until my toes skim the cold surface. My hand finds my left knee, rubbing at the ache that's settled deep in the joint. There's a fresh bruise from yesterday's fall in Fury's paddock, but the real soreness is from skipping the exercises the physical therapist set to keep my ACL strong.

The new bruise makes me smile. It feels like I earned it doing something that mattered.

This morning, Fury didn't bolt when I stepped into the paddock. His ears didn't flick back, and he didn't bare his teeth. He stayed where he was, watching me warily but not running. That's more than I ever expected when I raised my hand at the auction. That's progress. And the feeling blooming in my chest as I think about it is pure pride.

I never felt like this playing football. I loved it. I loved the adrenaline rush, the intuitive way I could read the opposing team, break up plays, make a difference for my team. I loved the high of the win! But it was fleeting, always shoved aside by the next challenge, the next game. Out here, even the smallest things feel permanent. These horses started as a mistake. But the more time I spend with them, the less I want to leave. And even though the thought terrifies me, I don't hate it.

I know what I want. I've known since the night of Moonlight's foaling. Watching Izzy deliver that foal—the tension, the stakes, the way she moved with confidence and control—something shifted. That night, I felt what it means to belong in a way that's different from a game plan or a tackle. And then Quicksilver took his first steps. That feeling? That was purpose. The kind I never felt playing football, even before my injury. It's a feeling I haven't felt since I was a kid, helping my dad.

I wade into the water. The contrast to the heat of the sun on my shoulders is sharp but welcome. I keep moving until the water's at my waist, then dip my head beneath the surface. When I come up for air, water droplets slide down my face and my chest. I ground my feet in the sandy bed of the lake and start the rotation of my leg, going through the motions of the exercises. I've been doing them for so long my body knows the routine by heart and my mind drifts back to the ranch.

Fury isn't showing interest in the other horses, still preferring to stay in the furthest corner of his paddock. I was too soon with the saddle yesterday. He might be the most stubborn horse in the world, but he's got a hell of a lot of spirit too. Talking of stubborn, I smile again remembering last night and seeing Izzy on the roof of her trailer. I've barely managed two minutes without thinking of Izzy today.

I was done with interruptions and wondering what might happen. I wanted to kiss Izzy, and from the way her eyes were burning into mine, she wanted it too and a lot more. I wanted the kiss to be unforgettable. And it was. Every part of me burned for more, but inviting her into my home and then into my bed hadn't felt right. So I walked away. Used what little willpower I had left.

Then, this morning, it was Izzy who pulled back. A reminder that there's a clock on all of this. That in a week, she's gone. I get it—Izzy's independent as hell. She loves these horses and I think she loves this ranch, too, but she's made it clear she doesn't rely on anyone and has other offers lined up. And maybe she hasn't brought up leaving again, but she hasn't said she's staying, either.

The truth is, she's the best damn person to run Oakwood. She's the only one I trust. The only one I want beside me. But I'm scared to ask her to stay. Scared she'll say yes for the wrong reasons. Out of duty to the horses. Out of loyalty. Not because she wants to. And mixed up with those fears are my growing feelings for this woman and whether asking her to stay is just as much about me as it is this ranch. So I've been making calls, setting up a backup plan.

But I've also been avoiding the conversation Izzy and I need to have. Madison's back today, and with Mama, Jake, and Chase arriving back from Dallas too, time's slipping through my fingers. Maybe that's what terrifies me most—not just screwing up the ranch, but losing Izzy. Watching her walk away without ever knowing if there could've been more. It's not just about needing her here. I want her here. For the ranch. For me. If she doesn't stay? Then I'll figure it out. I'll run this place on my own. But yeah—I want to build something real here. And I want her.

A noise from the shoreline drags me back to the lake and I catch Izzy striding toward me, those legs that go on forever and an expression on her face like she's going to kill someone. And by the way her eyes blaze as they meet mine, I think I know who.

"Ron's nephew, Travis, is barely out of high school. He can't run your ranch."

The words fire out before she even comes to a stop. Her fists are clenched by her sides, breath short like she sprinted here just to yell at me. I open my mouth to reply, but she barrels on.

"You think because you've been ranching for a month, you suddenly know all there is to know about these horses, but let me tell you, Sullivan—you don't. Not even close. The day-to-day stuff? Fine. You can stumble your way through that. Feeding, fixing. Good for you! But you need to be thinking ahead. We've got three pregnant mares who are due next spring. Are you planning to have a late foaling season next summer too? Because if you are, then you're already behind. And what about breeding decisions? Which mares are you putting to foal?"

She doesn't give me a second to respond, ticking off items on her fingers, her movements so exaggerated they'd be funny if she wasn't so angry. "You need to start lining up a vet check for the geldings, and Quicksilver is going to need breaking in before you know it—"

Tension snakes across my shoulders, my good mood disappearing. "You don't think I know all this?" I throw the question back at her, just as hard. "We need to make decisions, real ones, and start thinking long-term about what Oakwood Ranch is going to be. I get it, but yelling at me—"

"We?" She gives a harsh laugh. "Oh, you mean you and Travis? That should be fun. A high school kid and a washed-up football player who thinks getting thrown on his ass in a paddock qualifies him to run a breeding program?"

"That's not the 'we' I meant!" I yell back, the cool lake water doing nothing to calm my rising irritation. How does this woman always get under my skin so fast?

"And don't get me started on my trailer roof. You had no right to fix it. I'm more than capable..." Her words falter as she looks past me, her eyes narrowing on something across the lake. Then she points to a space behind me. "What the hell is that?"

I turn to where the rope swing I made yesterday hangs over the water. The thick rope is secured to a wide oak branch at the water's edge, just where the bank drops down to the deepest part of the lake. The perfect spot.

When I spin back toward Izzy, her face is still stormy but there's something almost amusing about her expression. I try to hold on to my resentment, but my next question lands more exasperated than anything. "Only you could be mad at me for building a rope swing for your daughter, Brooks. What's the problem now?"

Her lips press together and she's quiet for a second, eyes still snagged on the swing. When she finally looks back at me, her voice is quiet. "I thought you'd forgotten."

I shake my head. "Mad's expecting it, right? I wasn't going to forget. But thanks for having faith in me."

Izzy exhales. "I was just..."

"Just about to say, 'Thanks, Dylan. You're such a great guy.'" I mimic a high-pitched voice that has her rolling her eyes and biting out a laugh despite herself. "'You fixed my trailer and you built a rope swing. You're my hero.'"

The look Izzy gives me in the next second is teetering on a knife-edge between wanting to kill me and wanting to throw something at me. She opts for the second, crouching to the water, cupping her hand, and flicking it straight at my face.

A rumble of shocked laughter hits my chest as the cool

water rolls down my face. Slowly, I wipe it away. "You really just did that?" I ask.

Izzy is fighting back a smile, barely keeping the steel in her voice as she replies, "You were being ridiculous."

"Wrong move, Brooks."

I surge out of the water before she has time to react. She shrieks, turning to run, but I'm faster. In one movement, she's over my shoulder and I'm splashing back into the lake.

Fists hit my back. "Dylan, don't you dare—"

"Oh, I dare."

She tries to wriggle free, body warm against mine.

"If you—"

Before she can finish the sentence, I duck down, submerging us both before letting her go.

She's throwing expletives and threats at me the second her head breaks the surface.

I laugh, running a hand through my own wet hair. "Worth it."

In the next move, she tries to lunge for me, push me back, but I'm too quick, catching her arms in my hands. Without thinking, I pull her close, holding her steady. Our eyes lock. Izzy stops struggling and my hold on her tightens as I draw her closer. Her clothes are soaked through, clinging to her body. Her eyes fall to my lips. The teasing is gone. All that remains is rippling tension. And this time, there's nothing holding me back.

TWENTY-FIVE
DYLAN

Izzy's eyes are dark with need. The kind that's been tugging between us since she strolled onto my ranch like she owned the place. The kind that exploded between us at the back of The Hay Barn in that first drunken kiss and has been growing ever since. I lift my hand, trailing my fingers down the smooth skin of her face, pushing back a wet strand of hair. God, she's beautiful. There's something strong and wild about this woman, but the more time I spend with her, the more I sense a vulnerability beneath the surface. Izzy Brooks might not need anyone for anything, but as my arms circle her back and I draw her close, I can't help wondering if she wants someone. If she wants me.

The lake water is cool around us, and Izzy's top is see-through, clinging to her breasts and showing me hard nipples I'm desperate to run my tongue over. A bolt of need shoots through my body as I cup her jaw, tilting her face up to mine. "You still mad at me, Brooks?"

"Furious," she whispers, her eyes dragging to my mouth.

"Good," I say as I move my lips to hers. Slow—barely a whisper of a touch. I hold us there for a long moment until Izzy wraps her hands around my neck, her body molding to mine.

Then her tongue is in my mouth and mine in hers. A noise catches in her throat and it's all the invitation I need. I deepen the kiss as my hands roam over her body. My dick strains in my shorts, already hard as Izzy moves her body against my length, seeking friction.

Heat circles low in my groin. Suddenly there are too many clothes between us, the water another barrier. I slide one hand under her ass, the other around her back, and carry her from the lake. For a split second, I think she'll protest, but then she wraps her legs around me, tightening her hold. I don't break our kiss as I lay her on my towel over the soft sand by the shoreline.

"We need to get you out of these clothes, blondie," I say, sitting back on my heels. "Wouldn't want you catching a cold."

Her green eyes spark with mischief. "Such a gentleman," she breathes out like she wants me to be anything but, and I'm more than happy to oblige.

"Always." I fist the bottom of her top and tug it up and over her head before reaching behind her to unhook her bra, my eyes searching hers for approval and finding her more than willing. Then my fingers move to the button of her shorts, slowly pulling the wet denim down over her hips and dragging her underwear with them until she's lying naked on the towel, the sun glistening on smooth, tanned skin. My eyes rake over her body, devouring the swell of her breasts and the toned muscles of her abs. Those strong legs that seem to go on forever.

"Fuck, you're so beautiful," I breathe, scrubbing a hand over my jaw as I stare.

Like the kiss last night, I want to take my time. I've been waiting for this. I trail a hand to her breasts, the tip of my finger feather-light as it circles her nipple. She gasps. So responsive.

I lean down and rest my weight on my elbows, catching her lips in another long kiss as my rock-hard dick presses against her through my trunks. Her hands slide from my neck down my back, all the way to the waistband.

She breaks our kiss, eyes locking with mine. "Madison is going to be here in a few hours and I want you now."

I drag my lips down the column of her throat, my hands roaming her body. "I love that you think I've got a few hours in me after the way your kiss wrecked me last night."

"You should've stayed then," she replies. Of course, she wants to start a fight now, when she's naked in my arms.

"Maybe I should have." I brush a kiss against her collarbone, then lower, savoring the way she shivers beneath me as my tongue swirls over the hard tip of one nipple, then the other. I move lower, trailing kisses across her abs.

"You want this, Brooks?" I ask, murmuring the words against her skin, needing to hear her say it again.

She nods, breath hitching. "Yes."

"Don't worry, I won't assume it means you like me or anything. What was it you said last night? I'm barely tolerable, right?"

Her laugh is breathy, cut off by a gasp as my fingers skim her inner thigh, trailing close but not quite giving her what she wants.

"I'm suddenly warming to you," she murmurs, squirming.

I chuckle, moving my body lower. "Let me see if I can make you actually like me." My hands gently nudge those beautiful legs apart. But just as I move to press my mouth against her, Izzy tenses, shifting away, closing her legs on me. I draw back in confusion, taking in the hesitant look on her face.

"I thought you wanted—"

"I do," she replies as a flush spreads over her chest.

I tilt my head to one side, trying to figure out what's changed.

"It's..." Her cheeks flame, and when she finally speaks, her voice is barely above a whisper. "No one has ever..."

Realization dawns and I smile slowly. "You're telling me, Izzy Brooks, no man has ever had his mouth on your pussy?"

She groans, covering her face with her hands. "Do you have to say it like that?"

"But you were married. Hooper didn't..."

She shakes her head, her blush deepening.

"Oh, darling." I chuckle, pulling her hands away so I can see her face. "You married the wrong man." Izzy opens her mouth to reply, but I get there first. "And that's a damn shame," I say. "But it's something that needs rectifying. Right now."

Before she can argue, my hands catch her legs, pulling her gently back toward me. I push her thighs apart again, and this time, she doesn't stop me. I start my kisses at her inner thigh, working slowly closer. The first swipe of my tongue all the way along her center makes her whole body jolt.

"Oh my God," she gasps.

"I haven't even started on you yet," I say, the words murmured against her clit, making her heave in another gasp.

I groan at the taste of her. She tastes like heaven. I take my time, licking slowly, savoring her, teasing every inch of her with lips and tongue until she's arching into my mouth, breathless and desperate. I slide a finger inside her and she's so wet, so ready for me, it makes my dick ache to be inside her. I've never wanted someone this much. The need is raw, like something I've been starved of without even realizing it.

And the way she's responding to me now? It's wrecking me in the best way. I add another finger, sliding in and out and curling them to reach that sensitive spot just as my tongue flicks against her clit.

"Dylan," she moans, her hands fisting the towel.

I lift my gaze to watch her face, the way her lips part, the way her body quivers with every stroke of my fingers, every flick of my tongue. Izzy arches off the towel, another low moan escaping her lips. I vary the pressure, licking then drawing back so only a whisper of breath tickles her skin, then more, reveling in every cry of pleasure I draw from her. She's so fucking responsive. I love being the first man to have had his tongue on her like this.

"It's too much," she gasps as I press a firm kiss to her swollen clit.

"Let go, Iz," I tell her, redoubling my efforts, licking and sucking, pumping my fingers in and out.

"I can't," she whispers. "I..."

I lift my head just enough to catch her eye. "Darling," I say with a wicked grin, "you can, and you will."

And then I take my time proving it.

Fuck, I could make this woman scream all day.

TWENTY-SIX

IZZY

The heat burning through me is exquisite, almost unbearable. My legs are trembling, my chest heaving, head spinning as Dylan's tongue continues to work between my legs. Every touch causes electric shockwaves radiating through my entire body. I can't stop my back from arching, pressing myself harder against his mouth. I close my eyes as pressure builds deep in my belly, coiling tighter and tighter with each stroke of his tongue. I'm so close, teetering right on the edge, unraveling piece by piece under Dylan's mouth, his hands, his touch. I'm losing control in the best, most terrifying way. Hooper never—God, I can't even compare. No one has. No one has ever *wanted* to, not like this. Not like Dylan.

Fuck.

It's all-consuming, like I'm floating and falling at the same time. Coiled so goddamn tight. One more touch and I'll be gone, and yet... Dylan's mouth moves away, causing a desperate whimper to escape my throat that I don't even recognize. In seconds, his fingers are replacing his mouth, stroking gently over the sensitive spot. A fresh shot of heat pulses through me.

"Open your eyes, Izzy." The command in Dylan's voice has

my eyes snapping open. "Look at me," he growls, his mouth moving lower again. "Look at my mouth on you. I'm so fucking hot for you right now. I want to fuck you, but you're going to have to let go for me first." His words rip through my defenses and then his tongue runs over my clit once more and I gasp, my world exploding as I cry out his name and grip his broad shoulders, nails digging in. Any fight left in me shatters in crashing waves of pleasure and want. I shudder, clenching around his fingers as pleasure floods my body.

Dylan doesn't stop. He drags out my orgasm until I'm trembling beneath him, gasping for air, my entire body pulsing. By the time he finally lifts his head, I feel weightless. Brain fuzzy. My heart still hitting my ribs so hard I swear he can hear it.

Dylan smiles, lazy and smug, and runs his tongue slowly over his lips, like he's savoring every last drop of me. "You taste so fucking sweet, Brooks." His voice is low and rough, sending another tremor through me.

I let out a shaky breath, trying to pull myself together.

"Still just tolerable, am I?" Dylan asks as he kisses his way up my body, hovering over me, his weight delicious and warm.

"Maybe it's a bit more than that," I whisper.

He raises an eyebrow, moving up my body. "Just *a bit?*"

His lips brush over mine, teasing, coaxing, making my pulse kick up again. His kiss is slow, deep, letting me taste myself on his tongue, and I moan softly, pulling him closer.

I can feel his length pressing against me, hard and heavy in between my legs. I'm so hot for this man. He groans. "Fuck. I want you so much, but... I don't have a condom."

The world crashes back into focus. I blink up at him, his expression a mix of desire and apology. There's no way we've got this close only to stop here. I can't.

"I have an IUD," I say, my voice barely a whisper, my chest heaving. "And... it's been a few years since I've done this," I add, heat flaming my face.

"A few?" His head tilts, lips quirking into a smile that's equal parts teasing and reassuring.

"Like five." Even as I say it, I realize whatever came before, it wasn't like this. Hooper was my first. We were madly in love, but sex was slow, lazy, predictable. After him came the occasional dates ending in unsatisfactory fumbles. This—whatever this is—burns hot and raw. It's scary and thrilling and fuck I'm here for it. "I've been tested since the last time."

If I'm expecting laughter or teasing from Dylan, it doesn't come. Instead, his face softens, his hands sliding up to cradle my face, tender and reassuring.

"The truth?" he says. "It's been a while for me, too." His thumb brushes along my cheekbone. "I'm clean too, but we can stop," he says and I can tell he means it.

I shake my head. "I want you inside me," I beg.

A slow smile pulls at his lips. "Say that again. Say that you want to feel me bare inside that perfect pussy." His voice is as rough as the scratch of his beard against my skin.

I swallow, the fingers of one hand threading into his damp hair, the other moving down his body, sliding over his swim trunks. His dick is long and thick and oh my God, he's huge.

Dylan unleashes a strangled curse. "This isn't going to last very long if you keep touching me like that," he says, taking my hands and pinning them above my head as he slips out of his swim trunks. I'm used to being the one in control, but the weight of Dylan's body on mine makes a fierce need throb between my thighs.

"You want this, blondie?" he grits out, nudging my legs further apart, pressing his tip against my opening. "You want me inside you?"

"Yes," I whisper, no hesitation.

His dick nudges my entrance and I hold my breath, waiting to feel him push inside. But just as he starts to move, a series of loud barks carries through the still air—excited and continuous.

"Fuck," Dylan hisses, drawing back a fraction. "If Buck's barking like that, it means my family's home. And knowing Chase, he'll be heading out to look for us any minute."

I groan. "What is it with us and interruptions?" My body is still thrumming, my skin flushed and aching for more.

He pauses, eyes locked on mine. There's need there, but something else, too. Something deeper that makes my heart race for a very different reason. "What do they say about something being worth the wait?"

And then his mouth is on mine again, urgent and full of promise, telling me this isn't over. He pulls me up and we scramble to get dressed. Dylan throws me his dry tee to put over my damp cutoffs. My legs are still shaky, my head still spinning from the best orgasm of my life. I don't think I can walk straight, let alone think straight. But a minute later, we're heading through the tree line and back to the ranch.

Dylan glances sideways at me. "You OK?" he asks, voice softer now.

I start to nod, but stop. I can't keep avoiding asking questions because I'm too scared of what the answers might be. "Earlier, when we were fighting, what did you mean when you said 'we need to make decisions'? Because Ron's nephew, Travis—"

"Is coming by to lend a hand a few days a week," Dylan says. "At first, anyway."

I shake my head, tension knotting my stomach. "If you think you can manage on your own with only a part-time ranch hand, then think again because..." My voice trails off as I take in the amusement forming on Dylan's face.

"Maybe we wouldn't fight so much if you let me finish a goddamn sentence."

I bite back a smile and roll my eyes as I pull an imaginary zip over my lips.

"The 'we' I was referring to," Dylan continues as his hand takes mine, fingers tangling together, "was you and me. You know what needs to be done here. I've got a lot to learn, I know. And I haven't exactly been the best help, so I thought if I was going to ask you to stay, I'd better sweeten the deal. With Travis picking up some of the basic jobs a few days a week, it will free you—us—to make those decisions you so carefully listed off your hand earlier."

"Oh," is all I can say. "I thought you were replacing me."

"I mean... you did tell me you were leaving," Dylan teases and I swipe his arm. "You said you had plenty of other offers."

"Because you were being a jerk," I reply.

I wait for the next biting retort, but instead he scrunches his eyes shut. "Maybe I was."

It's the last thing I expected him to say. "Maybe I was, too," I reply. The rest of the words I want to say stick in my throat. A silence draws out and I know he's waiting for my answer. I want to tell him how much I love this ranch, this work, these horses. How, of course, I want to stay. And yet, I can't find my voice and I'm not sure why.

"Look," he says. "I'm not saying running the ranch together is going to be easy, and I know you've got Madison to think about, so I want you to know that if you don't want to stay, that's OK. I just figured if we were going to make something real out of Oakwood, we needed to build something that *we* could manage. Together."

My eyes widen, mouth dropping open. Run Oakwood together?

Waking every morning to the sound of the horses in the paddocks, the sun on the mountains, the smell of fresh hay, and Dylan bringing me a coffee. Working alongside him. It sends a buzz of something warm through me. But a cold fear chases that buzz.

"And what about this? Us?" I ask, hating the way I hold my breath but needing to know where I stand.

We're at the edge of the trees, the paddocks and ranch in

sight. Warmth spreads through me at this view and how much I love it. Dylan stops walking, tugging me into his arms. "I don't have all the answers," he says. "But I know I can't stop thinking about you, and whatever this is we're doing, I want to see where it goes. But if you want me to back away, I will. There's the ranch and there's us and it's not a package deal, Iz. If you want to carry on working here and for us to go back to..."

"Hating each other?" I finish for him. I shake my head, but no words follow. Already my thoughts are spiraling.

What if Dylan makes reckless decisions again? What if he gets bored of the day-in-day-out of ranching without the thrill of the game he's spent his life chasing? Or worse—what if I screw it up? An image of standing on the trailer roof last night flashes in my thoughts. I don't exactly have the best track record with decision-making either. If I screw this up, it will crush Madison.

Dylan must see the hesitation on my face because his voice when he speaks is soft. "It's fine if you need time to think. Or if you want to talk to Madison. I just want you to know that for me—I'm in. For the ranch and whatever this is between us. I'm in for it. I want you to stay."

It should be the easiest yes I've ever uttered. Staying at Oakwood Ranch with these horses. Isn't that what I wanted? But I can't ignore the new fear whispering poison in my ear. Staying at the ranch doesn't just mean staying with the horses anymore. It means facing whatever this is between me and Dylan. Staying means opening myself up to get hurt, and I'm not sure I can do that.

TWENTY-SEVEN

IZZY

MOM: *Your father and I thought we could visit your new ranch this weekend. Tomorrow evening?*

IZZY: *That would be nice. Madison is back from camp. She'll be happy to see you.*

MOM: *We have something to talk to you about too.*

The rumble of tires on the driveway snaps me out of my thoughts of Dylan. Thank God I've had time to shower and dress and make myself look presentable since the lake, even if I've wasted a lot of that time reliving the way Dylan touched me, kissed me. I finish tying my hair, slip on my boots, and rush out of my trailer in time for the door of Grandpa Joe's blue truck to fly open and Madison to rush at me, backpack bouncing against her shoulders, arms outstretched. Her wide grin matches my own. A rush of love hits me at the same time as my daughter. I scoop her into my arms, spinning her around, and when she laughs, I swear it's the best sound in the world.

Nothing compares to this. No matter the mistakes I've made

in the past, no matter how uncertain my future, this perfect human is my anchor. She's my reason for everything. I press a kiss to her blonde curls and breathe in the smell of her—wind and outdoors, and the fruity scent of the pink shampoo she loves. The second her feet hit the ground, she's wriggling out of my arms. "Mom! Look what I got."

She tugs at the tee she's wearing. It's dark gray and huge—easily a man's large, drowning her small frame and skimming her knees. Bold block letters stretch across the front, accompanied by a brooding face staring moodily into the distance.

"Dad gave it to me! It's from his last tour."

Something sharp and complicated tugs in my chest. Of course Hooper would give her a tee that's way too big. Of course he wouldn't actually think to give her a tee in her size, instead of just throwing one of his leftover merch pieces at her. And of course Madison thinks it's the best gift in the world. I push the feeling away, keeping my smile fixed in place.

The driver's door opens and I glance over, expecting to see Hooper's dad. But instead, stepping toward me is someone far too skinny, far too smug, and far too young to be Grandpa Joe.

"Only the best for my princess," Hooper says, flashing me that charming smile—the one that makes women fall at his feet wherever he goes. The same smile that once convinced me running away to Nashville to get married would be an adventure.

The one I'm now completely immune to.

He holds up another oversized shirt. "Got you one too, Iz."

"Hooper, hi." I bite out the greeting, forcing my hands to my sides. If Flic's assessment of me is correct—if I do look like I'm about to kill someone with a pitchfork—then the reason is standing before me in skinny jeans. What the hell do women see in this man? What did I? His hair is down to his shoulders, hanging limp like it hasn't been washed for a week. His skin is pasty and he's rake-thin.

"You didn't tell me you were coming." I try to keep my voice neutral, but a whisper of hostility sneaks in.

"Flying visit." His smile falters a little, like he's remembering his charm won't work on me. "I was missing my princess, so I swung by the camp to see Mad and offered to drive her here."

Missing her so much you haven't called for three months? I swallow the words because this isn't about me. This is about Madison. She's already bouncing on her feet, excitement radiating from every inch of her. "Mom, Dad's taking me out for burgers tomorrow night! The best ones in Denver."

Disappointment slices through me at Madison's words. During the summer months, with Mad at camp, these weekends are all I have with her. Without Hooper's parents and the land they bought out by Granite Lake five years ago, moving away from the same neighborhood as my parents to run summer camps for kids and winter hiking retreats, I don't know how I'd manage. The summers without her are only bearable because I know how much Mad loves spending time with her paternal grandparents and being part of camp life.

And now Hooper is swooping in, doing whatever he wants without a single thought for anyone else and their plans. I think of my mom's message just now. Their visit tomorrow night. A weight sinks inside me as I wonder what my parents want to talk to me about, already sensing I won't like it. Without Madison with us, there'll be nothing to distract my parents from sharing their thoughts on all the ways I could be improving my life.

But I force myself to smile, trying to match Madison's excitement as I remind myself that some attention from him will be good for Mad. Even though he doesn't deserve it, she adores him. "That sounds fun," I say.

"Dad says I can get a milkshake and fries, and a brownie for dessert."

Of course he did.

I keep my voice light. "Sounds like a lot of sugar."

Hooper laughs. "She deserves spoiling. Live a little, Iz. Your mom used to be so much fun, Mad."

"One of us had to grow up," I throw back, hating myself for falling straight into the groove of a fight that feels like it's been ongoing since the day Madison was born.

I'm grateful when the back door of the ranch swings open and Dylan appears, striding toward us. He's fresh from the shower, dark hair still damp. He's wearing a plaid shirt with the sleeves rolled up to show strong forearms. With the tan on his face and his work gloves tucked into the pocket of his jeans, he looks every bit the rancher. My pulse stutters at the sight of him. This man is so hot! All I can think about is what we did by the lake this afternoon—what Dylan did—and how much I want to pick up where we left off.

"Hey, Mad," he calls out, stepping toward us until he's beside me. Close enough that I catch the intoxicating scent of his leather and cedarwood aftershave.

"Dylan!" Mad rushes to him, wrapping her arms around his legs. From the way Dylan's eyes widen, he's as surprised as I am by the hug. But then he smiles and returns the gesture.

"Good to see you, Mad."

Then she's spinning back to us, dancing on feet that can't stay still. "Dad, this is Dylan. He bought the horses from Grandpa Bill. Remember I told you about Fury—Dylan's horse. He was going to be killed, but Dylan saved him. And he saved Moonlight's foal. I called him Quicksilver."

"That was all your mom, Mad," Dylan cuts in before extending a hand to Hooper. "Dylan Sullivan."

Hooper stares at the offered hand for a second too long before shaking it. "Hooper Greene." Hooper is already smiling, waiting for Dylan to make the connection to the famous country singer. I love it that he doesn't.

Then Hooper tilts his head. "Sullivan... Football Sullivan? Don't you play for the Stormhawks with your brothers?"

I wonder if I imagine the way Dylan's shoulders tense at the mention of football. The question leaves an uneasy feeling in the pit of my stomach, but Dylan simply states, "I'm retired."

"Oh yeah. Think I heard about that. So it's horses now. That's one hell of a career change," Hooper says, laughing like he's made the funniest joke.

There's a pause. I'm aware of Madison looking between us, but my eyes fix on Dylan. He makes a sound low in his throat, something close to a laugh. His eyes flick to mine, amusement dancing in them. And suddenly, I know exactly what he's thinking.

This guy. This is the guy you married?

This is the kind of man who never put his mouth on your—

A blush flares up my neck and I can't stop the laugh from bubbling up, biting out of me. I sense Dylan's shoulders shake from beside me and it only makes me laugh harder.

"What's funny?" Madison asks, wanting in on the joke.

"It's nothing," I splutter. "We should probably get inside."

Madison tilts her head. "Mom, you look different."

I make a show of looking down at my jeans and the dry tank top I just threw on. "Do I?"

"Yeah," she says, brow furrowing. "You look less grumpy."

Dylan barks out another laugh.

"Wow, what a compliment." I press a hand to my chest in mock offense.

Hooper smirks, arms crossing over his chest. "She's not wrong. You do look... different." His eyes flick between me and Dylan like he's making the connection.

"Yeah." I roll my eyes. "Don't tell me—I look less like I want to kill someone with a pitchfork, right?"

Madison nods eagerly. "Yeah! That's it!"

Dylan is full-on smiling now, and I shoot him a glare.

"I'm getting that a lot," I mutter.

Dylan leans in, breath hot on my neck as he speaks so quietly only I can hear. "Wonder why that is, Brooks."

I don't dignify that with an answer, but there's nothing I can do to avoid the heat burning beneath my skin.

"Can't I just be happy to see my daughter?" I ask.

From across the driveway, a horse whinnies and it's enough to bring us all back to this moment.

"I'd better get going," Dylan says. "Good to meet you, Hooper." He starts to stride away and I really love that Dylan didn't mention Hooper's fame. Didn't even let on he knew who he was. It's the kind of thing that will annoy the hell out of Hooper. But then, unexpectedly, he stops and turns. "Hey, Mad, do you wanna come meet Quicksilver?" Dylan asks.

"Yes!" Mad jumps in the air, throwing a wave back to Hooper. "Bye, Dad," she calls, already skipping toward the paddock, Dylan keeping pace beside her. She says something to him and he laughs. I want to follow, to drink up every second of Mad's time here, but then Hooper opens his mouth and it stops me in my tracks.

"Bye, princess. Hopefully see you tomorrow."

Heat streaks through me and I round on him. "Hopefully?" I say quietly. "What's that supposed to mean?"

He looks confused for a moment. "Nothing. I just meant—"

"Because it's been months, Hooper. Months since you've seen your daughter. You rarely call or text either. Do you have any idea how much she misses you? How much she wishes that today's the day you're going to call her."

Hooper exhales, like I'm being unreasonable. Like I'm the problem here. "Hey, you know how busy it is on tour."

"I'm pretty sure you're still finding time to fuck your groupies," I reply, tone cutting as I remember walking into our bedroom in the one-bed apartment in East Nashville, to find Hooper in bed with a brunette twice his age. I shove the image aside. I remember the rage. The way it scorched in my chest. Our apartment. Our bed! It wasn't like I hadn't suspected he was cheating, but it was like he wanted to be caught. Less than a year into a marriage that felt like it ended before it had even begun, with Madison still so tiny. It was surprising how quickly my feelings turned to relief.

It was the reason I needed to walk away. To stop limping through a relationship that never really worked. Even before I got pregnant, I think it was the idea of Hooper I fell in love with. He gave me a reason to rebel against the rules my parents set. A reason to run away from a life I didn't want. But that doesn't mean I wasn't humiliated. I'd just turned nineteen and I was alone, caring for a baby I loved so fiercely I cried myself to sleep every night over how much I was already letting her down.

Hooper sighs. "When are you going to let that go, Izzy?"

"I don't know, Hoop. When are you going to grow up and be a better father to Madison?"

Then, Hooper scoops his hair behind his ears and looks at me in what I'm certain he thinks is his smoldering look, but it just makes me want to punch him.

"She's not an occasional hookup," I continue. "She's your daughter."

For a moment, Hooper's shoulders sag, and I swear I catch regret flash in his eyes, but it's gone in an instant. "No one gets anywhere without making sacrifices. But you're right. It's why I came this weekend."

My mouth drops open. Hooper is like a cheap prize at the carnival. Shiny on the outside, worthless up close. This is the first time I've known him to admit he's anything less than perfect. Something sparks inside of me then. A tiny hope that things could be different for Mad. That even though it will drive me crazy, her dad could be in her life more.

And then Hooper reminds me of what a spineless prick he

really is. "But hey, seems like I'm not the only one who's been busy." He raises his brows, shooting a look to where Dylan and Mad are stroking Quicksilver and Moonlight. "Shacking up with a pro athlete pretending to be a rancher. How long's that gonna last? I thought you had more sense than that."

My spine snaps straight. Any hope that things could ever be different turn to ash. "Really?" I give a hollow laugh. "Because I married you, Hooper, so clearly my judgment was never great to begin with." I don't give him a chance to reply as I jam my finger in his direction. "You will be taking Madison out for burgers and milkshakes tomorrow. You will be here at six on the dot, and you will have her home by nine, or I will personally hunt you down and—"

He laughs. "I forgot how easy it is to push your buttons." He backs away to the truck. "See you at seven tomorrow."

"Six!" I yell back before stalking toward the paddock. I want to forget Hooper's existence and focus on Madison, but his words have burrowed under my skin like a splinter I can't dig out.

Shacking up with a pro athlete pretending to be a rancher. How long's that gonna last?

Of course, he manages to hone in on the main fear that's been circling my head since Dylan asked me to stay earlier. I shove the thought aside as I reach the paddock and see Dylan smiling as Madison talks at a hundred miles an hour. I step through the gate and across the paddock to where Quicksilver stands close to his mother, his little silver-gray body sleek in the early evening sun. He's growing stronger and more confident with each passing day. His dark, playful eyes dart toward Madison as she reaches out a hand.

"You're so beautiful," Madison gushes, voice full of wonder as she gently strokes his nose. Quicksilver flicks his ears forward, nudging her palm with his soft muzzle. "That's right. I gave you your name."

"I was going to call him Brian," Dylan jokes. "But I guess Quicksilver works."

"Brian?" Madison giggles. "That's a terrible name for a horse that's going to win the rodeo."

Madison turns to Dylan and I swear I can feel her energy vibrating in the air. "Dylan, can you come for dinner tonight? Mom always makes spaghetti on my first night back. And she always makes way too much."

"Because it's your favorite," I say automatically.

Madison scrunches her nose. "It used to be. My favorite is burgers now, but I still like spaghetti."

"Burgers have dethroned spaghetti? How did I not know this? Well, we'd better start cooking then."

Madison gasps as if remembering something important. "Oh! But first, I want to play on the rope swing!" She turns to Dylan, eyes wide. "Can you take me?"

I'm torn in an instant. This is motherhood. This is wanting to say no—because there's dinner to cook and bags to unpack and I want to spend time with Mad too—but knowing I'll say yes because my daughter's happiness is the most important thing. But Dylan must sense my hesitation because before I can reply he gets there first.

"Actually, Mad, I'd love to join you for dinner, but Mama, Jake, Harper, and Chase just got back from Dallas, and I was gonna cook something for them. Why don't you join us? That way, I can make dinner while you two go try out the rope swing?"

Madison hisses an excited "YES!" before sprinting toward the trailer. "I'll get my swimsuit!"

I watch her go before turning to Dylan. He's already looking at me, arms crossed over that broad chest, those dark eyes shadowed and unreadable—but locked on me like I'm the only thing he sees. "You don't have to—"

Dylan fixes me with a knowing look. "Go spend time with Mad. I'll take care of dinner."

I bite my bottom lip. "But the horses—"

"I got this, Iz."

There's that feeling again—that pull that makes me want to lean into it. Into him.

Then he's closing the gap between us, his hand finding mine, his thumb brushing once—just once—against my skin, before he's stepping back.

"Trust me," he replies, voice low.

And even though his touch is light, the feel of it lingers as I whisper a thanks and follow Madison to the trailer to get my swimsuit. My hand tingles from that thumb stroke, like my body is remembering every touch and kiss by the lake. I have no idea what's happening between me and Dylan. No idea if I should trust it and him or if I should run for my life. But for tonight, I shove my fears aside. Tonight is about Madison, I remind myself. Even as my body hums with the memory of Dylan's touch, and I know I want more.

TWENTY-EIGHT

DYLAN

I find Mama at the stove with a frying pan and Chase at the table eating pancakes when I step into the kitchen for my second coffee on Saturday morning. A smile tugs at my lips that I don't bother to hide. Hell, I'm almost chuckling to myself thinking about last night's dinner—Mad and Izzy with their matching wet hair, skin flushed from the lake, smiles wide and content. Mad declared my simple pasta the best she'd ever tasted.

Chase was quick to reply. *I like you, Mad, but you need to get out more if this is the best pasta you've ever eaten.*

Izzy sat beside me, our legs touching beneath the table, and all I could think about was how good it felt—how good she felt. She's under my skin and in my head. And the more time I spend with her, the more it never feels like enough. Especially when my thoughts drag to the time we spent by the lake yesterday and my dick stirs with a longing I've never felt for anyone before.

My thoughts disappear when I catch the tail end of Mama's voice. "You know you'll always have my support, Chase. No matter what you do."

Chase gives her a quiet, "Thanks," and I kick off my boots, heading for the coffee pot.

"I just told Mama I might look for Leanna," he says as I pour myself a cup.

I nod, glad Chase has finally opened up to Mama about his plans to look for his biological mom. "Still not sure?"

He shakes his head. "No. But Mama's got an old address in Nevada."

Mama steps across the kitchen, giving Chase's shoulder a squeeze. "Might not be current, but it's a place to start when you're ready."

Chase has a few weeks off before the season starts. That in-between time when the team is pumped up and ready, but left waiting. He could ditch some of the press events I know he's been signed up for and go find her. But it's his decision, and I don't push or try to understand the complexity of what he's going through. This is a woman who abandoned him on our doorstep in the middle of the night when he was two years old and hasn't tried to contact him since.

"You still heading to Florida next week?" I ask Mama.

She smiles. "Wouldn't miss my girls' trip. Two weeks of sitting by the pool, drinking mimosas, and swapping the same stories we've told for forty years. As long as you all think you can cope without me."

"We'll be fine," I say. The annual Florida holiday with her old high school girlfriends is the only time Mama takes for herself, and she deserves it. Mama looks to Chase, worry in her eyes, but before she can say any more, Buck rushes into the kitchen, tongue out and tail swinging furiously before he flops onto the cool tiles. He's followed a moment later by Jake and Harper, both wearing hiking gear.

"Hey, Dylan." Harper smiles. "Just the man I wanted to see. I was telling Mia about Fury, and she'd love to come by later and see him. Is that OK?" she asks, mentioning her best friend, who along with Harper was in the same grade in high school as Chase.

I smile. "Sure. She might be a corporate hotshot now, but she'll always be one hell of a barrel racer to me. It would be good to have her take on him."

Harper pulls her phone from her pocket, fingers flying across the screen. Jake pulls her back into his side with a kiss to her temple.

"Can you pretend you're here with me for like five minutes?" he teases.

"Hey, you've got me for a whole week in Hawaii starting Monday."

Chase looks over to them. "You guys aren't planning a secret wedding, are you?"

We all look to Mama and the almost comical look of horror dawning on her face. Jake is by her side in a second, giving her a hug.

"No way," he says, rolling his eyes at Chase.

Harper looks up from her phone. "When we finally find a place we like, you'll all be the first to get invites."

"Buck good with you while we're gone?" Jake asks me.

I crouch to ruffle Buck's ears. "What do you think, boy? Wanna play rancher with me?"

"Looks like more than playing," Harper says, nodding to one of Dad's old cowboy hats I've taken to wearing.

A swell of warmth spreads across my chest. "Yeah. I know it started as a drunken mistake, but it feels like I've got a purpose again," I admit.

The silence that follows is immediate and loaded. Chase shoots a look at Mama. Jake arches his brows. Harper looks like she'd rather be anywhere else. Something's up.

"What?" I ask, turning to Jake.

He gives a tiny shake of his head, then glances at Mama.

"Mama?"

Her eyes meet mine. "Coach Allen's been calling you."

"So? Probably just checking in."

"It's more than that," she says, still hesitating. "He wants you to join the Stormhawks coaching staff."

The words hit me like a gut punch. Coach wants me to join the coaching staff. I could be part of the Stormhawks again. For all my talk about finding purpose here, the thought of rejoining the team—even from the sidelines—sends a jolt of something electric through me that I'm not ready for. I open my mouth. Close it. Then finally I find my voice. "I... I've got the ranch now." Even I can hear the hesitation in those words.

Mama's warm hand rests on my arm. "And seeing you come out of yourself over the last few weeks has been wonderful. I want you to choose this life if it's what you want, Dylan. But don't choose it because you think your dad would've wanted you to or because you feel like it's all you've got. Don't settle. Remember—we don't give up on what we love."

The silence stretches again until Harper breaks it with a wave of her phone. "Mia says she'll be here by four."

Talk turns to plans—two weeks in Florida for Mama, Hawaii for Jake and Harper, and Chase's media days in the city. Everyone's going somewhere. Doing something.

Except me. I'm staying right here. And for the first time in weeks, I wonder if that's enough. Am I throwing myself into this life because it's truly what I want or because I thought it was all I had? I picture Fury—his progress, the pride that swells every time he takes a step forward. Football was my life. It isn't anymore, I tell myself, and maybe I even believe it—most days. But there's still something lingering. That last tether to the life I left behind. The way I come alive when I toss the ball with Mad. If raising horses was truly all I wanted, would one mention of an offer from Coach be enough to send me into this kind of turmoil? I've thrown myself into ranching, day after day, but deep down, something still feels incomplete. And I can't help but wonder if Izzy senses it. Maybe that's why she hasn't said she's staying.

I glance out the back door, my gaze falling on Izzy, like I can't stop seeking her out. She's by her trailer, kneeling in the dirt, arms wrapped tightly around Madison. Even from this distance, I can see Mad's face is buried in her mom's shoulder. Something's wrong. And seeing Izzy comfort Mad makes me want to be out there, kneeling beside Izzy in the dirt. I don't just want to help them—I want to be part of their unit, if they'll let me.

I push aside thoughts of coaching football and Coach Allen's calls and stride out the back door, beelining straight for them and catching the tail end of Mad's hiccupped words, her voice small and sad, nothing like the determined little girl I've come to know.

"Maybe Dad had something really important to do," she says through sniffs.

"I'm sure that's it," Izzy replies, running a soothing hand over Madison's back. But when Izzy glances up, her green eyes meeting mine, I see her sadness. Most of all, I see her resignation. Like she already knew this would happen and hates herself for being right.

Anger smacks into me so hard I have to take a breath. What kind of father lets his kid down like this? What kind of man? It isn't just that Hooper canceled—it's that Mad is trying to convince herself that it doesn't hurt when it clearly does.

I understand Izzy a little more in this moment. The sharp edges, the stubbornness, the way she doesn't let people in. She's been the one picking up the pieces for Madison since day one. She's had to be everything to her daughter. And right now, all I want to do is take that pain from Madison and smooth the sadness from Izzy's face. I want to fix it.

I crouch down next to them, nudging Madison's shoulder with mine. "Hey, Mad."

She lifts her face, wiping away her tears. "My dad can't make it tonight."

"That's a shame, but do you want to know something?"

"What?" she asks, pulling back from Izzy's arms as she turns to look at me.

"I'm actually really happy to hear you're going to be here tonight because I've got plans for us."

She looks up at me, tears still clinging to her lashes, but she's curious, too. "What plans?"

"How does a barbeque by the lake sound?" I ask. "Burgers, swimming, and maybe even s'mores if you can convince your mom."

Mad's eyes light up. "Can Jake and Chase come too? I bet they'll push me really high on the rope swing."

"Not too high," I reply. "We don't want you landing on the moon."

"Dylan!" She huffs, rolling her eyes and looking so much like Izzy in that moment I laugh. "That can't happen."

"Even so, sounds like we have ourselves a plan. I'm going to need your help getting it all set up. You game?"

She gives a fierce nod, wiping away the last of her tears. "I'll get my notebook. We need to make a list!" She whirls around and disappears into the trailer, and I move to stand as Izzy brushes the dirt from her knees.

"Hey," I say quietly. My fingers brush the bare skin of her arm, and damn if I don't feel the way she tenses—like she's caught between wanting to step back and move close.

The air shifts, charged with something unspoken between us again. Her eyes flicker to my mouth, and mine drop to hers. It would take nothing—*nothing*—to lean in. But she blinks, and it's like we both remember where we are and who's watching.

"You OK?" I ask, still not moving my hand.

Her nod is tight. "It's not me Hooper has let down. But

thanks for cheering Mad up. You really don't have to do a big barbeque thing. It's a lot."

"And you don't have to tell me what I don't need to be doing all the time, Brooks," I reply. "Mad deserves a fun night. Everyone's here for the weekend anyway. It's perfect."

Izzy makes a face, smacking a hand to her forehead. "My parents! They're coming tonight." Before I can reply, she continues, "I'll cancel on them."

"Why?" I shrug. "My family's here too. Might be easier with more people?"

"Easier?"

"Your poker face is terrible, Brooks," I reply. "It's obvious you're dreading seeing them."

Before she can reply, Madison reappears in the doorway of the trailer, wielding a fluffy pink notebook and matching pencil.

"Ready?" I ask.

She gives a firm nod, and before I can say another word, she takes a running jump from the trailer steps, throwing herself at me as Izzy cries a horrified, "MAD!"

I catch her mid-air, her little arms wrapping around my neck like a spider monkey. For a moment, I pretend to stumble, making her shriek a giggle.

"Do you know who's the best at making lists?" I ask, shifting her weight easily in my arm.

"Who?" Madison asks.

"Mama," I reply. "Let's go find her, monkey."

"Monkey," she says, giggling against my shoulder, and a glow of warmth hits my chest again. Madison deserves only laughter and sunshine and fun, and it feels good to be the one to give her that.

As we make our way back to the ranch house, I throw a glance over my shoulder to Izzy. "Stop worrying, Brooks," I call at her. "I'll bring her right back."

"Yeah, Brooks." Mad grins before Izzy gets the chance to reply.

There's something in Izzy's expression—the way she's fighting back a smile and no doubt a sarcastic retort—that feels different. Like maybe we're done fighting. I don't know what this is, but like this ranch and these horses, it feels like it might be real.

And yeah, that thought terrifies me right now. Yesterday I told Izzy I was all in. I meant it. Or I thought I did. But now, with Mama's words still echoing in my head—*a future with the Stormhawks*—I feel that certainty waver.

Because even as Izzy looks at me like I might be worth believing in, there's a small, treacherous part of me whispering, *What if?*

TWENTY-NINE

IZZY

FLIC: *Is Dylan still alive? You left the bar pretty angry yesterday.*

IZZY: *He is! In fact, he's throwing a barbeque tonight. Can you get the night off?*

FLIC: *If Jen hadn't just called in sick with a stomach bug, I'd be there. Just try not to get any more splinters.*

IZZY: *You love it really.*

FLIC: *And what the hell have you done to that man? I've barely known him to crack a smile and now he's throwing parties?*

FLIC: *Promise me you'll wear something nice. And by nice, I mean not the clothes you wear for ranching. And brush your hair!*

IZZY: *It's not a date!*

FLIC: *It's not nothing either!*

"When you said a barbeque by the lake, I thought you meant a few burgers. This is quite something..." I trail off, taking in the scene before me: the long foldout table and chairs near the tree line, buckets of beer and soft drinks, string lights and lanterns strewn in the trees, lit by a generator humming softly from somewhere nearby.

Dylan grins, taking in the same view. "Go big or go home, right?"

I roll my eyes. "I don't know why I'm surprised. You went from no horses to eighteen overnight."

He laughs—a low rumble I feel more than hear. The sun is sinking lower, streaking through the trees and over the lake in golds and oranges. There's still a muggy heat to the evening and I'm grateful I chose a simple white cotton dress. God knows why I listened to Flic, but I've left my hair loose and even added eyeliner and lipstick to my usual hurried flick of mascara, laughing off Madison's, "Why do you look so pretty, Mom?" as we left the trailer earlier.

My gaze roams to the lake every few minutes, to where Jake is pushing Madison on the rope swing. She shrieks with laughter before plunging into the water, Buck diving in after her every time. I feel a tightness in my chest ease at the sound of her happiness. Like the claws of my anxiety—the constant fears I'm letting Mad down—are loosening their hold on me.

A sudden lump forms in my throat. She deserves this—to be surrounded by people who are kind, who see how special she is. Who show up for her. I look at Dylan. He's watching Mad too, a bottle of beer in his hand, an easy smile on his lips. He's wearing a fitted white tee and black jeans that mold to his thigh muscles in a way that makes my gaze snag, my mouth dry. And then I'm looking at the sand beneath my feet, remembering lying on Dylan's towel. The way he kissed me—every part of me. Liquid heat burns in my core and I force the image away.

Family dinner, Iz. Thoughts out of the gutter.

I take a breath, catching the aromas of the meat cooking on the grill. Chase is taking his turn flipping burgers. He's swigging from a beer bottle and he's wearing bright pink swim trunks, a yellow tee, and an apron that reads, "Hot Stuff Coming Through." I watch him for a second, the easy way he moves, the lazy grin he throws over his shoulder at Harper as she pretends to scold him for drinking on the job.

He shouts a greeting as a group of two men and two women arrive and greet Mama.

"I wasn't expecting so many people," I say, pushing aside the urge to slip into the background.

"I didn't take you for the shy type, blondie." Dylan's voice is teasing, and now it feels like I'm not the only one thinking of lying naked on the shore. "There's no one here to be scared of."

"I'm not scared," I reply.

"Horses are easier to read though, right?" he says, like he's read my mind.

He lifts a hand, trailing one finger down my arm. The touch is light, lingering for just a second before it's gone, but it's enough to send a thrill zipping through my body. I glance back to the rope swing, watching Mad and maybe checking she's not watching me. Flic's right. This thing with Dylan, it isn't nothing, but I don't want to confuse Madison, especially when she's already fragile from Hooper letting her down again. For a second my fury at my ex-husband—a Hulk-like rage—threatens to split me in two, but then Dylan moves close enough for me to draw in that leather and wood scent, and my thoughts are his once more.

"She's fine with Jake," Dylan murmurs in my ear, so close his beard tickles my skin as he follows my gaze to where Madison is swimming confidently to the shore for another go on the swing. He turns me around and nods to the group that has just arrived.

"They're our two nearest neighbors and Mama's friends." He turns me a fraction so we're facing the next group. "You met Mia and Serena at the first pre-season game, right?" he asks. I nod, looking to where Harper is standing in a cute, cropped red tee and black denim skirt with the two other women. Mia is wearing cowboy boots and a bohemian skirt, black braids loose down her back, looking like she stepped right out of a country music video. And Serena is beside her. Where Mia is beautiful and Harper is petite and cute as hell, Serena is a goddess. The kind of stunning that shouldn't exist outside of one of Madison's Disney movies. Blonde hair that flows in silk waves down her back and an easy smile that makes her look both effortlessly cool and completely untouchable.

"Mia is the bigshot at Arquette Media, right?" I ask.

"Yeah, but before that she was Colorado's youth champion barrel racer."

As I'm staring, Chase steps over from the grill, throwing an arm around Serena's shoulder.

"Are Serena and Chase...?"

Dylan laughs. "Not even close. They've been best friends since middle school. God knows why she still puts up with him, but they seem to have the same weird sense of humor. She used to be a Stormhawks cheerleader, but now she's one of the coaches for the cheer team and choreographs the routines."

"Cheerleader—I can see that." I never thought of myself as insecure, but it's hard not to compare myself with someone as stunning as Serena.

"You'd think she'd be a total bitch, right?" Dylan adds. "But she's actually one of the nicest people you'll ever meet. Completely down to earth. All she wants is the white picket fence, the kids, the minivan..."

I raise my brows. "The line of guys waiting to give her that must be wrapped around the block."

"You'd think." Dylan shrugs. "Except she has a thing for the bad boys who treat her like shit and never commit." Dylan turns his attention back on me, something playful dancing in his eyes. "What about you, Brooks? What kind of guy do you go for?" His voice dips low, that teasing edge curling into something more, making my pulse thud in my ears. My throat goes dry, my mind dragging itself straight back to the gutter, remembering exactly how his hands felt on me, how his mouth—

"I'm not sure I have a type. But I know one thing..."

"What's that?" he asks, like he already knows my next words will be cutting.

I take his beer from his hand, enjoy a slow sip before meeting his gaze, let my words land between us like a challenge. "Definitely not former pro athletes pretending to be ranchers."

Dylan lets out a rough laugh, shaking his head like I drive him insane, but I don't miss the way his eyes darken. "Who said anything about pretending? I didn't hear you complaining yesterday. In fact," he continues, rubbing his beard like he's lost in thought, "I seem to remember you quite liked—"

"Don't you dare go there when we're surrounded by your family."

He flashes me a wicked grin. "I'll save it for later, then."

And just like that, my entire body is humming. Whatever he means by later, it can't come soon enough.

The lanterns cast the perfect glow of light over the table as we sit down to eat. Madison rushes in from the water and wraps herself in a towel, hair still wet, legs swinging as she takes the seat beside me and eyes the pile of burgers with a gleeful smile.

Madison fills her plate with a burger and then heaps of

vegetables as Mama reminds her she wants to be big and strong like her boys. I do the same, eating quietly as talk zigzags from football to childhood memories to Jake and Harper setting a date for their wedding. I pretend not to notice Mad slipping the occasional bite of food to Buck, lying patiently by her feet.

"Damn," Chase groans, rubbing his belly and reaching for another burger. "I wish the nutritionists would let me eat like this every night."

Jake huffs a laugh. "Yeah. It's almost like they want your arteries clear for blood flow or something."

"I like my arteries clogged with beef and cheese, thank you very much."

"Gross." Mia laughs, rubbing her flat stomach. "Now I wish I hadn't eaten so much."

Across the table, Harper slips her hand into Jake's. "If we're making wishes, I wish we could get married by this lake. It's so pretty."

Jake leans forward and kisses Harper's cheek. "Why don't we then?"

"Really?" She grins.

"Why not? We've hated all the venues we've looked at so far."

Harper pulls a pained face. "That one by the harbor was more like a funeral home."

"Dude!" Chase jumps in, slapping a hand on Jake's back. "That sounded way too casual for a proposal."

"I already proposed, and she already said yes," Jake replies. "A wedding is just a party, right? Why not have it in one of our favorite places on earth?"

Serena punches Chase playfully. "Leave them alone. Just because you don't have a romantic bone in your body. I think this would be the perfect spot for a wedding."

Harper stares across the lake, her eyes shining with the reflection of the water and something softer. "Buck would have his head in the wedding cake before we even said the vows." She turns to Madison. "Think you could keep him in line for us, Mad?"

My daughter's face lights up like it's Christmas morning. "I can do that!"

Part of me wants to protest—to say we might not be here, that nothing about the future is certain. But the words don't come and I just find myself mouthing a "thank you" to Harper. Because maybe for the first time in a long time I don't want to protest. Maybe there's something terrifying but beautiful about being pulled in by the gravity of this family, like I'm already part of it, even if I never meant to be.

"Seeing as we're making wishes," Mama says, her voice gentle but steady, "I'm going to tell you mine. I wish you'll always feel that Oakwood Ranch is your home. That you'll always have somewhere to come back to."

I don't miss the way she says it—not just to her sons, but to Harper. To me. To Madison. The words settle in my chest like an ache I didn't know was there. A hope I haven't dared to name.

"And," she continues, "I've decided I'm going to build three houses on the opposite side of the lake."

All three Sullivan boys splutter a, "What?"

"Who for?" Jake asks.

"For you. For all of us. Seeing Dylan working the ranch these past weeks, it's made me realize the house is part of that life. Which is how it should be. But I don't want to be woken at the crack of dawn by the sound of Dylan in the kitchen, and you"—she nods to Jake and Harper—"want your own space when you're here. I love it when all three of you are home, but you're grown men now and we're all living on top of each other. This way, we'll all get our own space but still have our homes on the ranch."

"You're still planning to cook dinner for all of us, though, right?" Chase asks, shooting a look at Dylan. "No offense, Dyl, but Mama's cooking is way better than yours."

"Says the boy who buys vegetable-flavored ice cream," Dylan retorts before turning to Mama. "The ranch house is your home, Mama. I don't want you to feel you have to—"

"I don't have to do anything. This is what I want. A gorgeous, newly built house overlooking the lake. My own space, too. You realize I've never lived alone? My first home was here with your dad. Then you boys came along. I like the idea of some peace finally."

"Anything to get away from the smell of Dylan after a day with the horses," Jake says with a chuckle.

"That too," Mama agrees, joining in the laughter before turning to Madison. "Seems like there's a lot of wishing going on tonight, Madison. What are you wishing for, honey?"

Madison tilts her head to one side, licking ketchup from her fingers. All eyes are on her, and I'm already preparing myself for whatever dessert-related answer is coming. Probably an entire factory of ice cream.

Except I'm wrong.

Madison lifts her chin, her eyes bright with certainty. "I wish Dylan and my mom would get married so I could stay on Oakwood Ranch forever."

"Mad!" I gasp, wishing the earth would swallow me up.

"What?" She shrugs, completely oblivious to the fact that she's just thrown a grenade onto the table. "That's what I wish for."

I rake over my thoughts for a reply, a way to make this less embarrassing without hurting her feelings, to squash her wish without destroying her.

Then Chase bursts out laughing. "Mad, come on. Dylan's way too grumpy to marry anyone but an old boot."

"Hey." Dylan shoots him a dark look that has the rest of the table doubling over.

Madison giggles, but there's a wobble to her bottom lip, like maybe she's thinking of her dad and what she was supposed to be doing tonight. Like maybe she's been let down enough times. Is it any wonder she's looking for a way to keep hold of the fun she's having tonight? My heart clenches.

I reach for her hand beneath the table and squeeze. "We don't need anyone else when we've got each other," I say quietly.

"People don't just get married, Mad," Dylan says. "Even if it's to old boots."

"Yeah," Harper says, shooting him a pointed look everyone but Mad sees. "They go on dates first and get to know each other."

Mad's lips twitch as she turns back to Dylan. "OK, then I wish you and my mom would go on a date."

Dylan raises his brows at me before focusing back on Mad. "If I ask your mom on a date, that would make your wish come true?"

Mad nods, her grin wide now.

"She might say no," he warns gently.

"I'm saying yes for her. When are you going on your date?" she pushes.

Dylan hesitates.

"Next week?" she asks.

"Sure," he says with a slow nod, sounding suddenly unsure.

"Where will you go?"

He shoots me a look that practically begs for rescue. And even though a part of me wants to let him stew in this, I owe him for cheering Mad up tonight.

"Hey, no one's asked *me* about this date," I say, trying to sound offended. "I can handle my own love life, thanks."

Madison lifts her chin. "You always say you make bad decisions. So I'm making this one for you."

My mouth drops open. "I do not always—"

"Will you go?" she interrupts, fixing me with the look that's won her plenty of extra cookies and late bedtimes over the years.

I hesitate as I look at Dylan. He's watching me, expression unreadable, like he's waiting for my answer the same as Mad, and before I can overthink it, I roll my eyes and fight back a smile. "Doesn't sound like I have much choice. But I'm picking the place."

"Yes!" Madison grins. "My second wish is for Dylan to come swimming with me before it gets dark."

And then she's gone, towel flying behind her like a cape as she races for the lake.

I barely have time to breathe before Dylan pushes back from the table. He glances down at me, eyes lingering on mine a second too long, and it feels strangely like Mad wasn't the only one to have won that argument.

"Smart kid," Chase says, shaking his head with a laugh.

Too smart.

I stare after them, the warmth of Dylan's eyes on me just now clings to my skin the same way every one of his touches does. Maybe a fake date with Dylan isn't the worst way to spend an evening. Only it doesn't feel fake at all. Not with the way he just looked at me. Not with the way I wanted to look back.

THIRTY

IZZY

Before I can think any more about my fake date, I spot two familiar figures cutting through the trees. I leap from my chair to greet them. "Mom, Dad, you made it." I smile, glad to see them, and yet my stomach is already knotting, wondering what they want to talk to me about. There's always something.

Mom is dressed in her usual pressed slacks and silk blouse. Dad is trying to brush the dust from his white shirt and chinos. Both of them look out of place and uncomfortable amid the rugged beauty of the ranch.

"Isobel, you look well," Mom says, pressing a quick kiss to my cheek. "Are you wearing makeup? Very pretty."

"Thank you," I reply, trying and failing not to hear the words she doesn't say. *For a change.*

I lead them over to the tables and make the introductions. The Sullivans are welcoming and friendly, and even though my parents are polite and thank Mama for the invitation to her ranch, I can tell they'd rather not be here.

"David got head of plastic surgery! Did you hear?" Mom announces when it's just the three of us. "We're all so thrilled for your brother. Now, how are things here?"

"Great," I say, launching into telling them about Moonlight's foaling and the success of the last auction. They nod along for a minute before Mom nudges an elbow to Dad's side and my words trail off.

"Show her the brochure," she says.

"What brochure?" I ask.

Dad pulls a glossy booklet from the inside pocket of his jacket. "We've found the most amazing school for Madison," he says, the words bouncing like he's found the solution to a problem I didn't know existed.

I swallow. Remind myself that my parents love me. They love Madison. They only want what they see is best for us both. My voice is light as I reply. "She goes to a school she likes already." Although even as I say it, I realize she'll need to move schools now anyway. Her old school is out near Bill's ranch.

"But this one is really something." Mom beams, cutting through my thoughts as she flips the brochure open and hands it to me, tapping the page before I've even looked. "It has an incredible academic program, the best extracurriculars, and it has a full equestrian center. Weekly riding lessons, show-jumping facilities. She'll still be around horses, which we know she loves." The last part is added like they're making a concession.

They fall silent as I stare at the pictures of happy children in immaculate uniforms and beaming smiles. "It does look amazing," I admit. "And expensive. I can speak to Hooper about the tuition, but he's always liked the idea of Madison having a normal childhood."

"Don't bother asking that boy for anything," Dad says as Mom jumps in.

"We want to pay," she says, grabbing my hand and giving it a squeeze.

"That's what we wanted to tell you," Dad continues. "We

want Madison to have the very best chance at an amazing future. And we think this school would be perfect for her."

I force down the resentment trying to rise to the surface. "It feels like what you're saying is that you don't think Madison will have an amazing future if she continues as she is." *With me. Here.*

Dad shakes his head, offering me a smile. "That's not it, Isobel. But you have to remember, I grew up on a ranch. You didn't. I know how challenging ranch life can be. It's commendable, Izzy, and we know you love it. Growing up with two parents working every hour of the day is hard enough. But only having one parent makes everything so much harder. This school offers Madison so many fantastic opportunities she can't have living on a ranch."

"We only want what's best for Madison," Mom adds.

Then I realize what they're really saying. They want me to stop ranching, and this school is what they're offering in exchange. "I'm assuming there are conditions?" I ask, because of course there are. Of course this kindness is really about them getting what they want.

Mom's lips purse for a fraction of a second before Dad answers. "We don't think of them as conditions, but..."

"We will pay for Madison to attend this wonderful school, and you take up our offer to move back home," Mom says simply, knowing I could never afford to send her to a school like this on my own. "Both of you come to live with us. Madison will have the best education money can buy and you'll continue your studies. It doesn't have to be medical school—though that door is always open for you—but you're a bright woman, Izzy."

"Just so we're clear," I say. "You're saying you won't pay for Madison to attend this school if we continue living and working on a ranch?"

Their faces say it all. This isn't about what's best for Madison. It's about taking control of her life and mine. Again. Doing what they think is best. "You have more than proven you're capable of doing things on your own," Dad says. "It's time to let us help you. To give Madison more stable influences in her life."

Mom looks past me to the lake, where Madison is shrieking with laughter. Dylan is scooping her into his arms, throwing her into the air, and letting her land with a splash. Both of them have water rolling down their faces, shoulders shaking with laughter.

"It's getting a bit late for swimming, don't you think?" Mom says.

I feel suddenly uncertain. Mad is safe with Dylan. Maybe it is late, but it's not dark yet. "I'll call her in soon. Why don't you get some food?"

A pained expression crosses Dad's face. "Sorry, darling, didn't we say? We already ate. Barbeque really isn't great for your gut health."

"But we'd love to spend some time with Madison," Mom adds, shooting another pointed looked at the lake. "And you'll think about the school? You'll let us know? The new school year starts soon."

The crushing sense of failure isn't new but it's no less sharp as I nod and stride to the shore to call Madison in. The feeling lingers through the rest of the evening—through watching Mom and Dad dote on Madison, urging me again to consider their offer before they leave, driving back to their dust-free suburbia. It stays through helping to clean up and through tucking Madison into bed. I watch her fall asleep in seconds but find myself too restless to do the same.

I step quietly from my trailer, the door clicking softly behind me. There's a soft glow from the ranch house, but it's the light from the barn's open door that draws me forward.

I find Dylan organizing some tools by the workbench. He turns when I step inside, offering me a smile that makes me feel lighter.

"You OK?" he asks, reaching for my hand. He brushes his thumb lightly over my fingers, just like he did earlier. Gentle and reassuring.

"Just my parents again," I say. "They think I'm failing Madison."

"That's bullshit, Iz."

"Is it?" I ask. "They're offering her everything I can't—structure, a good school, financial security, an actual bedroom. All I have is a trailer with a broken washing machine I can't afford to fix."

He draws me into his arms. "You offer her unwavering love. You give happiness, safety, and the space to be exactly who she is. I've never seen a kid more secure and confident in who she is than Madison. That's *you*. That's what you've given her. And no amount of money can buy that."

The words settle into the cracks where the doubt and anxiety have taken root. I nod, swallowing the lump in my throat. "Thank you," I whisper.

I let myself think about everything Dylan's done for Mad... for me. The way he listens. The way he *sees* me. The way he put tonight together just to make Mad happy.

"Dylan?"

"Yeah?"

"Your offer—for me to keep running the ranch with you. Is it still on the table?"

There's a fraction of a second where Dylan seems to hesitate, but I must imagine it because in the next moment he nods. "Of course."

"Then I'd like to say yes." And even though I mean it, it doesn't make it any less terrifying. Because as much as I love these horses, as much as I know ranching is carved into my bones, a part of me wonders if I'm staying because of the way this place makes me feel... or because of the way Dylan does.

"But the other offers..." he starts to say.

I make a face. "There aren't any other offers. I lied." I shrug. "I didn't want you to feel sorry for me or think I wasn't serious."

"Neither of those things could ever happen," he says as he smiles broadly. "Guess I'd better start hiding the pitchforks, then."

I laugh, feeling the tightness in my chest ease. And then his hands reach to cradle my face. Slowly, like he wants me to feel every second of this moment, he leans in and presses his lips to mine. His tongue slides into my mouth and mine into his. A jolt of pure desire shoots down my body. His hands move to my waist, anchoring me to him as our mouths move together.

When he finally pulls back, his eyes are dark and full of need. "Where's Mad?" he asks, his voice a low rasp.

"Fast asleep," I whisper.

And this time, there's no hesitation. No teasing slowness. Dylan's lips press hard against mine, deepening our kiss and the want in my core.

"Fuck," he groans into my mouth, his voice a low rumble that sends shivers skating down my spine. "You have no idea how fucking beautiful you are."

His hands roam from my waist to my ass, gripping me like he's afraid I might vanish. My fingers drag down his broad shoulders, over every hard line of muscle, before finding the buckle of his belt. I can feel him, thick and hard against me, and the thought of how ready he is so quickly makes me dizzy with want. I stroke the hard length of him through the denim, and my core coils tight. This man has spent the last month infuriating me with his arrogance, his walls, his refusal to admit he made a mistake buying Bill's horses. The way he carries the weight of the world on those shoulders like no one else could possibly help him.

But he's also the man who listened without judgment when I opened up about my past. Who coaxed me down from the roof of my trailer and made me hot cocoa. Who is kind and attentive to Madison, showing her how to play football, always listening when she speaks. Dylan has folded us into his family and this ranch like it's the most natural thing in the world, like it's no big deal—when really, it's everything.

And now? Now I ache for his touch. For the heat of his mouth and the rough slide of his hands on my bare skin. It feels like we've been circling this moment forever, like every lingering look and almost-kiss has been leading to this. My body is humming, pulsing with need. And nothing is going to stop us this time.

My hands fumble with the button of his jeans just as Dylan drops to his knees, tugging down the straps of my dress until my breasts spill free into the cool air of the barn. His eyes blaze and a second later, his tongue flicks over one nipple, swirling, teasing, until I arch into him.

"Dylan," I gasp.

He stands, lips meeting mine again in a kiss that steals the air from my lungs. Then his arms sweep beneath me, lifting me like I weigh nothing. My legs wrap around his waist as he carries me to the workbench and sets me down. Our clothes are gone in a blur of tugging hands and frantic kisses. Our bodies press together, hot skin on hot skin. I reach for his rock-hard length, sliding my hand all the way down, loving the way it makes Dylan growl. His beard scrapes deliciously along my collarbone as he kisses his way down to my breasts, tongue and teeth driving me wild. Then his fingers slide between my legs and he groans.

"Is this for me?" he asks, touching my slick heat.

"Yes," I breathe, hips bucking toward him.

"Lie back," he rasps.

Every inch of me is humming as I lie across the bench. His lips blaze a trail over my breasts. His tongue circles my nipples, biting and nipping as strong hands slide over my legs, pushing my thighs wide. His hand never leaves my center, cupping me, fingers stroking in teasing circles that drive me to the brink. A thick finger slides into me, pumping in and out. I gasp again, my body tightening, every nerve sparking.

"Dylan," I cry out.

His mouth lingers on my nipple before he pulls back, his hand still working me into a frenzy, firm and confident. "Open your eyes. I want to see you when you come."

My gaze locks on the dark pools of his eyes as his fingers continue to rub slow, urgent circles over my clit. Heat coils tighter, sharper, winding deep in my core. His dick is hard and ready and so close. My entire body aches for him, my hips tilting toward the thick length I'm desperate to feel buried inside me.

He slides a second finger inside me and I almost beg for him to fuck me. But the intensity is building fast. Every muscle is tight and vibrating with need. I'm teetering on the edge.

So close.

Then his thumb shifts the pressure and it's more than I can take. My breathing is ragged, his name is on my lips, and his hands—his strong, unrelenting hands—are touching everywhere, winding me tighter and tighter. His dick moves closer. He's right there at my opening and fuck if it isn't enough to shove me over the edge. With a final gasp, I shatter. My thighs tremble, my breath stutters, body shuddering. Pleasure crashes through me in deep, rolling waves, leaving me undone. His name spills from my lips in a desperate, gasping plea.

Only then does Dylan move his hands to my hips, dragging me closer to the edge of the bench and to him. His eyes bore into mine. "You sure you want this?"

I glance down at him—so big, so hard. A breathless laugh bubbles up before I can stop it. "Hell yes."

The corner of his mouth twitches, that cocky, self-assured smirk that so often infuriates me but only fuels the fire right now. Before I can say anything else, I'm reaching for him, legs wrapping around his waist, drawing him close. The heat of his body against mine sends another jolt of desire through me.

He groans as I guide the thick head of his dick to my entrance. His hands grip my hips as he begins to slide slowly inside me. The stretch is... fuck, it's incredible. It's everything I want and need in this second. Intense in a way that steals the air from my lungs. I cry out, my head falling back as he fills me inch by inch.

"Fuck, Izzy," Dylan says, voice strained as he pushes all the way in.

The fullness is overwhelming, quickly melting into pleasure as he starts to move, slow and steady. Each thrust sends another spark of electricity shooting through me until I'm clinging to him, nails digging into his shoulders, until all that exists is this moment between us.

He leans forward, his beard scratching my cheek as he growls in my ear, "You feel so fucking good."

I don't answer, can't answer, because all I can focus on is the way his body moves against mine, the way every thrust is hitting just the right spot. My nails rake down his back, and he groans again, his hips snapping harder, the rhythm picking up, the bench creaking beneath us. Tension builds low in my belly, sharp and insistent. I think I'm going to come again. What the hell? That's never happened before. My heart is pounding, my breath ragged.

And still, a thought presses in. Not just this hot need, but something deeper. And God, I want to trust that feeling. Trust this man. But I've been burned before. Left to pick up the pieces for myself and Mad. And Dylan? He might be all steady hands and scorching heat, but I still don't know if he's the man who stays. All I know is that no one has ever touched me like this, wanted me like this, made me feel this way. Dylan Sullivan knows exactly how to ruin me.

THIRTY-ONE
DYLAN

Izzy's long legs are locked around my waist as I thrust into her. Each movement causes a shot of pleasure through me that borders on unbearable. The only sounds are the creak of the workbench and Izzy's gasps. I stare down at her, naked before me, her hair falling in messy waves. Her green eyes meet mine, sending a fresh surge of need coursing through me; the next thrust pushes deeper still, making us both cry out.

I can feel myself stepping closer to the edge, every thrust pulling me tighter. I could give in, let go right now, but I'm not ready for this to end. It's been too long. Not just the years when I only really had space for football, or the months I spent tunnel-visioned on recovering from my injury, but too long since I've wanted my dick buried inside this beautiful, sexy woman.

Izzy's cries ring in my ears. I want to stay right here, where the rest of the world ceases to exist. Where there's only her, and this need, and the steady rhythm of our bodies moving together.

"Fuck," Izzy hisses. "Dylan, I'm... oh God..."

Just hearing that pleasure in her voice shoves me closer

toward unravelling. I fight the heat burning in my groin, desperate to hold on for just a little longer.

Not yet!

I force myself to slow down, drawing out almost the full length of my dick. My thumb moves between us, pressing against her center in the circles that had her screaming my name minutes ago. I slide back into her, taking my time now. She feels so fucking good.

I run a hand down her body, over her nipples. "You're so tight, Izzy. So wet for me."

My words are the final shove, pushing her over the edge. Her head falls back against the bench as the orgasm claims her. Her walls tighten as she moans, gripping me in place like her body doesn't want to let me go. I push into her again, deeper this time, loving the way her body shudders with her release. The sensation is almost enough to undo me, a relentless pull that has my dick throbbing for the same. But I hold back, letting her ride the wave, my thumb never breaking contact with her center. I can't tear my eyes away from her. She's so fucking beautiful. And right now she's all mine.

Her eyes open, focusing on me, clear and sharp, and I see it —the want still burning in their depths. I scoop her into my arms, her legs wrapping around my waist, her arms looping around my neck as I stand, turning us toward the nearest stall. I press her back against the wood and she grabs the hay hooks either side of us, steadying herself as I push back into her. She tilts her hips, meeting every thrust, her movements as urgent and desperate as mine. All I can think about is the pressure building inside me, the dizzying urgency pulsing so close to the surface, it feels like my skin is on fire.

Her name slips from my lips in a low groan as I thrust deeper, harder. My control unravels thread by thread with every roll of her hips, every moan of her hot breath against my neck. My hands tighten around her perfect ass, and when I can't take another second, when the pressure and pleasure are too much, I lose myself completely, my release tearing through me, hot and powerful, shattering the tension in my body as I spill inside her. For the first time in what feels like years, I let go completely—of the frustration, the resentment, the weight of everything I've lost.

I'm not sure how long we stay like that—our breathing uneven, our bodies wrapped around each other. Slowly, the world pulls back into focus. The quiet of the barn. The night air cooling the sweat on our skin. Gently, I lower Izzy to the floor until her feet touch down. My arms stay around her, unwilling to let her go, not yet. All I want to do is carry her into the ranch house, into my bed. Let her fall asleep curled up against me, skin to skin. I want to wake up with her tangled in my arms.

But the house is full—Jake and Harper, Chase, Mama. And Madison is asleep in the trailer. Right now, in this barn, is the only moment we have together. So we untangle. Slowly. Dress slowly. Then we're standing side by side in the barn doorway, not ready for this to end. I brush my thumb over her cheek. "I hope it was worth the wait," I murmur.

Izzy smiles wickedly. "Since the lake? Yes. Since the five years... Definitely, yes."

I laugh, pulling her in for another kiss. But then I feel a flicker of tension in her body, and my eyes search her face. "What are you thinking?"

She bites her bottom lip, that telltale sign she's wrestling with something. "This date..." she starts. "Mad... She was just... We obviously don't have to go."

I give her my best mock-offended look. "Oh, so you've gotten what you want from me and that's it?"

Her eyes go wide. "What? No! That's not—"

I laugh and she swats my chest.

"What if I want to take you on a date?" I ask softly.

And it's her turn to search for something in my expression. "Do you?"

"Yes, Izzy. I'd like to take you on a real date. One without hay in your hair and a pitchfork two feet away."

She hesitates. "It could complicate things..."

I shrug. "Easy is overrated."

That makes her smile. "I'm still picking the place."

"Of course you are," I say, and then I kiss her again.

Eventually, we step apart and Izzy walks back to the trailer. I watch her in the darkness until the trailer door closes, then I head into the ranch house, stripping off and collapsing into bed.

Somewhere in the back of my mind, I know I should be thinking about what Mama told me this morning—about Coach Allen, the offer to join the Stormhawks coaching staff, a second shot at the game I used to live for. But as I lie in the dark, staring at the ceiling, the only thing I can think about is Izzy. How she's rewired something in me. And whatever I choose next, there's no going back.

THIRTY-TWO
DYLAN

MIA: *Hey Dylan, thanks for inviting me to the barbeque. This might sound a bit strange, but if Fury ever settles and you think about selling, can you let me know?*

DYLAN: *Sure. Although I think it's going to be a while. You know someone who might be interested?*

MIA: *Maybe. And thanks!*

~

DYLAN: *You planning to tell me where we're going?*

IZZY: *Just be ready at 7.*

DYLAN: *I hate to sound like an insecure teen, but... what do I wear?*

IZZY: *What you normally wear is fine.*

DYLAN: *OK, but if you're wearing those tiny cutoffs, just know there's a very high risk we won't make it out of my truck.*

IZZY: *What happened to being a gentleman?*

DYLAN: *It's overrated!*

The knock on Izzy's trailer door feels loud in the quiet evening. I rub the palms of my hands on my jeans, feeling excited and nervous all at once. The emotion is wrapped in a big fat bow of stupid. We've spent three days working side by side after the night in the barn, stealing moments together—lingering kisses, a touch as we brush past.

I've played football in front of tens of thousands of fans, plus millions watching at home. I've led the team to victory just as many times as I've fallen on my ass and been crushed in front of those fans. Pressure is nothing new to me. And yet, none of that matters. Because standing in front of Izzy's door, I feel like a damn teen on my first date.

Maybe it's the knowledge that there's no job to hide behind tonight. Ranch life gives us cover. It gives us a distraction. A way to circle each other. But this? A date? It's just us.

Maybe it's how deep I feel myself falling for this woman— how much she's tangled into everything I do now. How I catch myself looking for her even when I know she's not there.

Or maybe it's knowing that when we come back tonight, the ranch is all ours. Chase is in the city. Jake and Harper flew to Hawaii yesterday. I dropped Mama at the airport for her girls' trip to Florida this morning. The house is empty—except for Buck, who's smart enough to stay out of the way when I need him to.

The trailer door swings open and my mind empties. All I see is Izzy wearing a black top that falls off one shoulder and a denim skirt that somehow makes those tiny cutoffs she wears look respectable. My eyes snag on those long, tanned legs. It's a fight not to lean over, pull her in, run my lips down the elegant line of her neck.

"My eyes are up here, Sullivan." Her voice is sharp but her lips are pulled into a teasing smile. Her dark blonde hair is loose and shining in tousled waves around her face and down her back. Her green eyes are sharpened by dark eyeliner. Her lips—those perfect lips—are painted a peachy red. The look is sexy as hell and has my dick twitching in my jeans.

"Damn, Brooks. With you in that outfit, I'm going to be spending the night trying not to sucker punch any guy who looks your way."

"I can take care of myself," she says with her trademark eye roll.

"Didn't say you couldn't. But it doesn't mean I'm not going to be looking out for you, too."

Her smile falters for half a second as my words land. It's the slightest crack in her armor, but I catch it. Izzy has had to stand on her own, face the world head-on while raising the sweetest little human I've ever met. With her parents trying to push her into a box she doesn't belong in, and her douchebag ex letting Mad down over and over, it's no wonder she doesn't trust people to have her back.

And the way I bought the horses and dragged her into my life wasn't exactly the best start to building trust. But if ranching's taught me anything these past few weeks, it's that trust takes time and patience. You show up, again and again, until the doubts have nothing left to stand on. Which is why it eats at me that I haven't told her about the offer from Coach Allen... I've meant to. More than once. But the truth is, every time we're alone, every moment her eyes lock on mine or she leans just a little closer, all my good intentions get buried under the need to touch her.

I could tell myself I'm waiting until I know more. Until

Coach calls again. Until I've made a decision. But deep down, I know I'm holding back. Because saying the words out loud might break whatever this is that's building between us.

"Come on," she says, stepping from the trailer, passing so close I catch the scent of her perfume—like the ocean on a summer's day, with something purely Izzy underneath. My pulse kicks up a notch.

"You gonna tell me where we're going yet?" I ask.

"Nope."

I hide my smile. "Fine, but I'm driving, blondie."

"Suit yourself, big guy," she throws back, using the nickname from the first time we met. The day my truck hit her compact feels like a different lifetime. The name—the memory of our exchange and Izzy using it now—makes me tip my head back and laugh. The last of my nerves disappear. Izzy was wrong the other night when she said this date would complicate things. Spending time with her is the easiest thing in the world.

We fill the drive talking about ourselves. Izzy tells me more about her family, the pressure she felt to become a doctor. I tell her about being drafted to the Stormhawks and my life before the injury.

"The problem with living the dream is the constant fear that you're going to mess up and lose it," I admit. "Seven years I spent playing tight end. Seven years of looking over my shoulder at newer drafts. Leaving it all on the field, knowing it could get ripped away from me any second." And then it did. My chest tightens at the memory, but I keep talking. "Looking back now, it feels like I barely stopped to draw in breath because I was scared if I stopped, it would end somehow."

"And now?" Izzy asks, her voice soft, like she knows this isn't an easy question.

I feel her gaze on me and the weight of what she's asking. She wants me to tell her again that I'm all in. That I know what I want now. For a split second, I think of the coaching offer again. Then I shove it aside. I haven't even spoken to Coach Allen about it. I'm not even sure if I want to.

"When I first got injured, I didn't know who I was without football. I guess I'm still figuring it out," I admit. "But yeah, I'm breathing a little easier."

It's not the all-in commitment Izzy wants, but it's the truth. And from the thoughtful look on Izzy's face as I glance her way, it's enough. For now.

An hour north of Idaho Springs, Izzy points to a field already filling with trucks. Beyond it is a small arena lit by bright floodlights. I shake my head, huffing a laugh as it dawns on me where Izzy has brought me. Not a restaurant or a bar, but the rodeo. Of course she has.

A grin lights up my face. "I can't believe you thought of this place. I haven't been here for twenty years." A pang of sadness hits my chest. The last time I was here, we were a family of five, with Dad behind the wheel of our old truck, Mama beside him, Chase squeezed in the middle between me and Jake.

"Is this OK?" she asks.

I see the sudden hesitation in her expression and throw her an easy smile. "It's more than OK." And it is.

"Nothing beats a local rodeo," Izzy says as I park and kill the engine.

I turn to look at her, drinking her in—just as fucking beautiful now as when she's hauling hay bales.

Izzy's eyes land on mine and suddenly the air between us is elastic pulled tight.

My voice when I speak is a low rumble. "Keep looking at me like that, Brooks, and this date ain't making it out of my truck."

The corner of her mouth quirks, and the glint in her eye tells me she might not have a problem with that. So I grab the door and jump out before I can give in to the need hammering in my chest. A second later, I'm opening her door, holding out my hand for her to take, but she jumps down on her own. Typical.

There's a muggy heat to the night, the promise of another summer rainstorm brewing. The air smells of grilled meats and cotton candy. The scents wrap around us as we make our way to the arena. "So do you bring all your dates to the rodeo?" I ask as we weave through the crowds.

She exhales a laugh. "If by dates you mean Mad and Flic, then yes. After Hooper, dating was the last thing on my mind for a very long time. And even if it wasn't, apparently my prickly 'might kill you with a pitchfork' personality doesn't exactly lend itself to dating. Which is fine by me," she adds quickly. "Madison, horses, and ranching—that's all I need."

Something about the way she says it makes me think she's convincing herself as much as she is me. My jaw tightens at the mention of Hooper and the pain he's caused Mad and Izzy over the years.

"What about you?" she asks, shifting the conversation. "Where do you take your dates?"

"I don't remember," I say truthfully. "For a long time, I couldn't think about anything but my injury. Before that, I was dating a fitness instructor. She was nice, but when I got injured, I couldn't focus on anything else."

Izzy shoots me a look. "'Nice.' Wow," she says in a teasing voice. "I can't imagine why it didn't work out."

"Maybe I just prefer pitchfork-wielders over nice." The back of my hand brushes against hers, sending a bolt of energy through me that makes me want to sweep Izzy over my shoulder and straight back to my truck. I squash the caveman thought. Right now, I'd settle for slipping my fingers into hers and pulling her close, but something makes me hold back.

We join the crowds of families, couples, and groups, wearing denim and cowboy hats the same way the Stormhawks fans wear their red jerseys. The small arena sits just beyond a wide-open gravel lot, where trucks and horse trailers are lined up and men and women are hurrying as they carry saddles and equipment back and forth. Floodlights light the wooden bleachers and country music hums through the speakers, barely cutting through the lively chatter of the crowd.

We grab popcorn and sodas before finding a couple of seats about halfway up the stands. The wooden planks creak as we take our seats just in time for the tinny-voiced announcer to introduce the first event. Izzy tosses a handful of popcorn into her mouth and nods toward the program in her lap. "I prefer this to the bigger shows. You get to see the younger kids starting out. It's great to spot the talent in the riders and the horses."

Her face lights up as she scans the lineup and taps her finger against one of the entries in the breakaway roping event. "Kevin Anders on Hunter—that was one of the first foals I birthed. I still remember how good it felt to see him sold to the Anders family."

Her pride is infectious and makes me think of the ranch and the future of the horses. Before I can reply, the gates below us burst open, and a bronc explodes into the arena, his powerful muscles kicking up clouds of dust as the rider fights to stay on. There's no saddle—just eight seconds of raw power and chaos where the cowboy tries to cling on, his body jerking with every violent buck.

I feel Izzy tense beside me, her whole body leaning forward like she's in the arena with the cowboy. Holding her breath.

Three seconds.

Four.

Five.

The crowd roars as the rider holds, but then—

BAM.

He's thrown clear, hitting the dirt hard, rolling to his feet as the rodeo clowns distract the bronc.

Izzy lets out a breath. "Damn. Thought he had it."

The evening passes in a blur of heart-stopping action, cheering, and talking. I don't bother fighting the smile as two huge blue barrels are hauled into place on the dirt for the barrel races.

"This was my dad's favorite," I say as a rider in a bright pink shirt flies out of the gates on a white stallion, hooves pounding hard against the dirt. She's good. Striking the perfect balance of speed and tight turns, the horse cutting close to the barrels, kicking up a cloud of dust as it thunders toward the finish line. "It's mine too, if I'm honest," I add, watching the horse cross the line in a time I can't see anyone else beating tonight.

My mind pulls straight to Fury. The strength in those muscles. He was built for this life. One day, I tell myself. One day he'll be back in an arena like this and I'll be in the stands cheering him on. Izzy glances at me like she knows exactly where my thoughts have gone.

"Fury's making progress," she says, her voice soft. "You were right to buy him. He's got something."

I turn my head, raising an eyebrow. "Izzy Brooks, you did not just admit I was right and you were wrong."

She pretends to look around like she's searching for someone. "I have no idea what you're talking about."

I laugh, taking her hand in mine. She lets me hold it for a moment before she pulls away, reaching for her soda.

"I don't know how much you remember..." Izzy starts, hesitating a little as she drags her eyes to the program. "But your dad had a horse called Dusty Star."

I glance at her, surprised at the name. "A gorgeous chestnut mare," I reply. "The white star on her nose. I remember."

She nods, chewing her lip like she's debating whether to say more. "When Bill bought those horses, Dusty Star was my favorite. A few years after she joined us, Bill bred her with a champion stallion." She gestures toward the arena, where a new rider is lining up at the gates. "The next horse about to take the arena? That's Dusty Star's foal."

"No way." I smile, but there's an ache stretching across my chest, too. A grief and a guilt I thought I'd come to terms with a long time ago.

We fall silent before Izzy speaks. "Should I not have said anything?"

"I'm glad you did," I say, meaning it. "My dad got a real kick out of seeing the horses he bred in action."

I feel Izzy watching me. "Must've been hard to say goodbye to them."

I take a long time to nod. "No one has ever said that before. With Dad dying, it was like I couldn't grieve the horses and that life on top of him. I'd have given anything to have my dad back, but the ranch was a huge part of my life, too."

"Do you wish Mama had hired ranch hands and tried to keep it going?" she asks.

I shake my head. "Selling was the right thing to do." I pause, my thoughts pulling back to the eleven-year-old boy who didn't know how to comfort his crying mama. "Jake and Chase think Mama sold the horses to focus on us, and that's true in part. But it was about money too. We might be set for life now with our NFL careers, but back then, the ranch had its share of good years and bad. She needed the money from the sale to keep us afloat. And the hardest part is..." I pause. Swallow. Not sure if I can go on but wanting to explain. To tell Izzy the one thing I've never told another living soul. Beside me, Izzy doesn't fill the silence and her quiet patience is enough for me to carry on. "None of it would've happened—Dad's death, selling the horses —if it wasn't for me."

"I'm sure that's not true," Izzy says carefully.

I keep my gaze focused ahead, staring into the empty arena. The noise of the crowd dies away as I think back to the night my dad died. "There was a rainstorm and the horses were still in the paddocks," I say. "Jake and I went out to help Dad get them into the barn. Jake got to the paddock first and made a move to get Dad's horse. He was a huge gelding—the biggest horse we had—and I almost stopped Jake, almost told him to get a different horse. But I let him go while I went for two other horses."

I swallow back the pain threatening to consume me.

"Dad's horse got spooked by the thunder and reared up at Jake. He slipped and would've been trampled if Dad hadn't pulled him out the way, getting knocked on the head in the process. Dad lost his life saving Jake. If I'd called Jake back that night, told him to get a different horse like I'd thought about..." My words trail off. The what-if is a burden I've carried for so long. It's a part of me.

"You were only a little boy, Dylan," she says quietly. "You couldn't have known what would happen."

"I know, but it still hurts."

Before we can say any more, the gates are opening again and a chestnut stallion streaks into the arena. He's fierce and wild, like Fury. I smile at the thought, about to say something to Izzy, when her hand slips into mine and stays there. Izzy leans closer, our arms touching, and I'm no longer thinking of the race or the past. I'm thinking about us.

There's still a part of me that wants to hold back because whatever this is between us, it's new and I'm scared of how fast it's happening. But with Izzy's hand in mine, I know this thing between us is real. It's not just the pull of desire, the want I feel when she's near. It's something deeper. A connection I've never felt before.

THIRTY-THREE

IZZY

The final rider leaves the arena and all around us people stand and start to move toward the exit. The announcer's voice crackles over the speakers, listing the dates of the next rodeos. Dylan and I stay in our seats, my hand wrapped in his, resting on his thigh. Leaving marks the end of our date, and I don't want that. It's like we've stepped out of ourselves, like this night is all there is to think about. Like maybe this isn't the mistake I keep telling myself it is.

Above our heads, the clouds have cleared, taking the muggy heat with it, and I shiver as I force myself to stand. Dylan moves too, but he keeps my hand in his, fingers entwined. Held tight. Before we leave, he turns to me, tilting my chin and lightly brushing his lips to mine. "Thank you for tonight." His voice is low, vibrating through my body along with the electric charge from his touch. The need for him—for his hands on my skin, his lips, to feel him inside me—is a physical ache. An exquisite pain.

Dylan pulls me close as we follow the crowd toward the parking lot, weaving through the stragglers and those waiting to greet the competitors. Dylan holds on to me like I'm something he wants to keep. And that scares the hell out of me. Because when I start to trust something is forever, it's usually when it falls apart. Like Hooper. Like running Bill's ranch. Like Oakwood? It feels too soon to believe this is forever, but I'm too far gone to imagine leaving. These thoughts make my heart stammer and my head spin as we reach a bottleneck in the crowd.

Dylan pulls his hand away, throwing his arm around me. He moves his lips to my ear like he's going to say something and already my body is tingling. But before he can speak, there's a shout, high-pitched and childlike. Filled with the fever-pitch excitement that reminds me of Madison on Christmas morning. Heads turn and the crowd parts to show a little boy, no older than Mad, jumping up and down, a finger pointed straight at Dylan.

"Dylan Sullivan. You're Dylan Sullivan!" The boy's face is bright red, his grin wide, as he breaks away from where he's standing and all but throws himself at Dylan, barely managing to skid to a stop in front of us. "You played tight end for the Stormhawks. You had over five thousand career receiving yards! And forty-two touchdowns."

"Hi," Dylan says with a smile, crouching down to greet the boy. "What's your name, son?"

"I'm Dylan too," he says proudly, his smile so wide I think his face might split in two. "But I was named after my grandpa, not you. I've watched all your highlights on YouTube. My favorite is the one where you caught the one-handed pass in the snow playing against the Desertraptors. That was so cool!"

Dylan laughs, warm and easy. "That was a good game."

"Can I have your autograph, please?" he asks breathlessly, thrusting out a pen and his rodeo program.

"Sure."

Little Dylan's eyes pop, and I stand back, watching the interaction. Watching this little boy have the best day of his life.

Watching Dylan smile in a way I've never seen before and it's the most natural smile in the world. An uneasy feeling twists in my gut. It's hard not to think that this is where Dylan belongs. In a world of football and fans. Not stuck on a ranch day after day with only me and the horses.

A man approaches us and places a hand on the boy's shoulder. He's tall with short, mussed hair and an open face. "Wow. Not every day you get to meet an NFL legend." Then his eyes land on me. "Hi, I'm Harrison, Dylan's uncle."

"Hi. I don't have anything to do with the NFL," I reply.

The man laughs. "With those arms, I think you're missing a trick." He smiles and it's nice, but it's also more.

"Are you coming back this season?" Little Dylan asks.

Dylan's smile falters for the smallest second, but he covers it quickly as he moves to stand, giving the boy a pat on the shoulder. "I won't be on the field this season, but I'll always be part of the Stormhawks family," he says smoothly.

"So," Harrison says, turning back to me. "If you're not part of the NFL, what do you do?"

"Ranching," I say.

"No way. I work in sales for Big Sky Feeds. I bet I could offer you a great deal on premium grain and custom-blended supplements." He pulls out a business card from the back pocket of his jeans and slips it into my hand. "Give me a call sometime. We could talk discounts over dinner."

I open my mouth to reply, but Dylan gets there first. He throws his arm around me. "Sorry, Harrison. This one belongs to me."

Belongs? Deep down I know Dylan didn't mean it that way, but my gut tightens anyway. I've belonged to someone before—I gave them my heart and lost myself in the process.

"Can't blame a man for trying." Harrison grins before disappearing with the little boy into the crowd.

Dylan's arm is still around me as he moves us out of the

arena and into the parking lot. The second we're outside, I step out of Dylan's touch, needing space. A prickling anger needles at my skin, my body. Away from the floodlights, stars litter the sky. A perfect night.

It was a perfect night. Until just now. Thoughts rush at me, Dylan's voice echoing in my head.

I'll always be part of the Stormhawks family.

This one belongs to me.

And suddenly I'm furious, my anger burning as I stride across the lot.

"Izzy..." Dylan's voice calls after me. A second later he's by my side.

I whirl around so fast he almost knocks into me.

"I don't belong to you."

Dylan's expression morphs from surprised to baffled. "That's not what I meant." There's a playful smile on his lips that only fuels my irritation.

"Sure as hell sounded like it," I snap. "You think you get to claim me like some prize?"

He runs a hand through his hair and looks at me. "That guy was hitting on you."

"And?" I throw my hands out. "I'm a big girl, Sullivan. I can handle myself."

"You don't think I know that? I see it every day, Iz," he replies. "You're so good at taking care of yourself you've built sky-high walls and you're not letting anyone in, least of all me."

"So what are we doing here then?" I throw back, my heart pounding in my chest. A voice inside my head is screaming at me to back away, like I'm on that trailer roof in the storm, knowing I'm making a mistake.

"Right now? I have no idea." He sighs. "I want you, Iz. And maybe I didn't say it right back there, but I'm not going to pretend I didn't feel something watching that guy flirt with you."

Suddenly, everything feels too much. Too intense. So I do the only thing I know how to do. I walk away. I yank open the truck door, climb in, and slam it shut.

The drive back to the ranch is silent. Anger hangs heavy between us. The second we're rolling to a stop in the driveway, I'm out. Striding across the dirt. Boots kicking up dust. My pulse hammering in my ears.

I don't belong to anyone. Least of all Dylan Sullivan.

The second I'm inside the trailer, the door slammed shut behind me, I press my back against the cool metal. I grab my phone and throw myself onto the bed.

My fingers fly furiously over the screen as I tap out a message to Flic, filling it with expletives and pitchfork emojis. I'm still breathing fast as I read it back. My thumb hovers over send, but I hesitate, already hearing Flic's mocking tone in my head.

So another man hit on you and Dylan stepped in. Did he punch the guy? Did he threaten to kill him? No! He just made it clear that the guy didn't have a chance.

Tears prick at my eyelids. I can feel the shadows of annoyance shifting to something else and I don't want to go there. I know where I am with righteous indignation. It's practically my default setting. But the other feeling is creeping in, taking over. I squeeze my eyes shut, allowing the first tears to fall as my mind races back over our evening. Our perfect evening I didn't want to end.

Then the little boy came over to us and Dylan lit up, like he was stepping into a role he belonged in. Like football was still his world. Like it always will be. A stone lodges in my chest. Sharp-edged and cutting. It's not anger I'm feeling. It's fear. Because no matter how hard I try, I can't stop seeing this ranch and this life as a distraction for Dylan. And one day soon he'll get bored and go back to his old life, and he and his friends will laugh about the time he played at being rancher.

Where does that leave me? And Madison?

The stone moves to my throat, blocking my airway.

No matter how much I want to deny it, Dylan is more than an itch I want scratched. He's more than the magnetic pull I feel around him. And that terrifies me more than I can voice. Because if I continue down this road, if I let him in and he proves me right, it will be Hooper all over again, and I'm not sure I have the strength to pick up the shattered pieces of myself a second time.

Maybe if this was just about me, I could go all in. But it's not. I have to think about what's best for Madison too. If Dylan lets her down like her dad, it will destroy whatever whispers of trust she has in men. She deserves better.

Silent tears trail down my face. Madison deserves... She deserves... A sob catches in my throat. She deserves someone who'll build her a rope swing. Someone who'll throw her a dinner with burgers because she's sad and it's her favorite food. She deserves someone who listens to her and treats her like she matters. She deserves all the tiny moments I've seen between her and Dylan in the time they've spent together, heads bent, talking and teasing. The way she lights up around him. The way I do. I press my palms to my eyes. I don't know if I can trust Dylan. But if I don't try—if I let fear win before I've taken a step—then I've already failed Madison. And I've failed myself.

I draw in a shuddering breath and push myself off the bed. I will not let fear be the reason I don't try. With that, I throw open the trailer door and head out into the night.

THIRTY-FOUR

DYLAN

I scrub a hand over my face as I pace my bedroom in long, impatient strides. I'm torn, furious. Confused. My mind stuck on a loop. I want to storm after Izzy and yell at her for being so infuriating. But another part of me wants to stay right where I am and leave Izzy to her irritation. What the hell just happened?

We were having a good time. No—the best time. It felt like we were really getting to know each other. Telling her about Dad and the night he died, her hand in mine, her eyes softening like she was right there with me. It meant something.

Then it went to shit over one comment. I head for my weights corner, needing the burn of a routine—a distraction. I grip the dumbbells tight in my hands, launching straight into a vicious set that has my pulse racing in seconds. I close my eyes, leaning into the burn of each rep, but all I see is Izzy—the fire in her eyes as we argued. The way she spun on me, ready to fight—because that's what she does. The way her voice wavered, just for a second, before she stormed away. I drop the weights with a frustrated growl, my heart pounding for reasons that have nothing to do with the workout. It's just one fight. Not our first, and it won't be our last, I'm sure, but I don't know what this means for us.

My feelings for Izzy are tied up with the ranch and the horses and this life I'm carving for myself. A mess I need to untangle. But I'm not giving up. She can push me away, pick fights, slam those walls up, but I know that beneath the cutting remarks, that temper that flares from nowhere, the jokes, and the eye rolls is a woman who is kind and funny. The way she loves Madison is fierce. She's a protector. Not just for her daughter, but for the horses too. I know without a shadow of a doubt that she'd burn everything to the ground to protect what she loves.

My thoughts spin as I strip off my clothes and stride to the bathroom, heading straight for the huge walk-in shower. I turn the shower to hot and step beneath the spray. The heat of the water pounds my shoulders, rolling down my back as I brace my hands against the tiles and try to empty my head.

Then I hear it. A noise that I think might be Buck coming to say hi, but when I turn, it's Izzy standing in the entrance to the shower. Her cheeks are flushed, her green eyes wide and glassy. She looks wild and so fucking beautiful.

"I'm sorry," she blurts, her voice soft but urgent.

I push my hair back, water dripping down my face, and step out of the spray, not giving a damn that I'm naked right now. "I shouldn't have said—"

She shakes her head quickly. "It wasn't really that. I... got scared. You were right before. I've put up some pretty high walls. I don't know how to not be this person." Her voice cracks and the confession is nearly enough to unravel me.

"Scared of what?" I know the answer, but I need to hear her say it.

She swallows hard. "Of this. Us." Her gaze locks onto mine.

The steam from the shower is billowing around us, the water still needling my back. "But you want to try?" I ask.

"Do you?"

My lips pull into a half-smile and I ignore the way my heart is pounding in my chest. "I asked first."

Izzy lets out a shaky breath before she nods. "I don't want to walk away from this."

I hadn't realized until this moment how much I needed to hear those words. How much I've been falling for this woman. My feelings for her might be tangled in the ranch, but I'm damn sure that whatever else happens, I want Izzy in my life. And I want to be something she fights for like she does Mad and the horses.

I move fast, hand wrapping around her wrist, tugging her fully clothed into the spray of water.

"I meant what I said the other day. I'm in." I tangle my fingers in her hair, my lips hovering close to hers. The tension stretches tight, like we're on a cliff edge, hands clasped. Ready to leap.

"And I'm wet," Izzy deadpans, rolling her eyes. But there's a smile pulling at the corners of her mouth.

And now it's my turn to smile. I drop my voice low before I speak. "Blondie, I haven't even started getting you wet."

She starts to laugh, but I capture her lips in mine before she can finish. The kiss is urgent. Her hands wrap around my neck, her body pressing against me. I'm rock-hard in seconds and tugging at her top and skirt until she's in her underwear—black lace, sheer and sexy as hell. I drop my mouth to her collarbone, tracing the damp skin with my tongue, savoring the way she shivers beneath my touch as heat burns in my groin.

I unhook her bra, freeing her perfect breasts, wanting to feel her skin against mine. To ravish every part of her until she's screaming my name.

"You gonna let me take care of you, Brooks?" I grit out.

She replies with a teasing smile. "I might, but first..." Her eyes darken and she drops to her knees and takes my dick in her hand, fingers wrapping around my length, firm and deliberate and so fucking good. Fire pools low in my belly.

I groan low in my throat as her eyes lock on mine. She strokes me slowly, her thumb brushing over the tip then down to the hilt. I press my hands to the walls, steadying myself as her tongue traces a path all the way up my length—slow and torturous—as the warm water beads down on my shoulders.

"Izzy," I groan. "You're killing me."

Her breath is hot against my skin, and I shudder under her touch. "Patience, Sullivan," she says before trailing her tongue over my tip, her eyes watching me come apart. "You're always so damn impatient."

She takes her time, teasing me with little flicks and sucks, and when she finally takes me fully into her mouth, I hiss out a long, "Fuck," as my hips jerk, pushing myself further into her mouth. She draws me in deep, my tip hitting the back of her throat and sending jolts of pleasure through my body. My hands tangle in her wet hair, needing to touch her. "You take me so well," I groan.

She draws herself up, her tongue moving in slow circles. I swear I grow harder in that second before she slides me back into her mouth. All the way in. Taking me as far as she can before drawing back. Over and over, she moves until the burn in my groin scorches. The pressure starts to build, but I want more. I want her. I want everything. And it's like she senses my thoughts because she pulls back slowly.

"You want me to carry on?" she asks, her hand stroking my length. "Or you want to play?" Her grin is wicked and has me pulling her to her feet in one movement.

"Oh, I want to play."

I press her back against the cool tile of the shower wall. The water rolls down her body, soaking her hair, her skin glistening. My lips press to hers, our tongues colliding as my hands roam every inch of her body. I trail my fingers over her breasts, rolling

one nipple between my thumb and forefinger until she's arching
into me. My mouth trails down her neck as my hand moves
between her thighs, brushing over the lace of her panties.

Her breath hitches as I lean in, my lips pressing against the
sensitive spot below her ear. "You wet for me, Brooks?"

"Yes," she gasps out.

I growl, nipping at her earlobe before trailing kisses down
her neck. My hands move to her hips and I push her panties
down over that perfect fucking ass of hers. She wraps her arms
around my neck, wriggling out of them, pressing her naked
body against me. I reach a hand between her legs, groaning as I
feel her wetness, how much she wants me. My dick is begging to
be buried inside her, but I'm not done playing yet. I circle my
finger around her center, finding her sweet spot. Her body
tenses, her head leaning back against the tiled walls as her hips
arch into my touch.

"Please fuck me," she gasps.

"Patience, Brooks. You're always so damn impatient."

She laughs, the sound ending in a hissed gasp, her name on
my lips as I slide a finger into her. I bury my head in her neck,
my mouth on her skin, kissing, sucking, wanting everything she
has to give. Her body. Her mind. Everything. I want it all.

THIRTY-FIVE

IZZY

Dylan's hands are everywhere. His mouth too. On my neck, my collarbone, trailing down to the swell of my breast. He slides two fingers inside me, his thumb circling my clit, making my knees buckle. I'm breathless, chest heaving, desperate and so close already. The air around us is heavy with steam, the water warm as it slides over us. My hands rake over his muscular back as my hips move on their own, grinding against his hand, chasing the pleasure he's teasing me with.

His mouth moves over one nipple, sucking and nipping until I'm gasping.

"Dylan," I breathe, my voice trembling. "I need more."

His laugh is a low rumble I feel all through my body. He moves his mouth slowly back to mine, kissing me deeply before drawing back. I whimper at the loss of touch as he slides his hands away from me, before taking my wrists and pinning them to the tiles either side of my head. I move my hips toward him, desperate to feel his body against mine.

"You ready for me to take care of you now, Izzy?" His eyes are dark with desire and focused entirely on me.

"Yes," I whisper.

"Say it," he commands.

I lift my chin and pull back my shoulders a fraction. "I want you to take care of me."

He smirks—that infuriating, cocky smirk that drives me crazy in the best way. "Good."

Then he moves. He drops my arms, moving his hands to grip my hips, firm and possessive as he lifts me effortlessly against the cold tile wall. I wrap my arms around his neck, my legs gripping his waist. I feel every hard inch of him pressing against me. His beard brushes against my neck, and I tilt my head back, a gasp escaping my lips as he nips at the sensitive skin.

"Dylan," I breathe again, but it's barely more than a whisper. My heart races as the tip of him presses against my opening. With a low growl that sends shivers down my spine, he thrusts into me in one smooth, long motion. I cry out as he fills me completely, stretching me in a way that makes my body tremble with pleasure as his heat sears through every nerve ending.

"Fuck," he murmurs, his voice raw like it's taking everything in him not to lose control right then and there. "You feel so good. So fucking good."

He supports my weight easily, driving deeper into me with each thrust. My breath is ragged. My nails dig into the hard planes of his muscles as he moves, each thrust sending waves of pleasure crashing through me. The water from the shower streams down on us, slicking our skin, making every touch, every slide of his body against mine, feel electric. I can't think, can't breathe, can't do anything but feel him—every inch of him —as he takes me to the edge and holds me there.

"I want you so much," he rasps, throwing a hand out to kill the water and carrying me effortlessly out of the bathroom and into his bedroom. He spins us around so I'm on top as he eases back onto the covers. Then I'm pushing down, taking every delicious inch of him until he's groaning my name. "I'm going to take such good care of you, you'll never want to leave my bed."

Then he's taking control again, guiding me deeper. My head spins with the pleasure coiling tighter and tighter. Dylan's eyes lock onto mine, like he's seeing straight into me. "Come for me, Izzy. Come all over my dick." His voice is rough with need. His thumb brushes against my clit again, causing a gasp to tear from my throat. "That's it," he growls. "Let go for me."

The pleasure notches higher until I feel like I'm losing my mind. My thighs tremble and I lean back, riding him hard, feeling the pressure build. Every thought empties from my head. All I can feel is this need. All I want is this moment. "Don't stop," I cry out.

"Never," he rasps. "Fuck, Izzy. You feel so fucking good."

"I'm going to come." I heave a breath as the pulse of the orgasm starts to spread through my body.

He grabs my ass, pulling me down on him over and over as he works my center. "Who do you belong to?" he asks.

"You." The word gasps out as I come undone, falling over the edge, the pleasure white-hot and all-consuming. My muscles clench around Dylan's length as I shudder with release. Dylan works me through it, softening his strokes, murmuring sweet words, slowing down our rhythm until I collapse against him.

Then gently, he flips me over, brushing my hair out of my face, catching my lips in a deep kiss as he begins to move again, thrusting into me hard and fast, and fuck if my head isn't spinning from it. The angle is deeper now and I swear I can feel him in places I didn't know existed. His pace quickens as he draws all the way out then back into me. He buries his face in my neck.

"Izzy." He groans. "Fuck, Izzy." His voice cracks, and then he's coming undone too, pulsing deep inside me with a groan that sounds almost primal.

For a long moment, neither of us speaks. The only sounds in the room are our breathing and the faint rustle of the covers as Dylan shifts to one side, tucking me close against him. I close my eyes, letting myself sink into the warmth of him, into this moment that feels too big for words.

Dylan props himself onto one elbow, looking at me in the dim light. His expression is open—like he's willing me to see the steadiness of him. The trust he's offering me.

A trust I'm terrified to accept. Because trusting anyone but myself means giving them the power to hurt me. Falling for someone means laying myself bare. And yet, this doesn't feel like falling. It feels like being caught. Like maybe I don't have to do this alone anymore.

I exhale, pressing my palm against his chest, feeling the steady beat of his heart. Then I voice the question I'm terrified to ask, but I have to know. "Can I trust you?"

He's quiet for a moment as the back of his hand strokes my cheek. "I can't promise we won't argue, Iz. I can't promise I won't mess up sometimes, but I can promise that I'm here right now. And I'll do my best for you and for Mad."

His arms tighten around me, and when he kisses me, slow and deep, like he's sealing his promise between us, I believe him.

THIRTY-SIX

IZZY

The next two days blur in a delicious haze of ranch work and being together. I spend more time in Dylan's bed than in my own trailer, and the more time I spend there, the less I want to be anywhere else.

Ron's nephew, Travis, has been a great help. He's young and green but doesn't shy away from hard work. I can already tell he's a natural with the horses. The gentle way he talks to them makes me think he'll be a great ranch hand one day.

When the work is done and Travis leaves, Dylan and I take long showers together and then I sit at the kitchen table in one of Dylan's shirts and not much else while he cooks a simple meal for us—pasta or grilled meats. We wash the dishes side by side. Every time our hands brush against each other, our conversation stops, replaced with heated glances, shots of electricity sparking between us. Then he takes my hand and leads me up to his bed, where we worship each other's bodies and talk long into the night. About horses. About the future. About the kind of rancher Dylan wants to be. He thinks he wants to keep the foals longer, break them in, give them the skills to be the best damn rodeo horses in the state. Selling them when they're stronger, more confident. I like that idea, too.

We both know this is a bubble. Tomorrow, Mad will be home from camp and Chase will swing by. Next week, Jake and Harper will return from Hawaii and then Mama from Florida the following week. And somehow, we'll have to figure out how to fit this thing between us into the chaos of real life.

But right now, lying in Dylan's bed, my limbs heavy with exhaustion and my mind buzzing like a live wire, I feel suspended between sleep and something that feels a lot like joy. There's a smile on my lips I don't try to hide. I don't know how this is possible. How something that started as a mistake could feel so right.

Beside me, Dylan's breathing is steady, but the slow, lazy path his fingers are tracing over my thigh tells me he's not asleep. For the first time in years, I feel safe. I feel settled. It feels like the walls I spent years building have crumbled, and in their place is Dylan's solid, steady presence. I don't want to be anywhere but here.

"Which mare do you think would be best for a late-summer foaling?" Dylan's voice is low, rough with sleep, but there's curiosity in his tone.

I turn my head on the pillow, finding him watching me in the dim light. "Callie would be my first choice. She'll be coming into season soon and I think she's ready for another foal. Are you thinking of breeding this year?"

His fingers trail higher, brushing over the curve of my hip. "If you agree, then yes."

I hum, thinking. "Buckshot is a great stallion for her. He's all speed and agility. Their last foal sold well at auction. And it's good to have the injection of cash later in the season."

Dylan nuzzles my neck. "I like hearing you talk like this."

"Like what?"

"Like this is your ranch too," he replies.

The words settle deep in my chest, and I arch into his touch, my body responding to the warmth of his skin, the slow scratch of his beard on my shoulder as he moves his lips to kiss my neck. His hand moves lower, fingers teasing, and oh God I'm ready to lose myself in him again. Until his ringing phone shatters the moment.

"That's the second call in an hour," I say, eyes still closed. "You gonna answer it?"

"Kinda busy right now," he replies, shifting over me.

I laugh, pushing him gently back. "Answer that phone, Sullivan, or we're not getting any peace tonight."

He groans, rolling onto his back and grabbing the phone from the bedside table. "It wasn't peace I was looking for."

I laugh at his words as they send desire curling low in my stomach, but the moment vanishes as he swipes to answer.

"Coach," Dylan says, his body tensing. He swings his legs over the bed, planting his feet on the floor. Awake. Alert.

The warmth between us—the safety I felt only seconds ago —vanishes in an instant. It's just one phone call. It doesn't mean anything. Doesn't change anything. And yet my heart starts to hammer in my chest as Coach talks, his gruff voice rumbling through the quiet, loud enough for me to hear every word. "Finally answering your phone, eh, son?"

Dylan rubs a hand over his face. "Sorry, Coach. It's been a busy few weeks."

"Mama spoke to you about the opportunity?"

There's a pause before Dylan replies. Unease streaks through me. *What opportunity?*

"Yeah, she did."

"Truth is, we could really use your help, Dylan," Coach Allen says. "The team is the strongest it's ever been. We've got a real shot of getting to the Super Bowl, and for that to happen, the coaching team needs to be at its strongest too. I've let Philip and Jason go and I'm rebuilding. I want someone who knows the team, someone who understands these boys and what we're doing here. I can't think of anyone better for the job than you."

My stomach tightens. Dylan is being offered his old life back. Or a form of it anyway. I feel sick and unsteady.

Turn it down!

The words are a whispered prayer in my thoughts. A rock seems to form in my throat. I can't swallow. He promised he was here for this ranch and for us.

"And selfishly," Coach continues, "I'm looking at retiring in five, maybe six years. I want to know I've left the Stormhawks in good hands. This isn't just a temporary gig, son. This is a future."

Dylan exhales slowly. "That's a fantastic offer..."

There's no escaping the excitement in Dylan's voice, which cuts into me as easily as a knife.

"But—" Dylan starts, hesitation thick in the air. I hold my breath.

Please remember your promise.

I trusted you!

"I know you've got something else going on now," Coach cuts in, his tone gentler. "I'm not asking you to make a decision tonight. Take some time to think on it. Come by my office sometime before the season starts if you're interested."

"I will. Thanks, Coach."

"You're one of us, Dylan. We need you," Coach says before ending the call.

The silence that follows feels like the moment before a storm—a stillness you can't trust. Just like Dylan, I realize. I sit up slowly, watching Dylan's broad shoulders tense, his phone still clutched in his hand. He's facing away from me, but I don't need to see his face to know what's there.

Hope.

The same hope I'd been letting myself feel about this place. About us. In one phone call, everything is shifting under my feet, the ground no longer steady but quicksand I'm sinking into. A rush of anger scorches through me, and I let it in. Let it drown out the pain threatening to crack open my chest.

I punch the lamp on, already scanning the floor for my clothes. "I knew this would happen," I bite out, jumping out of bed. "I fucking knew it."

Dylan twists toward me, his brows drawn tight. "Izzy, hang on. I haven't decided anything."

"Right. Keep telling yourself that." I reach for my clothes and dress fast. The space in this room is suddenly too small.

Dylan moves to standing. He's naked apart from a pair of shorts, and even in this moment, I can't drag my eyes away from the muscles of his chest. "Hey, just stop for one second, Izzy," he pleads. "Let's talk about this."

"Nothing to talk about," I bite back as I grab at the clothes I've left in Dylan's room, bundling them in my arms. Hiding the tremor in my hands.

His jaw tightens. The walls close in. "You don't get to push me away again and destroy us over one phone call," he says. "Nothing has changed."

I pause, drawing in a ragged breath. He's right. Even in my anger I can see that. I'm about to walk away from something amazing because of one phone call. Dylan could turn it down. He could stay. He could still be mine. *Don't run!*

And yet I have to ask: "How long have you known about the offer?"

Dylan's expression shifts like he's warring with himself. "Since Saturday."

Something cracks inside me at his admission. "Saturday. The same night we slept together for the first time, and you knew then you were going to sell the horses and go back to football."

"I told you, I haven't decided anything. Mama mentioned there might be a coaching offer coming. I didn't know anything about it or whether it was real until thirty seconds ago. Please, Izzy. Let's talk about this."

I force my feet to stay rooted and my voice to remain steady. "Answer me one question, Dylan. Are you going to meet with Coach?"

His hesitation is a thousand splinters, each one digging deeper. But I hold my breath, force myself to wait. To hear his answer.

"I..." He drags a hand through his hair before finally he looks at me. "Going for one meeting isn't me turning my back on this place. It's just one meeting."

The trust shatters. Our relationship shatters. Everything disappears so fast it gives me whiplash. I stare at the man I'd let myself start to fall for. The open face. The scowl. Dark eyes I've lost myself in countless times. That strong body I thought had my back. None of it was real. I was just another part of his distraction. I can't believe I fell for it.

I shake my head, my laugh harsh and broken. "You've been kidding yourself this entire time, Dylan." I gesture toward the ranch beyond the window. "These horses were a drunken mistake. And you've done a really good job of pretending they mean something to you. Hey, you even fooled me for a minute there. But you're still lying to yourself if you think taking this meeting isn't choosing football over the ranch."

"There might be a way to do both," he replies, his voice sharp, desperate.

I meet his gaze, holding back the tears burning at the back of my eyes. He will not see me break. "Before you were injured, when you were at the top of your game, if someone had come to you and told you that you could run a ranch in your spare time, would you have said, 'Sure, sounds great,' or would you have said, 'No way, there's no time for both'?" I take a step closer, my voice trembling. "Because there isn't time, Dylan. This is an all-or-nothing life. So do us both a favor and admit you made a mistake. Sell the horses and go back to your real life, because I'm done here."

I think Dylan will argue. Tell me I'm wrong. Beg me to stay. But he doesn't. He stays silent, irritation rippling from him with the same force as my own.

That silence is the final answer I need. I turn on my heels and stride away. Down the stairs, through the kitchen. Out of the back door, across the driveway. Into my trailer. Only when the door is closed and locked do I lean against the wall and let the first sob shudder through my body. Then the next and the next.

Tears blur my vision. I trusted him. I let myself believe this was different, that he was different. How could I have been so stupid? I should have known better. I should have kept my walls up, should have protected myself, protected Madison. But instead, I let myself fall. Not just for this life on Oakwood Ranch, but for Dylan too. I opened myself for him. Let him in. And now it's all slipping through my fingers like it was never real to begin with.

Fucked up again, Iz!

I bite the inside of my cheek. I cannot keep messing up my life. I have to think about Madison. It's that thought that forces me forward. I move on autopilot, opening cupboards, throwing clothes for both of us into bags. I'll get my trailer moved next week, but for now, I just need a few things. And then I need off this ranch.

For one gut-wrenching moment, I think about waking up tomorrow in a place that isn't Oakwood Ranch. This isn't just about leaving Dylan. Fresh tears spill down my cheeks, the pain of all I'm leaving behind. I think about not being the one to feed Quicksilver. I think about not being here for the horses I love as much as the work.

The guilt is fierce, but I swallow it back and fire off a message to Travis, asking him to take on more hours and days.

Dylan can sort out the finer details with him, but I won't leave without making sure these horses will be cared for. Until Dylan can find a buyer for them, anyway.

I pull my shoulders back and wipe my tears. Mad has to be my focus right now. My parents were right—Madison needs more than this. I shove the last of my things into the suitcase. Dylan hasn't been the only one to make mistakes and pretend this is working.

My six weeks are up. It's time to move on.

THIRTY-SEVEN

DYLAN

As the alarm drags me into consciousness, I find myself reaching instinctively for Izzy. Wanting to pull her close, feel her skin against mine. Except she's not here. It's been two weeks since our fight. Two weeks since she left the ranch. But I can't stop reaching for her.

The argument replays over and over in my head. She didn't even give me a chance to explain. Football was everything to me. Surely she can see that. Surely I get one goddamn minute to consider if there's a way to have both—the ranch and football. The offer from Coach Allen... it's big. Not just a slot on the coaching team, but a pathway to take over from him one day. A future in football again. Don't I get to even think about that?

I groan and turn onto my back. However much I might be frustrated with the way Izzy reacted, I can't really blame her. Mama told me about the offer days before that night. I should've said something. But when I'm with Izzy, it's like something slots into place. Like I'm not a man with shattered dreams or a past I can't rewrite—but someone with a future. Something I can build.

Still, she left. Packed up and disappeared like none of it

meant anything to her. Like the long nights in my bed, the tension, the heat, the connection I thought we had—meant nothing. Like Oakwood Ranch and these horses meant nothing. That part stings in a way I didn't expect. Because if she could walk away so easily, maybe I was the only one who thought this was something real.

I drag myself out of bed, throw on my clothes, and push a hand through my hair before heading downstairs. The smell of coffee draws me into the kitchen. Mama's already dressed for the day in business slacks and a crisp blouse, packing her laptop into her bag.

"Morning, Dylan. Sleep OK?" she asks, eyeing me like she already knows the answer.

"Fine," I reply, stepping to the counter and pouring myself a coffee. "You heading out somewhere?" I ask.

"New York. I told you yesterday." She raises a concerned eyebrow.

I nod, remembering something about a sports brand that wants Jake and Chase to appear together in an ad. "Right. The ad thing."

"We'll be back late tonight."

"You want a ride to the airport?"

She shakes her head. "Jake will be here any second. He wants to drop Buck off anyway."

There's a pause. Heavy with meaning. The same one that's been hanging between us since she got back from Florida. The unspoken question: What am I going to do about Coach Allen's offer? About the ranch?

Coach told me to stop by his office before the season started if I wanted to have a conversation about a future with the Stormhawks. Two weeks have slipped away and I haven't gone. The truth is, I can't think about it, and yet it's all I do think about.

The ranch isn't the same without Izzy, but there's something solid here. I know these horses now. The way Logan won't eat unless you talk to him. How Willow noses the latch of the gate when she wants out. The way Fury's ears no longer pin back the moment I step into his paddock. And Quicksilver? He's taken to the lead rein like a pro. Sometimes, when I'm working with him, I catch myself imagining more—converting the patch of back scrubland into an actual training arena. Installing a round pen for lunge rope work for when the foals are old enough. Then I pull back because those thoughts sound like the thoughts of a rancher and I haven't decided anything yet.

Outside, an engine rumbles. Jake's here.

"Season starts this weekend," Mama pushes, like I don't already know.

"Yeah, I know," I mutter.

"If you're going to see Coach, it has to be today. Sitting on the fence isn't helping anyone. Least of all you."

I nod, not trusting myself to answer.

I do miss football. It still feels like a part of me. But it's not the stadium or the cameras or being on that field I think about most. It's tossing the ball with Mad in the back pasture. It's her laughter when she scores a pretend touchdown. That's what I miss.

I'm saved from forming an answer by Buck clattering into the kitchen and galloping to me as I crouch to rub his ears. Jake steps in a moment later, his huge frame filling the doorway. His dark hair is pushed back from his face, his stubble trimmed to something that's never quite a beard. "Man, it's early!" He looks me over, the same unspoken question on his lips. "You heading into the city later?"

"Don't you start," I mutter. "I haven't decided anything."

"Harper said to tell you to get your head out of your ass and fix things with Izzy."

Hurt streaks across my chest. I miss Izzy more than I care to admit. "She left me," I remind him.

Jake doesn't flinch. "Harper said you'd say that. And to remind you it's probably your fault. Also, she said to ask if you want to spend the rest of your life as a grumpy, washed-up ex-pro."

"Those her exact words?"

Jake grins. "I might've paraphrased."

"We all miss having her and Madison around," is all Mama adds as she kisses my cheek and heads out to the truck, leaving Jake to linger in the doorway like he knows there's more for us to say.

"What would you do?" I ask.

He shakes his head. "Only you can answer that. Just don't make the call with a bottle of bourbon in your hand."

And despite everything, I chuckle. "Thanks. You've been no help at all."

Jake takes a step before turning back. "Remember what Mama says. We don't give up on what we love."

"What does that mean?"

He gives a short laugh, like I'm the dumbest man in Colorado. "Figure it out, cowboy."

I wait for the sound of the engine to fade along the dirt track before stepping outside.

The first hints of fall are in the air—a shift in the wind, a scattering of orange in the treetops. The kind of morning that announces football season is here. I breathe deep as my eyes scan the paddocks. Quicksilver breaks from Moonlight, trotting toward the fence, nose lifted in greeting—a demand to be fed first. Pride flares in my chest at the sight of him. Then my eyes snag on the empty spot where Izzy's trailer used to sit. She didn't come back. Just sent a truck to tow the trailer a few days after she left. We haven't spoken since our fight, but Travis let slip she checks in with him every day, sending him reminders of what to do around the ranch.

The hollow ache in my chest deepens. Every task feels strange without her beside me. I miss her eye rolls. Her smart mouth. The way she made even feed runs feel like a team effort. But the weekends—they've been the worst. Too quiet without Madison's chatter. Too still. I scrub a hand over my face and wonder not for the first time if I should've called. I wish I had.

I drag open the barn doors and lose myself in the rhythm of feeding. The sound of buckets, the shuffle of hooves, and the greetings from the horses who are starting to feel like a part of me. Izzy could've called me. Could've stayed. She didn't give me a second to explain. This job offer—it's one meeting. One conversation. She can't expect me to build my life around a mistake without a second thought.

For the first time, I try to think seriously about Coach Allen's offer. What it would mean. A life back in football. With my team. But more than that, it's a chance to undo the failure I've felt since Coach sat me down in his office and cut me from the team. It would be a second chance. A shot at proving I still belong in football.

Travis shows up just in time to save me from my spiraling thoughts. Dirty-blond hair shoved under a cap, his smile all nerves and eagerness. A face too young for the facial hair he's trying to grow.

I nod toward the stalls. "Check the water lines and then saddle up Rusty and Bramble."

"We riding?" he asks with an undisguised excitement that has my thoughts running to Mad.

"Yeah. I wanna measure a bit of land out by the football field. Might as well ride up there."

He nods and heads off. I lean against the barn wall, breathing in the heady scent of hay and horses. Today, I need to decide who I am. A coach. A rancher. Maybe a man Izzy thinks is worth fighting for.

I don't stop again until the afternoon, when my back is aching, my knee is screaming out to take the weight from it, and I'm too damn tired to be thinking of anything but the task in front of me. And right now, that task is Fury.

The black stallion stills as I step into the paddock with the lead rein. His ears prick. "Don't be getting spooked," I say, voice soothing. "We've done this before. It's just a little walk around the paddock."

Fury shifts his feet but doesn't bolt as I clip on the rein and start to walk him in a large circle, talking the whole time. "You got this, see? You're doing great. You can trust me."

Each step I think will be the one he resists, pulls back. But we keep going, completing two full circles of the paddock. "Good work, Fury," I say, running a gentle hand over his neck. His muscles tense, but again he stays with me. "Wanna try outside the paddock? You must be getting bored of the same view every day."

I lead the stallion to the gate and we walk through. Fury's head is high, his eyes alert. When we reach the paddock separating the other stallions, Fury halts, ears forward. He gives a low whinny, like he's saying hello. My heart lurches at the sound. He's snorted plenty since he's been here, but that's the first time I've heard him call out a greeting. It's the first interest he's shown in being around other horses.

"You wanna try hanging out with them?" I murmur.

When he doesn't pull back or shift his legs, I carefully open the gate. Fury hesitates for a moment before stepping forward. With slow movements, I unclip the lead rein, watching Fury for any sign of panic or aggression. Instead, he simply dips his head to graze like it's the most natural thing in the world.

A grin spreads across my face as I back away and close the gate. This is progress. This is huge. This is Fury accepting his place on the ranch. OK, so he might be way off taking a saddle, and he still eyeballs the hell out of me and any other human when we're too close, but he's also no longer fighting me every step of the way. He's choosing to stay.

I spin around, ready to tell Izzy. To see her face light up like mine is right now.

But there's no one to tell. She's gone.

The win turns to dust in my mouth. I swallow hard, the ache in my chest deepening. She didn't stay. She didn't fight for us. Or let me choose to fight for us. She just packed up and left. That's what really gets me.

So what now?

I've been clinging to this place like it's the only future left for me. But if Izzy can walk away from it so easily, maybe I need to stop pretending this ranch is the only place I belong.

What if there is a place for me with the Stormhawks after all? What if I have more to give? Why the hell shouldn't I go talk to Coach?

Fuck it. I'm going.

THIRTY-EIGHT

IZZY

IZZY: *Are you sure you're OK to pick Mad up from school?*

HOOPER: *I said I would, didn't I?*

IZZY: *Let your mom and dad know if you can't, so they know to go!*

HOOPER: *I got this!*

~

FLIC: *How are you holding up?*

IZZY: *The same as when you asked me yesterday and the day before that.*

IZZY: *I'm OK, I promise!*

FLIC: *You wanna hang out at the bar while I clean the beer pumps?*

IZZY: *Tempting as that is, I can't. I'm on a tour of the new school my parents want to send Madison to.*

FLIC: *What's it like?*

IZZY: *Impressive.*

FLIC: *Is it right for Mad?*

FLIC: *You know I've got your back no matter what. But I need to say this before you fuck up your life completely... Making decisions your parents (or anyone else for that matter) don't agree with doesn't mean they're mistakes! It means they're the right choices for you.*

The school grounds are immaculate. Neatly trimmed grass and pruned flower beds—not a weed in sight. The buildings are three stories high and grand, like they've stood for a hundred years, except they also look brand new. As we approach a court-yard, a class of children moves in a quiet, orderly line, their ironed blue uniforms pristine under the late afternoon sun. Their teacher smiles politely at our tour group of prospective parents as they pass.

From beside me, Mom shoots me another of her *See? See how perfect this life will be for Madison?* looks. I barely contain my eye roll. She's already annoyed I'm wearing my black sundress instead of the blouse and skirt of hers she'd laid on the bed for me. I hide a smile as I think of her face if I'd worn the denim cutoffs that drive Dylan wild. *Drove,* I correct with a slice of pain that comes from nowhere, ambushing me just as it has done countless times since I left Oakwood Ranch two weeks ago.

As we round a corner toward the tennis courts, Mom shoots a pointed look at my phone as Flic's final message arrives. I read it fast before shoving my phone into my bag and swallowing down the lump of anxiety that's been lodged in my throat since I arrived at my parents' house in the middle of the night after the call from Coach Allen. After my world fell apart.

For days afterward, I stared at my phone, willing Dylan to call and tell me he'd chosen the ranch. Beg me to come back. Tell me he was falling for me like I was him. The silence has stung almost as much as the knowledge that he knew about the coaching offer and didn't tell me.

I think of Flic's final message, wishing it was that easy. The right choice for me? Or for Mad? And are they one and the same? Because this school really is amazing. Routine. Stability. Exactly what Madison needs. I just wish it didn't feel like I was struggling to breathe.

I try not to think about how hard the weekends have been for Madison. Her sadness when Grandpa Joe dropped her at my parents' house instead of the ranch. The way she asked a hundred questions about Oakwood, about the horses, about Dylan—questions I couldn't answer.

But why can't we stay there?

Why can't we go back?

What about Quicksilver?

When can we see Dylan?

I'd forced out words that felt all wrong. *I know it's hard, Mad. One day you'll understand. Here, we can have a routine. A normal life.* I hated how much I sounded like my mom.

We spent last week playing in the park, helping cook dinner, and coloring in Mad's room while I flicked through the stack of college courses Mom had left so helpfully on my old desk. I smiled for Mad, read her stories at bedtime, told her I loved her, and tried to ignore the suffocating feeling of being back in my parents' house.

I hoped school starting and seeing her friends would help, but she's still quiet. Nothing like her usual bubbly self. I thought I was doing the right thing by agreeing to live with my parents, but now I'm not so sure. I can't shake the feeling that I'm still failing her. It's one of the reasons I agreed to this school tour. And for Hooper to collect Mad from school today. Maybe some time with her dad will lift her spirits.

We round the corner and another class of children passes us. They're about Madison's age, each clasping a basketball in their hands. A ball slips and the little girl who dropped it starts to run, chasing it down, but the teacher is quick to stop her, reminding her to walk, not run. The girl nods solemnly before continuing after her ball, slower now.

I try to remember a single moment in Madison's life when she hasn't skipped, jumped, or sprinted her way through the day. I try to picture her in this place—standing in a neat line, silent and composed. But the Mad who fills my thoughts is the one in the lake, her high-pitched squeal of delight when Dylan threw her into the air. Wild and free. Happy.

I think of the way her face lights up around the horses, the same way mine does, and a tightness grips my chest. Even before Hooper, trust never came easy to me. I grew up feeling like the odd one out, like the decisions I wanted to make for my life were wrong. It made me doubt myself, not trust my own feelings. Like the feelings now telling me this school and this life aren't right for Mad or me.

Flic's right. I have to start trusting my instincts, and right now those instincts are screaming at me to get the hell out of here. Madison doesn't belong in a world of strictness and structure and being told not to run. She doesn't belong in a world closed in, away from the land she loves. And neither do I.

My feet slow, the tour group moving on without me. Mom stops too, nudging me forward. I take another step but then stop completely.

"I'm sorry," I tell her quietly. "But this place isn't for Mad."

Sadness flickers across Mom's face. I feel bad for a moment.

Then she purses her lips. "Madison will benefit immensely from a place like this. Your father and I—"

"I know," I cut in. "And I'm grateful for the offer, really I am. But you and Dad think if you can squeeze Madison's bubbly, curious, fun personality into the box this place is offering, she'll magically become the kind of person who grows up to be a doctor."

Mom shakes her head. "That's not what this is, Isobel."

"It is," I reply. "And I know that because it's exactly what you did to me as a child. But I never fit and neither will Mad. This life you're offering us... I know it's coming from a place of love. But I can't keep pretending I belong in a world that makes me feel like I'm failing just for being myself. It isn't for me. And it sure as hell isn't for Mad."

Mom sighs, resignation in her expression. "I told your father this would happen." She must see the surprise on my face because she raises her brows. "We may not be perfect parents for you, Isobel, but we've always wanted what's best. We want you to have something stable. And we love you. And we love Madison."

I reach out, giving her hand a gentle squeeze. "I know. Thank you."

The disappointment still lingers in the air. Maybe one day they'll accept my choices, but I'm not sure they'll ever be proud. And that stings. But it only makes me more certain that this isn't the life for Madison. I will always support her choices, always be proud.

"You don't have to move out," Mom says then. "Whatever you choose to do, you and Mad can always stay with us."

"Thank you," I say, grateful she doesn't try to stop me.

"What will you do?" she asks.

Oakwood Ranch flashes into my mind—sunlight spilling through the barn doors, Quicksilver's whinny, the sound of hooves hitting the dirt. The foothills rising from the land. The lush green of the spruce trees by the lake. The dewy scent of the air first thing in the morning, like it's rolled straight off the mountains. I shake the image away. "I... I don't know yet, but we'll figure it out."

I turn and walk away, cutting across the lawn, grinning at the sign that tells me not to. I feel the wind in my hair, the giddy relief of making a choice that feels right.

HOOPER: *Dropped Mad at the ranch. I'll let you know the next time I'm in town.*

I'm in the parking lot of the school when Hooper's message lands. His words suck the air from the day. What the hell does he mean he dropped Madison at the ranch? He was supposed to take her to my parents'.

"Hooper," I say as he answers with a drawling hello. "Where's Madison?"

There's a pause and I swear I can hear the lazy smile stretching across his lips. "Didn't you see my message? I dropped her at your boyfriend's ranch."

I ignore the dig. I will not be dragged into a fight right now. "You were supposed to drop her off at my parents'. We're—"

"Yeah, I know, but Mad told me it would be fine to leave her at the ranch. She said you were meeting her there."

"And you believed an eight-year-old girl without checking with me?" My voice rises as the first streaks of panic pound through me. Why has Madison gone to Oakwood Ranch? She knows I'm not there.

"Was Dylan there?" I ask.

"I didn't see him."

"Mama?"

"Who?"

"Did you see anyone?" I ask.

"Er... no, but I was in a rush to catch my flight. Mad seemed fine when she got out."

My heart pounds a rapid drum in my chest. My hands start to shake. I think of how sad Madison was this weekend. How many times she asked about the horses.

"Hooper." His name comes out in a rush. "Turn around right now and get Madison. I'm not at the ranch."

"What? Where are you?"

"I'm in the city. You have to go get her."

"I can't." His tone turns whiny, bringing with it memories of our marriage. All the times I begged him to stay home with me when Madison was a screaming newborn and I was so tired, strung out, and scared. "I'm already at the airport and through security," he says.

"What? How long ago did you drop her at the ranch?"

"About an hour or so."

The scream rises up, barely contained. The next words I speak are fierce. "You abandon our daughter without bothering to check if there's anyone to take care of her, and you don't think to tell me for an hour? You're a selfish prick, Hooper."

I end the call. My heart continues to pound as reality sets in. This is all my fault. I shove away the anxiety and the guilt threatening to consume me. Neither will help me now. I'm on the east side of the city. Oakwood Ranch is west. I'm on the wrong side, and it's the start of rush hour.

I'm hours away.

Madison needs me. She needs help. I need help.

I tap my phone screen, and as the ringing fills my ears, the truth hits me with the force of a sledgehammer. There is only one person I trust to help me—Dylan. I can't pretend it's not true. I trust him with everything. With my life. With Madison's. I know he'll help me.

THIRTY-NINE

DYLAN

DYLAN: *Don't forget the feed delivery is arriving this after-noon. I've cleared space in the store for it.*

TRAVIS: *Got it!*

DYLAN: *And check the alfalfa bales for mold before stacking them.*

TRAVIS: *Will do.*

DYLAN: *I'll be back in a few hours.*

The parking lot of the Stormhawks stadium is nearly deserted when I pull my truck into a space and kill the engine. The last time I came to meet Coach Allen in his office runs through my mind.

Your time with the Stormhawks is over.

Coach Allen's words don't slice through me like they used to, but my chest still tightens as I glance up at the massive stadium. Concrete and steel rise against the skyline—the heart of the city. The red banners of the Stormhawks hanging proud. I was part of this once. For a huge part of my life, this was everything.

I step out of the truck, the noise of the city crashing in. Traffic, horns, and the drill from a construction site a few blocks away. A pang of longing for Oakwood Ranch hits me deep in my gut. I've only been gone an hour and already I'm longing to see the sun hitting the paddocks. The peace of watching the horses graze. I pull out my phone and fire another message to Travis to remind him to check on Fury. The kid is good, but he's new and he's no Izzy.

The longing for the ranch twists into a nervous energy. Is this how new parents feel leaving their child for the first time? The constant worry. The what-ifs. The feeling that I've forgotten something. Not at the ranch, but here with me, like a piece of me is missing.

My thumb hovers over Izzy's number.

You've been kidding yourself this entire time, Dylan.

The nerves tangle; my pulse kicks up. It's just one meeting. I haven't decided anything. But even as I tell myself that, something still feels off. I just can't figure out what that something is.

"Hey? Excuse me?"

The voice pulls me from my thoughts. A man in his forties waves at me from across the lot, a young boy bouncing beside him in a Stormhawks cap nearly too big for his head.

I smile, recognizing the boy. "Reece, right?" I say, remembering the kid from one of the Stormhawks outreach programs in the spring. A way to help kids from all backgrounds and walks of life get a taste of football.

Reece's mouth drops, eyes bugging out. "You remember me?"

"Of course I do. You caught a twenty-yard pass like a champ."

"It's his birthday." The dad beams. "We thought we'd drive

by the stadium. Couldn't afford tickets, but he still wanted to see it."

I look up at the stadium, remembering what it was like to be a fan when I was Reece's age, and Mama and Dad brought us to the games some weekends.

"I'm working on my throwing," Reece blurts out. "I want to be just like you when I grow up."

I smile at the kid. See myself through his eyes. This whole time, it has felt like getting injured then being dropped from the team was me failing. I couldn't see past it to the seven good years I had playing at the top of my game. This, right here—this isn't failure. It's change. It's moving on. The thought eases the tension in my chest.

"We'll let you go about your day," the dad says, starting to pull Reece away.

"Tell you what," I say. "How would you like to come to Sunday night's game against the Skychargers? You and your dad can sit in the skybox with my family. Meet the team after."

The kid's face explodes with joy. His dad looks like he might cry or hug me or both. We swap numbers, and I text their info to the team coordinator. "Just tell them who you are at the gates and they'll let you right in. But any problems, you give me a call."

As they walk away, I feel it settle inside me—a flicker of something solid. This... this is what I love. That moment. That connection. That hope.

I head inside the stadium. The halls still smell of cleaning products and old sweat. *This is an all-or-nothing life,* Izzy's voice echoes. *So do us both a favor and admit you made a mistake. Sell up and go back to your real life.*

Except... what if this isn't all or nothing? I don't want to leave football behind, but I don't want to live this life anymore, either. I don't want to chase the noise or the spotlight. What I want is quieter. Closer. Real.

Coach Allen's office door is ajar. I knock once and step inside.

"Dylan," Coach says, heaving himself up from the chair, a broad smile lighting his face.

"Hey, Coach. Thanks for making the time."

We clasp hands before he motions me to the chair opposite his desk.

"I hope you've come to tell me you're ready to be part of the team again?" he asks with a smile.

I take a breath. "Coach, I appreciate the offer. Really, I do. But I don't think the coaching team is the right fit for me."

His brows lift, but he stays quiet, letting me talk.

"But I want to stay involved. What if instead of coaching the pros, I lend a hand in the youth outreach program? There are kids out there who need football and what this game gave me when I lost my dad. It's an outlet. A place for them to feel like they can belong. The program is good, but it can be so much better, and I want to help make it that."

He studies me for a long moment. Then a slow smile spreads. "You sure about that?"

"Yeah. I am." Since Coach called me, I've been thinking of my future as either running Oakwood as a horse ranch or going back to the Stormhawks to be part of the coaching staff. Football is a part of who I am. Turning my back on it completely isn't the answer, but that doesn't mean there isn't another choice. A way I can do both.

Coach leans back, nodding. "I'm proud of you, son. That's one hell of a thing you're proposing. Let me speak to management, but I have a feeling they'll be biting your hand off."

We clasp hands again and Coach pulls me in for a manly half-hug. And when I walk away from his office this time, it feels like I'm walking toward my future.

~

I'm climbing into my truck in the parking lot when my phone rings. Izzy. Seeing her name light up on my screen causes my pulse to race, my movements urgent. There's so much I have to say. I answer with a rushed, "Izzy, I need to tell you—"

"Is Mad with you?" Her words cut over mine, just as rushed but laced with a panic that stops me dead. "Are you at the ranch?"

"No. I'm at the stadium, but I'm leaving now. I'm half an hour away. What's—"

"Is Mama there or Jake or Chase?"

"No, they're in New York. What's going on?"

Her next words come in a frantic rush. "Hooper picked Mad up from school and she asked him to drop her off at the ranch and he did and now she's there and I think... I think she's run away, Dylan. She's been so upset about not being there." Her voice breaks before she heaves in a breath. "I'm on the other side of the city. It's going to take me hours to get to the ranch."

I start the engine and throw it into drive. "I'll be there in thirty minutes and I'll call Travis. Don't worry, Iz. Mad is a smart girl. She'll be OK."

"Call me as soon as you get there," Izzy replies.

"I will," I promise, already moving the truck to the parking lot barriers. They rise with an infuriating slowness, but then I'm out, heading for the highway, my phone on speaker as I call Travis. The second time it goes to voicemail, my eyes flick to the clock on the dash. The feed delivery is due now. Travis will be unloading it to the feed stores.

What was Madison thinking? My heart refuses to slow as I hit the highway and gun the accelerator. Images of the night my dad died fill my head. The horse rearing at the sound of the thunder. The hooves coming down. The sickening thud of impact. My pulse races, breath short. What if Madison tries to talk to Fury? What if he's spooked? What if she falls?

My hands grip the steering wheel. I can't lose her. My whole world feels like it's shifting beneath me. Madison has to be OK. I'll make sure of it. Because just as I'm certain that my future lies with the ranch, there is no possible version of that future that doesn't have Izzy and Mad in it.

FORTY

DYLAN

I hit the dirt track to Oakwood Ranch in a cloud of dust, skidding to a stop on the driveway and running straight for the open barn.

"Madison?" I call out, my heart sinking at the sight of the empty space.

There's a movement behind me and I spin toward it, but it's Travis, not Mad. He's carrying a bag of feed and looks surprised to see me. "Hey, Dylan. You're back early."

"Have you seen a little girl?" I blurt out. "Dark blonde hair. Eight years old."

His brow furrows as he shakes his head. "No, but it's funny though because I was in the paddock with the mares, and..."

"What is it?" I push, willing him to get to the point.

"I think one of the mares is missing. I was just going to call you."

"The little one, Rosie?" I ask.

"Yeah, how did you know?"

I glance over to the paddocks. Mad has taken Rosie. She knows she's not supposed to go out without one of us. Izzy was right. She's run away.

I'm already sprinting to the ranch house to get Buck as I yell at Travis, "Grab me Rusty's saddle."

It takes minutes before the orange gelding is ready and Buck is by our side. I don't know how much use he'll be, but Madison adores him. If anyone can coax her back to the ranch, it's Buck. I swing into the saddle, my pulse hammering. It feels like the most natural thing in the world to be on Rusty's back, urging him toward the lake with nothing but a gentle squeeze of my thighs. We slow to a fast walk as we hit the trees. I'm breathing fast, barely registering the dewy pine scents and the cool of the shade before we're by the lake and I'm scanning the water and banks for any sign of Madison or Rosie.

My heart drops into my stomach for a second time. She's not here.

Where else would she go?

My thoughts race back over the weekends Madison was here. Swimming and rope swings, football on the field, dinners at the ranch table, in the paddocks helping Izzy. Spending time with Quicksilver, and riding the ranch with us. Then it hits me, and suddenly I know exactly where to look.

I fire off a message to Izzy before pushing Rusty into a canter, Buck keeping pace by our side as I guide us past the football field to the edge of the ranch and the foothills, praying I'm right. Praying Madison is safe. The sun is dipping in a sky washed with cotton-candy pink, but it's not the beauty I see, it's the time Madison has been on her own and the nightfall that's coming. My mouth is dry. My breathing quick. Rusty's coat is slick with sweat, but I don't slow down. We hit the trail leading into the foothills, only slowing as we come to a steep incline and a sharp turn, where the path is overgrown with shrubs.

Please be there!

Another turn and there's the cave. The one I used to come to when I thought I was in trouble as a kid. The one I showed Madison on one of our rides. I heave a sigh at the sound of a horse's whinny and catch sight of Rosie tethered to a tree root. The mare is here. But where's Madison?

Buck barks, galloping ahead now, disappearing into the cave before barking again. My feet hit the ground, my heart refusing to slow as I force myself not to think of Mad fallen, injured. She has to be OK!

"Madison?" My voice echoes against the rock face, but all I hear in response is the pounding of my own heart in my ears.

"Mad," I try again, softening my voice. "It's Dylan."

Then a noise. A rustle. A muffled sob.

Relief floods me so fast my knees almost buckle. She's here.

I yank out my phone and, with shaking fingers, send a three-word message to Izzy:

DYLAN: *I've got her.*

Securing Rusty beside Rosie, I drop down, crawling into the mouth of the cave. It's smaller than I remember from coming here as a kid. My head is grazing the top of the cave at a crawl. My eyes adjust to the gloom and there's Madison, sitting on a blanket with a backpack and a teddy tucked by her side. There's a notebook open on the blanket, like she's making one of her lists, but her face is streaked with tears and she's hugging Buck tightly to her body, crying into his soft fur.

I smile, swallowing down the rock lodged in my throat as relief continues to skip through me. "Hey." I smile.

Mad lifts her eyes and fresh sobs shake her tiny frame. She scrambles across the dirt and throws herself into my arms. Her body is solid and warm, and I wrap her into me. "It's OK, Mad. It's all OK."

"You weren't at the ranch," she sobs. "I thought you'd left me too."

Guilt slams into me worse than any defensive lineman ever

has. I tighten my hold on her. "I'm sorry. I'm here now. I'm not going anywhere."

"Promise?"

"I promise." And it's the easiest promise I've ever made. One I want to make more than anything else right now. Mad, Izzy, this ranch. All of us together. I just hope I'm not too late. I promised Izzy I would be there for the ranch and her, and I wasn't. Not fully. My head was still on the Stormhawks and what I saw as my failure. But this promise to Mad is one I will keep if it's the last thing I do.

Beside me, Mad sniffs and wipes at her tears with her hands. "I didn't want to go back to Grandma and Granddad's house. I wanted to come home, but I didn't know where that was, and it made me upset, so I came here to talk to you. But you were gone. And then I realized I was in trouble because I wasn't supposed to be at the ranch, and I knew Mom would be mad, so I..." She hiccups, patting her backpack. "I got Rosie and I came to live here. But I've already eaten all my snacks." Her little voice wobbles.

A soft chuckle escapes me as I catch the next tear with my thumb, wiping it away before it can run down her cheek. "I used to do the same. But Mad, this is your home. Oakwood Ranch is your home if you want it to be."

Her lower lip trembles. "Mom said we couldn't stay here anymore."

I wish I could take the weight of her sadness as my own. How do I explain the mess and the mistakes I've made to this little girl who thinks adults have all the answers?

"Your mom and I had a fight, Mad," I say. "I thought I wanted to go back to a life in football, and she thought that meant I didn't care about the two of you or the horses. But that's not true. It just took me a little time to realize what was most important in my life." I rub a hand over my beard, wondering if I'm making any sense. "Grown-ups make mistakes too."

Madison's voice drops to a whisper. "Like Mom and Dad having me?"

I shift back, making sure Madison is looking right at me, hearing what I'm going to say. "No, Mad. You were never a mistake. Your mom and dad love you so much."

"But over the weekend, I heard Granddad tell Grandma I was a mistake."

My jaw clenches, but I keep my voice steady. "I'm sorry you heard that. People say things they don't mean sometimes. And also? People can be dicks."

Her eyes grow wide. "Dylan!" She gasps, her horror quickly melting into a giggle.

I grin, tucking a loose strand of hair behind her ear. "I'm sure your grandparents love you very much. What they probably meant was that your mom got married really young. But your mom loves you more than I've ever seen anyone love anything or anyone, and I know for absolute certain that you are her entire world. She's really worried about you."

Madison's mouth forms an "O" as fresh tears gather in her eyes. "I want to go home now. I want to see my mom."

"Me too." I smile. We crawl out of the cave and I scoop Mad into my arms and carry her to Rosie.

We take the ride back steady, Buck trotting at Rosie's side. Madison is quiet and I leave her to her thoughts. The sun has almost disappeared as the ranch comes into view. The last rays stretch over the paddock in faint streaks of gold and pink.

"Dylan?" Mad says, voice barely more than a whisper. "Is this really my home now?"

"I want it to be, but we need to talk to your mom."

"Don't mess it up then," Madison replies, and I'd laugh if I didn't feel the weight of her hope pressing down on my chest along with my own. I've been so stupid. I've been clinging to my past, grumpy as hell because I thought a life without football was failing. But letting go, moving on, it doesn't mean losing. It means making room in my life for something else. Something bigger and better than I ever imagined possible. And it's taken me too long to realize that the something is this ranch.

We don't give up on what we love.

Mama told me that. Jake told me that. I thought they meant football, but now I think of the look on Jake's face. *Figure it out, cowboy.* He knew before I did. I love the horses, the work, the peace of the land. But most of all, I love Mad and Izzy. And I'm never going to give up on them again.

The thought lands as Izzy comes into view. She's running toward us, her hair wild. A new kind of fear takes hold, grabbing me by the throat. Izzy gave me her trust and I stomped on it with my own fears for my future. Have I ruined everything? Am I too late? The sight of her, like the first time I saw her—like every time since—steals my breath, makes my heart leap and my body long for her touch.

FORTY-ONE

IZZY

The second I see Dylan and Madison riding side by side, my heart feels like it will burst open and I'm running as fast as my legs will carry me, not caring that my dress is swirling at the tops of my thighs and there's dust on my sneakers. Madison trots with Rosie to meet me by the barn, sliding down from the small mare with a sheepish smile and watery eyes. I scoop her into my arms, crouching to the ground, crying, holding her tight, pressing kisses into her hair, whispering how much I love her over and over again.

Buck shoves his head into the embrace, licking our tears and making us both laugh as we pull apart. From the corner of my vision, I see Dylan take Rosie's rein, leading her and Rusty toward the fence to secure them. He steps back, giving me and Mad this moment, and I'm grateful for it. I hold my daughter tight, breathing in the fruity smell of her shampoo and wiping the tears from her face.

"You OK?" I ask.

She nods, her bottom lip trembling. "I'm sorry I ran away."

"And I'm sorry I thought for a single second that living with Grandma and Granddad was right for us."

"I don't like it there," she whispers.

"Neither do I." I smile, brushing away a stray tear from her face. She reaches up and brushes away one of mine, too. "We'll figure this out," I say. "But no more running away. You talk to me from now on, and I'll talk to you. We're a team, Mad. I'm sorry I forgot that."

She nods, her arms wrapping around me in another tight squeeze. I hold her close. Every ounce of fear I felt in the last few hours crashes into me at once, and I have to squeeze my eyes shut to keep from crying again. She is my world, my reason for everything, and I will never let her feel alone again.

A throat clears, and we turn to find Travis shifting from foot to foot in the doorway of the barn, looking sheepish. "Since you're both here now, would one of you mind showing me how these bridles are supposed to hang?"

Madison is out of my arms in seconds. She shoots me an exaggerated eye roll that has me holding back a sudden burst of laughter, before striding toward Travis like she owns the place. "I'll show you. This way."

Travis throws me an uncertain look before following Madison into the barn. And then it's just me and Dylan and the weight of so many unspoken words, I don't know where to start.

I take my time rising to my feet, brushing the dirt from my dress as I turn toward him. My heart lurches in that now familiar way as I take him in. Broad shoulders, strong arms, the kind of height that makes me feel small in the best possible way. The beard I love to feel against my skin. The thick, dark hair I love to run my hands through. But it's more than that. It's the steadiness of him, the quiet strength. The way that when he sets his mind to something, he gives it everything, whether it's football or this ranch or—God, I hope—me.

The truth hits me, deep and absolute. For the first time in my life, I finally feel what it is to belong. To feel like I have a home. And yeah, it's Oakwood Ranch—the beauty of the land

and these horses. But more than that, it's Dylan. He is my home.

"I don't care if you go back to the Stormhawks," I blurt. "If you want to be a coach, if that's your life, then OK. We'll make it work."

"Iz—"

I hold up a hand, shaking my head. "No. Let me say this. I said it's all or nothing—the ranch or football—but I didn't mean that. I realize now I meant us. It's all or nothing with us. And I want all, Dylan. I want you. No matter what you do with the ranch, it's you I want. I'm all in. Wherever you go, I go."

A smile pulls at his lips. "Will you be bringing your temper and your pitchforks?"

I laugh. "Never leave home without them."

"And Madison, of course," he adds.

"We come as a pair." My voice catches on the emotion tightening in my throat.

"That's good to hear." Dylan takes a slow step forward, closing the space between us until we're inches apart. The pull between us is electric, but I keep myself still, hold my breath, waiting for him to speak.

"Because I'm crazy for you, Izzy," he says. "Head over heels. Give me the eye rolls and the standing on a trailer roof in a rainstorm in your underwear. Give me your death glares when I'm doing something wrong and that little noise you make in your throat when my lips touch the side of your neck." He trails his thumb over the sensitive spot and I inhale sharply. "I want it all. And I want us to live here together and run this ranch and build our life here with Madison. I'm sorry I made you doubt that. I'm sorry that I made it hard for you to trust me—"

"And you were grumpy," I add.

"That was both of us." He grins and I laugh again. "It took me a bit longer than it should've to see it, but I'm certain now. You, me, Mad, this place, it's all I want."

Emotion surges through me, stealing my breath. "Really?" I whisper as he cups my face in his hands. "But football—"

"Will always be a part of who I am. I can't pretend it isn't. But what I really want to do is coach kids. Help those who need it find an outlet in football. And I think I can do that alongside this place. If you're OK with that."

My eyes rake over his face, taking in the honesty in his dark gaze, down to his lips, hovering so close to mine I swear I can taste him already. "Yeah, I can be OK with that. But this doesn't mean I like you, Sullivan."

His grin spreads, and he laughs, the sound rumbling through me, filling every last corner of my heart. "Don't tell me—you tolerate me?"

"I love you," I breathe.

The biggest smile spreads across his face as he whispers, "I love you too."

And then he's kissing me. Deep and consuming, like every unspoken word, every moment we've lost, every promise of our future is sealed between us. My hands slide up his chest, around his neck, holding him close. Knowing I never want to be anywhere else but right here.

TWO MONTHS LATER

FORTY-TWO
DYLAN

JAKE: *You ready, Dyl?*

DYLAN: *I think so.*

JAKE: *Don't mess this up!*

DYLAN: *You need to work on your pep talk.*

CHASE: *Try not to scowl.*

DYLAN: *More worried I might tear up.*

JAKE: *Me too. Gonna be bawling like a baby!*

CHASE: *Dudes! What has happened to the two of you?*

DYLAN: *Your turn next, Chase!*

CHASE: *Never gonna happen.*

The late-afternoon sun glistens over the lake as I take my place beneath an archway of wildflowers and vines set on the shore. There's a chill to the air that promises winter and snow are not far away. String lights twinkle in the trees and ahead of me rows of white chairs are filled with smiling guests.

Mama is in the front row, wearing a purple wool dress, already dabbing a tissue at her eyes. Flic is beside her, wearing a black dress, light blonde hair loose down her back. She catches my eye and she gives me a wink before mouthing, "Never thought I'd see the day," and I can't stop the grin from spreading across my face. There was a while there where I didn't either. But so much has changed in the last year. In the last few months.

The scrubland beside the football field is gone. It's now a training ring, perfect for groundwork with the yearlings. Quick-silver is staying for a while. And Fury is still making progress. Slowly. He has accepted the saddle but not the rider and seems to enjoy working on the lunge rope. His confidence is growing day by day. Mine too. I feel it every time I step into a paddock—a contentment deep in my soul I never thought possible.

This is where I belong.

On the edge of the clearing, the harpist starts to play the first notes of a melody and I take a steadying breath, glancing a final time over the lake. In the far corner, through a gap in the trees, are the signs of construction and the houses Mama is building for her, Jake, and Chase. She hopes they'll be ready in the new year.

The ranch house will feel different without Mama living in it, but Izzy, Mad, and I are making it our own. Madison chose Chase's old bedroom, keeping all the Stormhawks memorabilia and declaring herself their biggest fan. She even joined the kids' football league I coach on Sundays in Idaho Springs, and comes with me when I run the outreach practice for the Stormhawks.

She may never be a professional quarterback, but she's got fire in her veins. She's got heart. One of the best times of the day is when she gets home from school, bringing that fire and energy with her.

I turn back to the wedding party as Jake steps up beside me on one side, Chase on the other, all three of us in matching suits. Behind us, the wedding officiant waits patiently.

Jake adjusts his cufflinks and shoots a look at Chase. "Damn, Chase, why do you look so much better in your suit than us?"

"I look good in everything, Jakey. And nothing as it happens."

"Gross," I mutter, shooting him a sharp look that has him cracking up.

Jake rolls his eyes before his gaze snaps to the top of the aisle and the biggest smile I've ever seen lights up his face. I watch as Harper takes her position, radiant in an ivory silk dress, her chestnut hair falling in loose waves around her face, her lips painted in her signature red. Her eyes are locked on Jake's, her smile matching his.

A rush of pride swells in my chest as I glance at Jake. He's always been the charmer, the flirt, the one with a smart comment. But standing in his suit, eyes locked on Harper like she hung the stars, I see the man he's become—steadfast and grounded in love. I spent so many years feeling like I had to look out for my little brothers, pulling them out of scrapes, calling them out on their bullshit, and they didn't turn out half bad. Seeing Jake about to marry a woman who fits him so perfectly is one of the best things I've ever witnessed.

I clap a hand on Jake's shoulder, leaning in and fighting my own wave of emotion. "Bawling like a baby yet?" I whisper.

Jake's voice is thick, but his eyes never leave Harper. "Any second now."

I chuckle and reach into my pocket, fingers brushing over the ring box, ready to do my duty as a groomsman.

I glance toward the front row where Madison sits, wearing a red dress and fluffy white jacket, her hair neatly braided, not a smudge of dirt in sight. She looks adorable holding Buck's leash, the yellow retriever sitting proudly, watching Harper at the top of the aisle like every other guest. Madison also looks like she's counting the minutes until she can ditch the dress for her new Stormhawks jersey and jeans. I don't blame her.

She catches me looking and gives an exaggerated wink as she pats the matching red bag on her lap—the bag holding the small velvet box I gave her earlier as we made our plans to surprise her mom. My heart tightens at the sight, the lump catching in my throat as my eyes draw to Izzy.

And like always, the rest of the world fades away.

She's sitting beside Madison, the golden light of the setting sun catching in her hair. She's wearing a deep green dress, the fabric clinging to her curves like it was made just for her. I swear, I could spend a lifetime staring and never get used to how beautiful she is. But it's more than that. It's the way she watches me, like she sees right through to my soul and isn't afraid of what she finds. It's the way she makes me laugh. The confidence she has in this ranch. In me. Maybe we haven't known each other long, but it doesn't feel rushed. It feels right. Izzy has become my home as much as this land has ever been.

My thoughts draw to later. After the ceremony and the reception we're holding in a huge, heated wedding tent beside the house, and after the toasts and the music and dancing, Madison will take Izzy's hand and lead her toward the little clearing in the trees we decorated with lanterns earlier. And I'll drop to one knee and ask her to be mine, just like I've done every night since the day she came back to the ranch. And just like every time before, she'll laugh, press her lips to mine, and say—

"I already am."

A LETTER FROM BELLA

Dear reader,

If you've just finished this book, I hope your heart is full and your Kindle is slightly overheating.

If you enjoyed *Game Over*, please consider leaving a review, telling a friend, or shouting, "DYLAN SULLIVAN IS MINE," on social media (I won't judge). Reviews really do help books reach more readers—and they mean so much to authors like me. If you want to stay up to date on future releases, you can sign up for my newsletter here:

www.bookouture.com/bella-north

I have LOVED writing Izzy and Dylan's story. All that stubborn energy really came down to them both searching for where they belong and finding their home in each other. (Be still, my swoony heart.)

Beneath Dylan's scowls and Izzy's fiery retorts is a story about second chances in love and in life. It's about the courage it takes to risk your heart and let someone in. I had a smile on my face writing every word. Especially the barn scene!

Please come and say hi on Instagram, TikTok, or Facebook and let me know what scene made you swoon the hardest.

With love, gratitude, and barn dust in my boots,

Bella x

facebook.com/BellaNorthAuthor

instagram.com/BellaNorthAuthor

tiktok.com/@bellanorth_author

ACKNOWLEDGMENTS

Massive thanks to the readers, bloggers, BookTokers, and bookstagrammers who've shared their love for Oakwood Ranch —you keep this author's heart full and fingers typing. Every shout-out, message, and review means the world. I hope you loved *Game Over* as much as *Score to Settle*—and if you haven't read that one yet... go, go, go!

To my editor, Lucy Frederick: Thank you for helping me deepen the heart of Dylan and Izzy's story. I love our shared joy for the swoon, the angst, and—of course—the spice! And to the phenomenal team at Bookouture—thank you for loving this series as much as I do. Special mention to Richard King for your excitement over Oakwood Ranch.

Amanda Preston—my agent and cheerleader—thank you for always backing my wild ideas (even the 6 a.m. Monday ones that start with "What if we..."). You're the best kind of chaos wrangler.

To Lila Whatley, for your insights on football, ranch life, and everything in between—you've been invaluable. Any errors are mine, but I blame Dylan and his growly voice for being far too distracting in the best way. I'd also like to give a special mention to DeAndra Lupa, my copyeditor for this series. You are nothing short of a superhero in my eyes.

Big love to my village gals—Sarah, Carol, Catherine, and Kathryn—for dragging me away from my writing desk. Thanks too to the wider village gang for sharing in the cowboy hype.

The process of writing *Game Over* was made so much more

fun by the endless memes, spice support, and gorgeous energy of Pippa Nixon. Quick shout-out to Avery for bringing the fun.

To Zoe Lea, Nikki Smith, and Laura Pearson—thank you for all the "I just had to tell you this..." voice notes that keep me laughing, inspired, and sane most days. I wouldn't want to do this without you.

And finally, to my family—thank you for giving me the space to live in fictional chaos. I love you endlessly.

PUBLISHING TEAM

Turning a manuscript into a book requires the efforts of many people. The publishing team at Bookouture would like to acknowledge everyone who contributed to this publication.

Audio
Alba Proko
Melissa Tran
Sinead O'Connor

Commercial
Lauren Morrissette
Hannah Richmond
Imogen Allport

Cover design
Ink & Laurel

Data and analysis
Mark Alder
Mohamed Bussuri

Editorial
Lucy Frederick
Melissa Tran

Copyeditor
DeAndra Lupu

Proofreader
Becca Allen

Marketing
Alex Crow
Melanie Price
Occy Carr
Cíara Rosney
Martyna Młynarska

Operations and distribution
Marina Valles
Stephanie Straub
Joe Morris

Production
Hannah Snetsinger
Mandy Kullar
Ria Clare
Nadia Michael

Publicity
Kim Nash
Noelle Holten
Jess Readett
Sarah Hardy

Rights and contracts
Peta Nightingale
Richard King
Saidah Graham

Dear Reader,

We'd love your attention for one more page to tell you about the crisis in children's reading, and what we can all do.

Studies have shown that reading for fun is the **single biggest predictor of a child's future life chances** – more than family circumstance, parents' educational background or income. It improves academic results, mental health, wealth, communication skills, ambition and happiness.

The number of children reading for fun is in rapid decline. Young people have a lot of competition for their time, and a worryingly high number do not have a single book at home.

Hachette works extensively with schools, libraries and literacy charities, but here are some ways we can all raise more readers:

- Reading to children for just 10 minutes a day makes a difference
- Don't give up if children aren't regular readers – there will be books for them!

- Visit bookshops and libraries to get recommendations
- Encourage them to listen to audiobooks
- Support school libraries
- Give books as gifts

There's a lot more information about how to encourage children to read on our websites: **www.RaisingReaders.co.uk** and **www.JoinRaisingReaders.com**.

Thank you for reading.